Plotting at the PTA

"Cozy readers will truly delight in the fact that this is the third in the series of these super-fun books, and with each release the plots just keep getting better and better.... Strong characters and monumental surprises, this cozy is a definite keeper!" —*Suspense Magazine*

"Laura Alden has written another delightful mystery. The plot is fast-paced.... Just wish I wouldn't have to wait so long to read the next in the series." —MyShelf.com

"An engaging whodunit.... Fans will enjoy Laura Alden's complex murder mystery, thankfully without a recall in sight." —Genre Go Round Reviews

Foul Play at the PTA

"Well-crafted." —*Publishers Weekly*

"Beth Kennedy gives amateur sleuths a good name.... For those of us who appreciate good characters, it's just as satisfying as her first book." —Lesa's Book Critiques

continued ...

Murder at the PTA

"Alden has strong talent and a well-skilled use of language that brings the story alive and gives vitality to each character . . . an excellent start to a new cozy series."
— *Fresh Fiction*

"A terrific debut." — *AnnArbor.com*

"*Murder at the PTA* is well worth your time."
— *Mystery Scene*

Also Available from Laura Alden

Murder at the PTA
Foul Play at the PTA
Plotting at the PTA
Curse of the PTA

POISON at the PTA

Laura Alden

OBSIDIAN
Published by the Penguin Group
Penguin Group (USA) LLC, 375 Hudson Street,
New York, New York 10014

USA | Canada | UK | Ireland | Australia | New Zealand | India | South Africa | China
penguin.com
A Penguin Random House Company

First published by Obsidian, an imprint of New American Library,
a division of Penguin Group (USA)

First Printing, February 2014

ISBN 978-0-451-41507-3 5324 2789

Printed in the United States of America 1/14
10 9 8 7 6 5 4 3 2 1

For Jon.
Always.

Chapter 1

"Beth?" A firm hand gripped my elbow. "Are you all right?"

I was pretty sure the hand belonged to Lois Nielson, the sixtysomething manager of my children's bookstore. At least I hoped it belonged to her, because there wasn't another soul in the building.

My eyes had closed during my short spell of dizziness, but now I opened them and beheld a vision. Winter white pants, shoes, and socks. Winter white sweater with a snowflake pattern woven into the fabric. A slightly smushed black top hat. Long bright red scarf wrapped multiple times around a skinny neck, and, dangling in amidst the scarf ends, a piece of fraying twine from which hung a carrot.

Yes, it was Lois. Being one with the snowman season, she'd said when she'd waltzed in earlier that morning. My own black pants and maroon sweater looked almost boring in comparison. Not that I cared. As long as I could present my medium-height self and my medium brown hair in a way that didn't cause me to be an object of scorn and ridicule, I was a happy camper.

For a minute or two, I'd been relying on the support of the front counter to keep myself upright. I lifted one hand away. Slowly. Since I didn't see any black dots dancing around the edges of my vision, I lifted the other hand. Still no spots. *She's cured, Doctor! It's a miracle!*

"I'm fine," I said. "Just a little tired, that's all. We had a busy Christmas."

"Very," she said.

"Did I tell you it was our best season ever?"

"Once or twice."

I looked closely, checking for sarcasm, but couldn't see any floating around. It was there somewhere, but I disregarded it and talked on.

"Plus, here we are, in the second week of January, and the returns are way down." I was very proud of both those facts. Running a children's bookstore was not the most reliable way to earn a living, yet the Children's Bookshelf was living proof that it could be done, even here in small Rynwood, Wisconsin. The close proximity to the far larger city of Madison helped, of course, but in the main my customers were locals. And for now, at least, many of them liked to shop in my store.

"Yes, here we are, in the second week of January, and here you are—" Lois stopped abruptly. Opened her mouth, then closed it before any more words blurted out.

"Here I am what?"

"Nothing," she muttered, and stomped off toward the middle-grade books.

I took a step after her, because there was obviously something she wanted to say, but a glance at my watch made me change direction and head to my tiny office in the back of the store. If Lois wanted to tell me something, she'd tell me when she was ready. Right now there was a long To Do list waiting.

*   *   *

Yvonne poked her head into my office. "Beth, have you had lunch?"

I rubbed my hands over my face, turned away from the computer, and tried to focus on my employee. Surely she wasn't normally that blurry. I blinked hard a few times and her dark hair, brown eyes, and calm expression came into focus. "Not yet. I'll go out for something after you and Lois eat."

"We already did."

"You did?"

"An hour ago. It's almost two o'clock."

That explained the empty feeling in my stomach. I smiled. "Time flies when you're doing monthly projections. I'll run down to the Green Tractor in a minute."

Yvonne hesitated, then said, "I could call in an order for you. I could get it, too, if you want."

What I wanted was to finish the mountain of work in front of me. And the secondary mountain that waited for me at home. In addition to all the chores that a single mom had to tackle, I was also president of the local PTA. The Tarver Elementary PTA was turning eighty years old this month, and the scheduled festivities were next week. The muscles at the back of my neck went tight. How was I ever going to get everything done?

I turned back to the computer. "Thanks, Yvonne, but you don't need to do that."

"Really, I don't mind. It's almost nice out."

Which was an odd thing for her to say. Last I'd checked it was twenty-two degrees with a fierce wind. Yvonne was a native Californian, and while she loved snow, she didn't care at all for the cold. But I didn't have time to puzzle it out; the To Do list wasn't even half crossed off.

"Thanks, anyway," I said vaguely. "I'll go out as soon as I get this done."

"Eat this." A small plate slid across my desk and came to a rest between my shirt buttons and the keyboard. On it were a ham sandwich, a scoop of cottage cheese, and a small heap of broccoli.

I looked up, but Flossie Untermayer, former owner of the downtown grocery store and my most recent hire, was already out the door. Even at eighty-two, she could move faster than most adults. Part of that ability was due to her earlier career as a professional ballet dancer, part of that was due to her determination to be active until the day she died, and part of it was just the way she was made.

"Thanks," I called, and reached out for a piece of broccoli. Dear Flossie, I thought, then pushed the plate aside. I'd finish this one thing; then I'd eat.

"Hi, Mom." My twelve-year-old daughter, Jenna, dropped into the guest chair, which was surrounded by stacks of books destined for the sale table. "Did you do anything fun today?"

I looked up from the checking account I was trying to reconcile and pushed back from the computer. Jenna and my nine-year-old, Oliver, were the lights of my life, and I would always give them all the time in the world. "Didn't do one single thing that was fun. How about you?"

She shrugged. "Got an A-minus on my math test. My math teacher says I should talk to you about taking algebra next year."

"That's the accelerated program, isn't it?"

Another shrug, but my Mom Sense detected the pride

beneath her offhand demeanor. It also detected a small amount of anxiety, and I decided to let it go. Someday we'd have a talk about the valuable life skill of not worrying about the future. And we'd have that talk just as soon as I figured out how not to worry about the future.

"What's for supper?" Jenna asked.

An excellent question, and one for which I didn't have an answer. MAKE DINNER PLANS sat there on the To Do list, but like the entire bottom third of the list, it remained pristine and pure and uncrossed-off. Last night the kids had stayed with their father, my former husband, Richard, and dinner on Wednesday Nights with Dad was usually submarine sandwiches from the deli close to his condominium. It was tempting to order pizza, but I knew myself well enough to know that pizza was a lure to the edge of a slippery slope, one that I dared not approach without danger of fast regaining the twenty pounds I'd so laboriously lost last spring.

"How about eggplant casserole?" I suggested.

Jenna squinched her face. "Ick."

"Pea soup?"

"You hate pea soup."

I slapped my forehead. "How silly of me to forget." Over Jenna's giggle, I said, "On the other hand, all three of us like tacos."

She tipped her head to one side, considering. "Okay. Does that mean you want me to go to the grocery store for ground beef?"

"And here you thought walking here after school instead of going to Mrs. Neff's for day care was going to be nothing but fun and games."

"Not after the third time you sent me to the grocery store."

"Ah, but I also send you to the antiques store to get cookies."

"Cookies?" She jumped out of the chair. "Can I get cookies, too?"

"Tomorrow. Friday is cookie day, not Thursday."

"But I got an A-minus on my math test."

"And we'll celebrate tomorrow with a big pile of cookies. Life is about delayed gratification, my darling daughter. I wouldn't be doing my job as a mother if I didn't teach you that."

"Being a mom means not letting your kids get what they want?"

I beamed. "Exactly. Now be off with you. Do your homework. Then we'll see about a grocery run."

"Can I have a snack first?"

"Check in the kitchenette. I think there are some crackers in the cupboard."

"How about that?" She pointed at my desk. "I mean, if you don't want it."

"Oh." I looked at the plate Flossie had left me. I'd eaten the broccoli, none of the cottage cheese, and not quite half of the ham sandwich. "The cottage cheese has been sitting out too long, but the sandwich is all yours."

"Cool." She snatched it away and stuffed a corner in her mouth. "Thanks, Mom. You're all right, for a mom."

Smiling, I watched her walk off, her shiny brown hair bouncing. She'd be thirteen in June. Her legs were growing long and her waist was starting to narrow. Soon she'd want to . . .

I forced my thoughts away from their most favorite subject—my children—and went back to the checking account. A dollar and eighty-three cents had gotten tangled up and it was up to me to track it down. It was here, somewhere. All I had to do was find it.

"It's time."

Marina Neff—my best friend, my children's day care provider, my former neighbor, and the person who was always coming up with ways to improve me—marched into my office, her red hair flying hither and yon in the dry winter air.

"What are you doing here?" Both my left and right hands held invoices. My desk was covered with invoices. My keyboard was covered with invoices. One of my New Year's resolutions was to organize the invoices beyond the sheer urgency of due date. At the time it had seemed like a wonderful idea. Now I was pretty sure that resolutions were remarkably silly things to make. "Time for what?"

"For you to come with me." With her plump fingers, she tugged the papers out of my hands. I lunged to grab them back, but she held them out of my reach. "Nothing doing," she said. "It's closing time, Lois is locking the door, and we're going to talk to you."

I cocked my head. "For a store that's closed, there's a lot of noise out there." There was a rumble of voices, mostly female, but some male.

"Mom?" Jenna sidled into the room, her arms filled with the homework she usually did on the large workroom table. "Hi, Mrs. Neff. Mrs. Nielson told me to come in here."

"She did?" I pushed back from my desk. Something very odd was going on. "And did Mrs. Nielson tell you why?"

Jenna's gaze darted from me to Marina and back to me again. "Um, not really."

Hmm. "You can work here, Jenna." I stacked up the invoices willy-nilly, slid them into a folder, and gave Marina a hard look. "I am curious as to the whereabouts of my son."

"Uh-oh." Marina jabbed my daughter in the ribs. "She's going all formal, did you hear? 'As to the whereabouts.' You can tell when she's getting mad when she does that."

"I know," Jenna whispered, but her smile dimmed when I shot her a look.

"The question remains unanswered," I said. "An answer would be welcome."

"Your son is with my Devoted Husband. Now, come on, and don't be mad." Marina hooked her arm through mine and steered me out of the office and into the store. "Happy happy, right?"

The store's overhead lights were off, but the workroom's lights were on, bright and shiny. Marina towed me in that direction, talking nonstop. "The DH will feed your Oliver and my Zach some atrocious dinner. They're into 'all bacon, all the time' these days, and while not much tastes as good as bacon does"—she made noises of pseudogustatory pleasure—"the bacon love has gone a little too far, I think."

She babbled on, and I let her. The sooner we finished whatever it was she had planned, the sooner I'd get home and be able to start working on the household version of the day's To Do list.

". . . and so here we are." She all but pushed me through the door of the workroom. "Ten is a nice round number, yes? One big happy family and tonight is all about Beth, so no changing the subject."

I stopped cold. The large worktables had been collapsed and leaned up against the back wall. Ten chairs sat in a large circle, seven chairs occupied by people, one occupied by a laptop computer, two empty.

"Sit." Marina prodded me in the back.

I looked at the seven people. Lois. Yvonne. Ruthie, owner of my favorite diner, the Green Tractor. Summer Lang, the PTA vice president. Gus Eiseley, my good friend and the local police chief. Winnie, his wife. Pete Peterson, owner of a forensic cleaning service and the man I was dating. One by one, each of them met my straight gaze.

The only bookstore employees not present were Flossie and my part-time employee, Paoze, a University of Wisconsin senior. Though there was bound to be a reason they weren't there, I wasn't sure I wanted to know.

A movement on the laptop caught my eye and the Skyped image of my sister, Darlene, came into view. "Is she here yet?" her electronicized voice said.

"Just walked in," Lois said.

"Bet she's not happy." Darlene snorted. "Is she sitting down?"

"Not yet."

"Make her."

I folded my arms. "Not until I know what's going on."

"We need to talk to you," Summer said.

"I'm listening."

"No, you're not," Darlene said. "You're standing there with your arms crossed and a cranky look on your face and you're getting all stoked up. Next thing you're going to start talking like an English teacher who has never recognized e-mail as a real form of communication. Now sit, will you?"

Stubbornness set in. "Not until someone tells me what this is all about."

Pete stood and came over and took my hand. "Please, Beth. That's what this is all about, to talk to you."

I eyed him suspiciously. "Feels more like a kidnapping."

"You can leave if you want," he said, then kept talking over Marina's squeak of protest, "but please stay." The earnestness in his face was plain to see. "Please?"

"Please, Beth?" Ruthie asked.

"Yes," Winnie said. "Please stay."

"What about her?" I nodded at the computer. "Darlene, did you say please?"

A heavy sigh made the computer's speaker go all fuzzy. "Fine. Pleeeeeeease?"

Any victory over a sister, no matter how much I loved said sister, was a good one. "Yes. Thank you." Pete pulled out a chair, and I sat primly as Marina took the chair next to the laptop. "Okay, what's so important?" I asked. "Did I manage to win the lottery without ever buying a ticket?"

All eyes, even Darlene's, swiveled around to focus on Lois, who put her folded hands on her lap and started talking. "I began to be concerned . . . well, years ago, really, but more so since you became secretary of the PTA. It's even worse now that you're president."

Marina's shoulders hunched forward and she looked at the floor. "I'll take the blame for that. I'm the one who convinced you to be PTA secretary in the first place. I thought it would do you good to get out of the house."

"This isn't the time and place for blame," Gus said. "This is about what's best for Beth."

Ruthie stirred, her gray hair and lined face showing every one of her seventy-one years. "We're worried about you."

Yvonne looked at me apologetically. "We all are."

"It's getting scary," Summer said, "watching you. You're not eating, you're not getting outside, you've got these blue smudges under your eyes all the time, and when was the last time you did anything other than—"

"Wait a minute." I waved her to silence. "This is an intervention."

A large collective breath blew through the room.

"Exactly," Darlene said. "Anyone else would have known it the second you walked in the room. You really don't watch enough TV, kiddo."

I watched everything that was worthwhile, but this probably wasn't the time or place to start a *Downton Abbey* fan club. "Interventions are about addictions, and I'm not addicted to anything. I have maybe one glass of wine a week, I don't smoke, and I certainly don't do drugs. What on earth are you intervening about?"

Silence.

"Right." I hitched forward in the seat and stood. "Well, since there's clearly nothing wrong here, I have a lot to do tonight."

"Bingo!" Marina called.

I sat down hard and blinked at her. "Excuse me?"

"You have a lot to get done."

Of course I did. Dinner, laundry, a driveway to shovel, and there was a whole slew of details left dangling for next week's PTA in Review event. After the PTA had voted to hold an event to celebrate the group's eightieth anniversary, we'd eventually decided to have a summary done of each decade by someone who'd been there. Or as close as we could get. The kids would be with Richard this weekend, so maybe that's when I'd catch up—

"She's doing it now, isn't she?" Darlene asked.

"Doing what?" I asked.

But all the other heads in the circle were nodding. "You get this special look," Marina said, "when you're working on your mental To Do list."

"I do not."

"Oh, you do, too," Darlene said. "We all know it, so quit with the denial. You're as bad as Bill thinking Max was going to be a scientist. The kid's had English Teacher written all over him for years."

It had taken a combination of Darlene, me, our mother, and the passage of time to soothe the troubled waters at our physicist brother Bill's house when his son, Max, had announced his intention to attend a liberal arts college. Everything had worked out, eventually, but it had taken a long, long time.

"You're wearing yourself to a frazzle, hon." Winnie's hands gripped each other. "We don't want you so busy that you don't take care of yourself."

"And you're not," Marina said flatly. "You haven't in years and you're so darn preoccupied with saving the world you don't even eat right. What did you have for lunch today, anyway?"

"I had lunch." Sort of. I slumped down in the chair, wanting to pout and cross my arms, but settled for staring at the floor. "I'm busy. Everybody's busy. How can we not be? It's the way life is these days."

"Have you ever considered you're carrying it a bit too far?" Gus asked.

No, I hadn't. I was trying to be a good mother and a successful business owner, not to mention trying to steer the PTA in a constructive direction. Then there was church and church choir . . . The list went on and on, and there wasn't any way to make it shorter.

"You're tired," Ruthie said. "It's all through your bones. I can see it."

My bones straightened and my chin went up. "I could do with a little more sleep, sure, but who couldn't?"

"When was the last time you got eight hours of sleep in a row?" Gus asked.

"No working adult gets that much sleep," I said.

"Seven, then." He waited for my answer. "How about six?"

"When was the last time you did?" I challenged.

"Last night," he said calmly. "Winnie makes sure I get my beauty rest."

"And, boy, does he need it!" his loving wife said.

A laugh ran around the room, lowering the tension a small notch.

"You haven't looked rested since September," Yvonne said softly. "Ever since . . ."

I looked away. Ever since that dark September night I'd almost been killed. Ever since I'd been instrumental in catching a murderer but had had to endure the black feeling of betrayal. So many nights I'd woken, sweating, gasping with fear from how close Jenna and Oliver had come to growing up without their mother.

"Don't get sick on us, Beth," Lois said. "We can't do without you."

"Your children need you," Summer said.

"We need you," Marina said, her voice catching.

Pete kept quiet, but reached out and touched my arm.

It was his touch that did it. Dear Pete, who deserved so much more than I'd had time to give him. "All right," I said, deflating. "I'll make it a priority to get more rest."

"Oh, yeah?" Darlene asked, her sarcasm riding high. "Going to put that on one of your lists, are you?"

Marina, sitting next to the computer, flapped it shut with a bang. "We were hoping to help with your lists."

I frowned. "What do you mean?"

"We want you to take it easy," Lois said. "We're all going to pitch in a little."

I started to puff up again. I was doing fine, thanks so very much. I didn't need their charity. I could run my own life without their interference. This kind of help was help I could do without.

Pete took my hand in his and squeezed it gently. For a second time, my anger deflated. If I kept hanging around with him, I'd never be able to sustain a good mad. "How?" I asked cautiously.

"For one thing," Ruthie said briskly, "I can help with your dinner menu. Every night you leave the store, I'll put together a nice, healthy family meal. Jenna can run over and pick it up. All you have to do is put it on plates and Bob's your uncle."

I smiled at the old-fashioned expression. And a meal from Ruthie every night sounded like heaven, but . . . "I can't afford that." A dinner out every night? Not a chance.

"Won't cost you a dime," Ruthie said. "Jenna eats like a horse, but you don't take in enough to keep a bird alive, and Oliver doesn't eat much more than that. It's my contribution, hon, and I'm glad to do it."

Comprehension dawned. "Each of you has a contribution?"

"Sort of," Lois said.

Marina carefully opened the laptop again. "We're listing contributions," she whispered. "Now, be nice."

Darlene grinned. "Ready? What I'm going to do is keep Mom off your back about coming up for winter break."

"You . . . will?" I hated driving up to Mom's in February. Every time I did, there was a horrible snowstorm and the drive took twice as long as on dry roads and the tension left me exhausted for days. Mom didn't see it that way, of course; she just wanted to see the grandchildren.

"We're hiring extra help for the inventory," Lois said. "No arguing. It won't cost hardly anything, and I'll take care of it all."

"And I know the PTA in Review is your baby," Summer said, "but I have someone lined up to take over the legwork."

Winnie said she had plenty of time to stop by twice a week to help with my housework, Gus said he'd come over with his pickup and plow blade to take care of the driveway when it snowed, Marina said she'd pack lunches for the kids, and Pete said he'd help put away the Christmas decorations that still festooned the house and get my car's oil changed and the brakes fixed.

Tears stung at my eyes. I didn't deserve friends like this. "Okay, I admit I'm tired. Maybe I am trying to do too much. Do we have a time frame?" I asked. "A couple of weeks?" There was a lot of shifting in seats.

Gus quirked up a small smile. "Two months would be ideal."

"Two months!" Not a chance. "That's too long. I'm a little run-down, but two months is excessive. You guys are great to want to help me, but that's too much to ask."

Gus waved off everyone else's comments and concentrated on me. "What would you think is suitable? We've all committed to two months."

"Well, I really think one would be more than enough." Marina snorted. "Have you looked in the mirror lately? Those bags will take more than a month to go away."

"Fine," I almost snapped. "Six weeks. And not a day longer."

"Six weeks?" Marina hmm'd, looked at the ceiling, looked around the circle at the other faces, then nodded. "Deal."

Pete squeezed my hand, Gus clapped me on the shoulder, and Winnie tugged on my other hand and pulled me onto my feet for a hug. As she did, I watched Marina and Lois exchange a slapping high five.

I suddenly got the feeling that it might be a very long six weeks.

Chapter 2

That night Jenna and I went home with a pile of foam containers heavy with mashed potatoes, mixed vegetables, turkey and gravy, and a small paper bag of hot rolls. Marina's DH brought Oliver home and during our meal Jenna and Oliver told me that Mrs. Neff had told them that they needed to start taking better care of me.

I raised my eyebrows. "Oh, she did, did she?"

Oliver nodded, his eyes open wide with concern and his spoon filled with mashed potatoes. "Are you sick? When we're sick, you put us in bed and read to us and put cool cloths on our foreheads and bring us ice cream." He looked at his overflowing spoon. "I guess mashed potatoes are kind of like ice cream. Vanilla, anyway," he said uncertainly.

I laughed. "Don't worry. I'm not sick. I'm a little tired, that's all. You don't need to take care of me." I ruffled his hair. "I'm the mom. I take care of you, not the other way around."

"My friend Alexis said she makes dinner once a month at her house." Jenna stuck her knife into the butter dish and put a generous amount on a roll. "Maybe that's something I should be doing?"

I blanched. The few times I'd tried to give Jenna cooking lessons, the results hadn't been what anyone might call outstanding. It was one thing to worry down an overcooked biscuit, but a whole meal? "That's a lovely idea, honey, and maybe someday we'll do that, but Mrs. Ruthie is taking care of meals for us."

So that was another thing to add to my To Do list: teach Jenna how to cook. It wouldn't do to send her off to college without knowing how to fend for herself. She was already doing her own hockey laundry, and I had plans to teach her simple mending tasks. I added these to my mental list, then sighed and erased them. No list making was one of the requirements for the next six weeks.

With dinner coming to us already cooked, cleanup was a short task. In no time at all the dishes were washed, dried, and put away. It was barely six o'clock and the rest of the evening stretched out ahead with glorious emptiness. Smiling, I started a load of laundry. Doing a couple of loads of clothes hardly counted as work, not with dinner so easy. It felt good, not having the weight of a thousand chores on my head. My friends were right: I did need a rest and—

"It's my turn!" Oliver yelled.

"It is not," Jenna shouted.

"Is, too!"

"Is not!"

Before the litany transmogrified into a physical attack, I marched into the family room. "What are you two fighting about?"

"She's using the computer!" Oliver stood in front of his sister, rage showing in his wide stance and balled fists. "It's my turn!"

"But, Mom," Jenna said, turning to me, "we only take

turns when it's for playing. I need to use the computer to look up stuff for my homework. That doesn't count as a turn, right?" Papers and books were spread across the coffee table as she sat comfortably on the couch with the computer on her lap.

From the minute my former husband proposed buying a laptop for the kids for Christmas, I'd known this moment was coming. Richard had chuckled when I'd pointed out the problem of two kids and one shiny new toy. "Why on earth would they fight over using the computer? I'll make sure the parental controls are installed — that's the important thing. Don't worry so much."

Technology was a wonderful thing. Sometimes.

I looked from one flush-faced child to the other. "If you can't learn to share the computer, you know what's going to happen."

"You'll take it away," they said in unison.

Jenna kept going. "I have to use it for my science project. He just wants to play."

"Why can't she use the computer in the study for her homework?" Oliver asked.

"Why can't he use the computer in the study to play?" Jenna countered.

I made a T with my hands. "Homework is more important than playing," I said, and Jenna smiled. "But since homework is so important" — I picked up the remote and turned off the television — "you shouldn't let TV interfere with your concentration."

"But, Mom —"

"No 'buts,'" I said. "Oliver, I know you have math homework. Go upstairs and take care of it."

"Alexis gets to use her computer in her room," Jenna said.

Hooray for Alexis. "And you don't, do you?" My calm gaze locked on hers, and she soon blinked, turning away.

"No," she muttered. "I have to use the computer where you can see what I'm doing and make sure I'm not sneaking off into some social networking site and making friends with people who could be bad guys."

It was for their own protection—they were too young to have to know that mistakes made now could last forever—but I didn't expect them to understand for a few years. Like maybe twenty. "Exactly." I looked at my son. "Did you have something to say, Oliver?"

"Just that . . . that . . . it's not *fair!*" He stomped off up the stairs, each small foot thudding down on the oak risers with all the force he could muster.

I sighed and went back to the nice, quiet laundry that had no interest in computers. Not even the socks.

The next morning, Lois had just served me a second cup of tea when Mary Margaret Spezza bustled in.

"Give it over," she barked, "and no one will get hurt." She held out her hand.

Mary Margaret and her husband, Lou, owned a fellow downtown business. Made in the Midwest had opened strong last summer and had had the typical fall lull, but then it had caught the eye of a Chicago magazine and been featured in an article in their December issue.

All the downtown merchants had benefited from the ensuing uptick in the tourist trade, and I wasn't alone in having a greatly expanded e-mail list. Hopes were running high for a good year of retail, and much of it was due to the energy of the fiftyish woman standing in front of me. Her black curly hair was as unruly as ever, and her stout body looked as if it could stand up to a category-five hurricane.

"Give it over?" I asked. "Okay, sure. Here." I tried to give her my tea mug, but she ignored the offer and settled into the guest chair.

"Your To Do list for the PTA in Review. We know you have one, so hand it over."

I stared at her. "You're the one Summer recruited?"

Her smile was wide. "You bet. Business is slow at the store. Lou's happy enough putzing around, doing inventory, but that tiddly stuff drives me nuts. He'll get along faster without me, God's honest truth, and I'm glad to help."

When I'd discovered that the Spezzas' daughter and family would be moving to Rynwood next summer, I'd mentioned the local PTA and Mary Margaret had practically begged to become a member. Since it wasn't the Tarver PTA's policy to turn down any member—if you could breathe, attend meetings, and pull some committee duty, you were a keeper—Mary Margaret had instantly become an integral part of the group. Some rumbled that she was a little too enthusiastic, but I'd rumbled right back that enthusiasm was better than apathy, and the rumblings had faded away.

Now I dug around on the desk for the PTA in Review folder. Since it was bright red it wasn't hard to find, but I flailed about anyway, making pointless motions whose only purpose was to give me time.

Finally, I couldn't put it off any longer. I pulled the folder from where I'd known it was all along, right underneath Rick Riordan's new book, and held it out to Mary Margaret, who took it with alacrity.

"You're sure you want to do this?" I asked.

"Can't wait to get going," she said, paging through my notes. "You've made a great start."

A start? Everything was almost done. Representative speakers for each of the decades had been chosen, time limits had been given, e-mail invitations had gone out, Tarver's gymnasium was reserved, and the refreshments had been chosen.

"You don't have anything about decorations," Mary Margaret said.

"Well, no." I frowned. Who needed decorations for an event like this?

"Hmm. Leave it to me." Mary Margaret slapped the folder shut. "I'll take care of everything. Any phone call you get about the event, just send it on, okay?"

There was an abyss to my left, a deep and dark one that I could easily step into, one that would let me drown in self-pity and let me feel useless and incompetent and—

Voices broke into my attack of self-pity.

"You don't know everything, Lois Nielson, and I'm not afraid to say so."

"Yeah, well, you don't scare me, Flossie Untermayer. Just because you lived in fancy-pants Chicago for all those years doesn't mean you know everything, either."

I jumped out of my chair and hurried out of my office. Flossie and Lois were fighting? Not once had I ever heard Flossie raise her voice. Lois, sure, but not Flossie.

"What is going on out here?" I called. The two women were toe-to-toe in the Young Adult section, both with their hands on their hips, jaws jutting. At the sound of my voice, both instantly relaxed into a friendly pose.

"Why, nothing, dear Beth," Flossie said, a smile in her voice.

Lois laughed. "Just a friendly discussion."

I narrowed my eyes. "Didn't sound very friendly."

"Well." Lois laughed again. "You know how we book-sellers can get when we talk about books."

"Is that so?" I leaned against the early reader nonfiction. "What books were you discussing?"

Flossie said, "Those graphic novels she's always going on about."

Lois's head bobbed rapidly. "That's right. I've finally gotten her to appreciate that they're more than just comic books."

Flossie looked as if she'd bitten a toad. "I said I *might* appreciate it."

"Whatever." Lois waved a hand. "That's a lot closer than you've ever been before."

I didn't believe a word of their story, but it was obviously the one they were sticking to. "Well," I said, "if you're going to argue like that again, take it outside, okay? I don't like it when the books hear us shout at each other."

While what I'd said was fanciful, there was some truth involved and we all knew it. I patted a shelf of dinosaur books—"There, there, it's all over now"—and went back to work.

That was Friday, the start of a weekend that the kids spent with their father. It was a makeup weekend, so to speak, because of a weekend in November that Richard had been out of town helping his parents move to an assisted living facility. Easy enough to switch weekends, for a reason like that. Friday night, Marina and I ordered out pizza and watched James Bond movies. So Friday was a good day. Saturday, not so much.

Saturday morning started off with Claudia Wolff thumping her snowy feet into the store. "Wow, it's getting cold out there. Global warming is a bunch of hooey, I tell you what." She gave one more thump, then looked about with a frown as she pushed her frizzy hair behind her ears. "Where's all the Christmas stuff? Don't tell me it's gone already."

I smiled politely at my fellow PTA board member. The vice president, to be exact. "Sorry, Claudia, but we got rid of the last Christmas item a week ago.

"It's barely January!"

It was almost the middle of January, but I wasn't going to quibble with Claudia. She and I had never seen eye to eye on much of anything, and since none of my New Year's resolutions mentioned Claudia, I didn't anticipate that fact changing anytime soon.

"I've talked to that Mary Margaret of yours," she went on, unzipping her coat and revealing hips that had put on more than their fair share of holiday pounds. "Quite the go-getter, isn't she?"

I made a noncommittal nod. Mary Margaret had called multiple times already, clarifying and questioning.

"But it sounds like she's really charging ahead with these plans. It's all going perfectly smooth, from what I hear." Claudia flashed me a full-wattage smile. "It's almost like you're not needed at all." She laughed, tootled a wave, and left.

"Was that Mrs. Wolff?" Paoze asked. Brown-skinned and brown-eyed with impossibly white teeth, Paoze had been born in Laos and moved to the United States with his parents when he was still a young pup. Now he was an English major with the goal of writing his people's history. The original intent had been to write his family's history, but somehow the manuscript was expanding to be a Michener-length epic, and I wasn't sure when he'd be able to stop.

"Yes," I said, "that was Mrs. Wolff."

He looked at the snow she'd left on the carpet, and, since his mother had clearly taught him that if you couldn't say anything nice you shouldn't say it at all, he kept quiet. Instead, he asked, "Have you chosen a code?"

One of the results of the previous September was my vow to get a store security system. Gus had recommended a local company, and by the middle of October, the electronic system was in place. The installer had gravely walked me through the steps of arming and disarming the system, and who to call if anyone accidentally set it off.

"Here's the code," he'd said, handing me a piece of paper with four numbers. "You should change it today. And please, please don't write the new code into instructions you post by the back door. You wouldn't believe how many people do that. Sure, it's easier, but you might as well hand a car thief your car keys."

I'd taken his words to heart and drilled my staff until we could all run the system without a second thought. Then, after reading up on security issues, I went a step further. It was easy enough to find an Internet application for a random number generator, and almost as easy to change the code once a week on random days. There was a small amount of Lois-led grumbling at the annoyance, but I was firm and we'd soon become accustomed to learning a new set of four numbers once a week.

After getting the new code to Paoze, I wandered around the store, straightening books and checking book alphabetization. It was Saturday. Two days since the intervention. Two nights in a row that I hadn't had to cook. Winnie had vacuumed my house on Friday and washed the kitchen floor. Mary Margaret had taken away anything I needed to do for next week's PTA in Review. The kids were with Richard this weekend. I felt rested and relaxed and ready to tackle the world.

Two days had been enough and it was time to release me from that silly promise. Six weeks? Please.

As soon as I flipped the store's OPEN sign to CLOSED, I moved into high gear. There wasn't much time. I shooed Paoze and Yvonne out the door, rushed through tallying the cash register, gave a cursory glance to the status of the store, pulled on boots and hat, set the store alarm, and left.

I parked in Marina's driveway. Made it! Marina's DH and youngest son, Zach, had made a new habit of bowling on Saturday afternoons, and they hadn't returned. I knocked on Marina's kitchen door and walked in.

"It's me," I announced to Marina, who was sitting at the kitchen table. I stood on the mat just inside the door and leaned down to pull off my boots. "It's been two days and I have to say thanks because I feel much better but it's been two days and I feel great, so can we call off the intervention dogs?" Boots off, I stood up straight. "So now let me get back to . . ." I stopped.

There had been signs that something was off, but I'd been full of myself and hadn't been paying attention. Marina hadn't greeted me, hadn't said anything, hadn't even waved. She was sniffling, and her head was down on the kitchen table, her right hand clutching the cordless phone to the point of white knuckledom.

I sat in a chair next to her and took the phone from her

hand. Phones. I'd never really liked them. Book covers, at least, gave you a clue to their contents. When a phone rang, you never knew if it would be good news or bad.

"What's wrong?" I asked softly. The cowardly part of me, the biggest part, didn't want to know. I'd never seen her like this. Whatever it was, it had to be bad. "Is it Zach? The DH?" Bowling accident, car crash, random kidnappings . . . my thoughts flashed on all sorts of horrible possibilities. "One of the older kids? Are they okay?" Zach had been a surprise baby; he had three older siblings in various stages of college and postcollege activities.

Marina grabbed my hand. "Fine," she said through her sobs. "They're fine."

Okay, her immediate family was fine. "And the rest of your family?"

"What?" She sat up and pushed at her face with the heels of her hands. "Everyone's fine. What makes you think there's anything wrong?" A grimace of a smile appeared on her face.

I pulled a small package of tissues from my coat pocket, drew one out, and handed it to her. "Because you're sitting here at the kitchen table with the phone in your hand, crying your heart out."

She honked her nose into the tissue. "Do you have another one?" Wordlessly, I handed her a fresh piece. Another honk, another tissue to dry her eyes; then she said, "On the phone just now, it was a wrong number."

"A wrong number," I said slowly.

"Sure." She dabbed at her eyes. "And it made me sad. All those people out there calling numbers that are wrong, and who knows if they'll ever reach the person they really want to talk to?"

It was making me a little sad, too, but I wasn't bawling my head off over it. "And that's what made your eyes so red?"

She squinched them shut, then opened them again. "I needed a good cry. Haven't had one in a while."

I studied her. She was lying. "You're sure that's all it was?"

Her smile was a horrible fake. "Why would I lie? Now, what was it you wanted? Oh, yes. You want off your six weeks of taking it easy. No way. I don't care how good you feel, you agreed to six weeks and that's what you're going to get."

She talked on, but I was still considering the question that she herself had posed: why would she lie?

I didn't know, but Marina was my best friend. Something was troubling her, and I was going to find out what.

That evening, Pete stood in the doorway, holding out a bouquet of brightly colored daisies. "For you," he said.

"They're beautiful!" I took the flowers and ushered him in out of the cold. "What's the occasion?" In the few months we'd been seeing each other, Pete had brought us pizza, an amazing knowledge of card games, and a laugh that warmed us all, but never once had he brought flowers.

He grinned. "Figured they'd help if you were mad about the other day."

The other day ... ah. "The intervention, you mean? Not mad, exactly," I said, thinking through my emotions of the last two days. "Disconcerted, sure. Unsettled. Thrown off balance. Flustered, even. But I don't think I'm mad."

"Well, good." He held out his arms and I went into

them gladly. "We're just trying to help," he said. "You know that, right?"

Into his shoulder, I said, "Yes, and I appreciate it." But that seemed incomplete, and therefore not totally honest, so I added one more word. "Mostly."

Pete laughed. "I can imagine." He gave me a hard squeeze, then released me. "You see the upside, though, don't you?"

"Well, not cooking is okay. And Winnie's promise to do some of the heavier cleaning is a huge bonus."

He was shaking his head. "That's all good, but the best thing is you get to be guilt-free for six weeks. If we're not letting you do anything except what you have to, there's no need to feel guilty about not doing everything else." He smiled, obviously proud of his reasoning.

I wanted to pat him on the head. Such a nice man, yet so clueless about women. "Let me get these flowers in some water," I said, kissing him on the cheek. "Come on back to the kitchen and we can talk about what we're going to do tonight."

"What do you say to dinner at Ian's Place, then an eight o'clock showtime?" He reached into his inside coat pocket and pulled out two tickets. "A client gave them to me: two seats for that traveling Broadway show you've been talking about. It's in Madison for a couple weeks, I guess."

My eyes went wide. "You have tickets for *Wicked*?"

He squinted at the small printing. "Yeah, that's it. This, uh, is okay with you, right? I mean, if you're tired we don't have to use them. We can stay in and order out—"

I flung my arms around his neck. "Pete Peterson, you are the most wonderful man in the entire world!" A meal at Rynwood's newest restaurant and a show I'd been wanting to see for years—maybe this intervention thing wasn't so bad after all.

The only cloud on the horizon was Marina and the phone call that had spurred her to tears. Tomorrow. I'd work on that tomorrow.

Chapter 3

But by Wednesday, the night of the PTA in Review, I was no closer to finding out what Marina's phone call had been about than I'd been on Saturday afternoon. Up until now, her life had been an open book to me. If anything, I knew more than I really needed to about her hot flashes and digestive issues. This, however, was different.

"It was a wrong number," she said again as we walked into the school. "How many times are you going to ask me? Because it's been about a hundred times already."

Until you tell me the truth, I thought. Then I decided what the heck? and said it out loud. "Until you tell me the truth."

"Well, it's getting a little old." Her voice was tight. "If I was going to say anything different, I would have said it already, okay?" She hurried ahead of me, waving at a couple down the hall. "Hey, Carol. Nick. Cold enough for you out there?"

I stared after her, troubled.

"There you are!" Mary Margaret seized my arm. "Let me show you what we've done." Her eyes sparkled with excitement as we neared the entrance to the gymnasium.

"You're going to love it. I just know you are."

I hated it when people said that. It inevitably resulted

in me disliking or being ambivalent about whatever it was, and, knowing that I was expected to like it, I would have to be very careful with my reactions.

We stepped into the gym and my mouth actually dropped open.

"Pretty good, eh?" Mary Margaret jabbed me lightly in the ribs.

"This is . . . fabulous." My wondering gaze drifted from the small trees in large pots flanking the stage, small white lights strung through the branches, to the vases of flowers lining the front of the stage, to the twig wreaths twined with white lights hanging on the walls, to the array of ferns in the back corners by the open window to the kitchen.

The decorations transformed the room from a slightly dumpy and decades-old elementary school gym to a show hall. It was gorgeous. For fifteen seconds, I appreciated the transformation. Then the left side of my brain kicked into gear. "How much—"

"Did it cost?" Mary Margaret chuckled. "Not one thin dime. The flowers up there were all headed for the trash at Faye's Flowers. I offered to take them off her hands, and by golly, she ended up letting us borrow those trees and the ferns, too. The wreaths are from our store; we had them up at Christmas. I just stripped them down, tossed some lights on them, and shazam!" She smiled proudly.

"You've done a marvelous job," I said, giving her a quick hug. Decorating the gym for this event had never occurred to me. And how she'd convinced the cranky Faye of Faye's Flowers to do anything for the PTA was a minor miracle.

"Aw, it was nothing," Mary Margaret said, blushing.

"Maybe it was nothing for you, but I never could have done it," I told her honestly. "Have you ever thought about running for the PTA presidency?"

Grinning, she made a cross of her index fingers and backed away. "I'm a worker bee, not a policy person. You take that back right now."

I was a policy person? What an odd thought. I'd never imagined myself as anything but a slightly inept forty-two-year-old woman trying to bumble her way through life with as few mistakes as possible. Funny, what other people thought about you.

"We're open for business!" called a voice from the kitchen. Immediately, the twenty or so people in the gym moved en masse to the back of the room.

I frowned. "Refreshments beforehand?"

"Yeah," Mary Margaret said. "We talked about it the other day at our last committee meeting. I figured what the heck, let's try it and see what happens."

"Try what?" I asked cautiously.

"See that?" She pointed to the end of the long counter that lined the opening to the kitchen. "A money jar."

"You're charging for refreshments?"

"Ah, don't look so horrified." She grinned. "We're asking for donations, is all. We made a few extra goodies and we're having tea and lemonade, plus the regular coffee. And we're going to have a short break between every decade where people can get more stuff. Maybe we'll make a few bucks, eh?"

It would also make for a very long evening. But it never hurt to try new methods of making money. And, anyway, if people drank a lot of coffee now, they'd need the breaks to hit the restroom.

The chairs in the gym were slowly filling up. In the

crowd were current PTA members, past PTA members, a few Tarver teachers, the new vice principal, and some people who, as far as I knew, had no connection to the PTA whatsoever. Alan Barnhart, for instance, was a retired teacher, but not from Tarver. He did, however, own the antiques mall downtown, so perhaps it was a sense of history that drew him here.

At ten to seven, Isabel Olsen, a member of the event committee, encouraged me to take my place on the stage. "If we get everybody up there and ready beforehand," she said, "maybe we can start this on time."

I climbed the stairs to the stage and joined the other presenters. May Werner, known to all as Auntie May, was ninety-two years old and the terror of Rynwood. Her most potent weapon was her rock-solid memory of every embarrassing incident in every Rynwood resident's life.

Even more terrifying was that her favorite thing in life was to catch people lying. It was the very real possibility of hearing Auntie May's cackle of "Liar, liar, pants on fire!" that had kept falsehoods in the entire town to a minimum for decades.

It hadn't been an easy decision to call Sunny Rest Assisted Living and ask Auntie May if she'd talk about the first two decades of the Tarver PTA, but, really, there wasn't anyone else. Auntie May might be ninety-two, but her mind was sharper than mine.

Two PTA fathers, Todd Wietzel and Kirk Olsen, had carried the bird-light woman and her bright purple wheelchair up onto the stage and she was now circling around the other presenters like a border collie rounding up cattle. "Almost time, chicks. Look at that crowd!" she crowed. "I haven't had that big an audience since I got up in church at Raymond Pratley's funeral."

"Who's Ray Pratley?" Erica Hale asked. Erica had been the PTA president before me. I knew I could never measure up to what she'd done during her tenure, but she reassured me I was doing just fine.

Auntie May snorted. "Some good-for-nothing lawyer. He was my cousin, died young from not enough fun, if you ask me. He was okay when he was a kid, though." She smirked. "Want to know what he did under the bleachers with Dolly Duncan in eleventh grade?"

"No," the rest of us said.

But I had the crawly feeling that Auntie May had told that story at her cousin's funeral. If she'd done that in a church, what was she going to say tonight? Frantically, I tried to think of a reason to call Todd and Kirk and haul her bodily off the stage. Could I pretend she was sick? Say she'd had a fainting spell? Fake an emergency phone call for her?

"Beth?" Isabel was at my side, a clipboard in her hand. "It's time to start."

I approached the podium, tapped the microphone to make sure it was on, and started. Not so very long ago, I wouldn't have dared to stand in front of a large audience without a word-by-word script to read verbatim. Today, I was fine just winging it. Who would have guessed?

"Good evening," I said. "If you're here for the seminar on analytical auditing procedures, you're in the wrong room." Smiling, I waited for the chuckles to die down. "We're here tonight to celebrate the eighty years of the Tarver PTA's existence. Eighty years, folks. There's been a PTA in this elementary school for eighty straight years."

There was a smattering of applause, and I nodded. "It is something to applaud and I'd like to salute all those who came before us." I turned and looked at the group of women sitting to my left and clapped my hands hard and loud. The audience joined in. Then, in what felt like a single surge, they all got to their feet, giving these women the recognition they deserved.

I sniffled back some unexpected tears and turned back to the podium as the audience sat back down. "Sadly," I said, "we don't have anyone who can talk to us about the Tarver PTA's first decade, but we do have a Rynwood resident who knew women from that first decade. The same woman was a PTA member in its second decade, from the end of World War Two to the boom years when Rynwood almost doubled in size. Ladies and gentlemen, please welcome Auntie May Werner."

The audience clapped politely as Auntie May wheeled herself to the podium. I handed her the microphone, sat down, and thought positive thoughts. There was no reason to think Auntie May would spend her allotted twenty minutes—ten minutes per decade—dredging up ancient gossip. I'd told her to stick to PTA agenda items and she'd agreed easily enough. She had no reason to slide sideways from straightforward history to sixty-year-old scandal.

Did she?

"Thanks, Bethie," Auntie May said. "You're a sweetie for inviting me. Lots of people wouldn't, you know. But just because I'm old don't mean I don't remember things."

I tensed. Not the story about catching Flossie's younger sister running around without any clothes on—please, not that. She'd been all of four years old, and it had been ninety degrees; who could blame her? But the poor woman was still carrying that story around with her.

"Like when the first Tarver PTA came about," Auntie May went on. "My momma's friend, Ethel, she'd moved here from out east and brought with her this idea about a group of parents getting together and trying to help the teachers."

Perfect. I relaxed. This would be fine. At last, Auntie May's prodigious memory was being put to productive use. Long may it reign.

We listened to Auntie May's tale of the first bake sale. "Made all of two dollars and thirteen cents and they were happy to get that much." Listened to her heartbreaking stories of children losing fathers to the war and the PTA doing what they could to help, and her account of the PTA's growing pains.

I glanced at the clock on the gym wall. She was right at the twenty-minute mark, but it sounded as though she was wrapping it up.

"And that's how that second PTA decade ended," Auntie May said. "Not only had Rynwood doubled in size, but Tarver had nearly tripled."

Assuming she was done, I started to stand so I could introduce the next speaker.

"Which reminds me of a story." Auntie May cackled, a high, scratchy noise that was nearly inaudible to the human ear. "Did I ever tell any of you about the time Walter Trommler was seeing three girls at the same time? It turns out that — "

I snatched the microphone from her hand. "Thanks for your memories, Auntie May." Smiling grimly, I gave her wheelchair a gentle push with my free hand. I had no great love for my former employee Marcia Trommler, but she didn't deserve to have stories about her father running all over town. Light applause followed a glowering Auntie May back to her place at the end of the row.

"We'll take a short break," I said, "and ten minutes

from now, we'll have the great pleasure of hearing
Maude Hoffman talk to us about the PTA's third decade." I clicked off the microphone and immediately entered a staring contest with Auntie May. My chin was up
and hers was down, which made the angle difficult, but
we were managing nicely.

Mary Margaret saved us from staying frozen like that
forever. "Nice job, Auntie May," she said, leaning on the
edge of the stage. "I'd love to hear that story about Walter Trommler. What say I stop by your place tomorrow
and hear all about it?"

Auntie May sent me a dagger-laden look. "At least
some people appreciate my stories."

Pick your battles, I told myself, and escaped.

The rest of the speakers didn't present any problems. We
laughed at Maude's anecdotes about fallen angel food
cakes and were moved to tears at her story of the entire
student body singing "My Country 'Tis of Thee" to a
packed gymnasium—the very room we were in—the
Monday after JFK's assassination.

A woman I didn't know spoke about the PTA during
the end of the civil rights movement and the Vietnam
War. I tried to listen while Cookie Van Doorne, a long-
time teller at the local bank, talked about the late seventies and the early eighties, but I spent more time
wondering why Cookie and I had never progressed beyond the acquaintance stage. Though I'd known her via
the bank for almost twenty years, I knew nothing about
her, besides the bare bones of widowed with two children moved out of state. Well, that and the fact that she
was rarely more than five feet from a cup of coffee,
morning, noon or night.

While I pondered the chemistry that makes up a friendship, other women described the PTA through to the twenty-first century. The always-elegant Erica Hale spoke about the most recent decade, and then it was my turn again.

I named each of the speakers, thanking them one by one. Auntie May grinned and waved, Maude Hoffman blushed prettily, Erica looked as regal as ever . . . but Cookie looked pale and unsteady.

I'd planned on talking about the projects the next eighty years might bring, but I skipped that and finished with "And I can only hope that the next eighty years of the Tarver PTA will be as productive as the last. Thank you and good night."

The applause was enthusiastic. I nodded, smiling, then went to Cookie's side. I crouched in front of her. "Are you all right?" I asked softly.

"No." She closed her eyes and swayed in her chair. "I really don't think I am. Beth, could you take me home, please?"

When I said I was driving Cookie home, one of the PTA fathers said he'd drive Cookie's car to her house and leave it in the driveway. Kirk Olsen offered to pick him up. "Got a hot new ride to show you," he said, grinning. "Nothing like heated leather seats this time of year."

Cookie gave a wan thank-you and I helped her into my car.

"I'm sure I'm just coming down with a little something," she said. "I thought a few cups of decaf would help, but they didn't seem to."

Light from the dashboard let me see Cookie push at her shortish gray hair, then see her thin hand fall to her lap. "It's that time of year," I said. If you can't make interesting conversation, that's no reason not to make inane remarks. "There's a flu thing going around." There always was, if you looked hard enough.

"Yes, I've heard that." Cookie sighed and I felt, more than saw, her relax into a slouch. Which was unusual since Cookie had been raised in the era of good posture makes for good girls. "I'm sure that's it."

Since I couldn't think of anything else to say, I kept quiet and reflected that this was always the case regarding conversations with Cookie. Once she'd finished whatever banking transaction I'd slid over to her, we had nothing left to say. She didn't read, didn't follow sports, not even the Green Bay Packers, didn't attend church, didn't garden. I wasn't sure what she did in her spare time. Maybe she cooked. Or knitted.

I was busy envisioning every shelf in Cookie's house crowded with adorable knitted animals when she said, "Beth, I've been meaning to talk to you for some time."

"You . . . have?" I tried to the keep the surprise out of my voice, but I was pretty sure I hadn't done a very good job.

"It's all those murders you've solved."

I stifled a sigh. For a number of odd reasons, I'd made contributions to tracking down a number of killers, and each time I'd vowed it would never happen again. Too dangerous and too stupid. That's why we had law enforcement. They hadn't needed my help then and they wouldn't in the future.

What Cookie probably wanted to know was one of three questions people typically asked me about those experiences. One: had I been scared? Absolutely. Two: what did a dead person look like? Sorry, but that's something I try not to remember. Three: were they going to make a movie about my life? Not a chance. But if they did, I'd like Sandra Bullock to play me.

"Don't you think," Cookie went on, "that the punishment doesn't always match the crime?"

"Excuse me?"

"I mean, if someone kills someone, premeditated, in cold blood, shouldn't they be killed, too? Isn't that the fair thing?"

"Um . . ." Getting into an argument about capital punishment was not high on my list of things to do with good friends and relatives, let alone with someone I barely knew.

"I know life isn't fair," she went on, "but shouldn't we be trying to make sure life is as fair as we can make it?"

"That's a good point," I said, trying to find a comfortable fence to sit on. "My children are always telling me what's fair and what isn't."

"Yes, I knew you'd agree," she said with satisfaction.

I hadn't, not exactly. Not at all, in fact, but since there is a strong tendency among humans to believe what they want to believe, I decided not to fight this particular battle. Skirmish. Whatever it was.

"I'm glad we had this talk, Beth," Cookie said. "My mind is at ease now, truly."

Fever, I figured. She was probably running a slight temperature and it was steering her to say things that didn't make a lot of sense. "We'll get you home in a jiffy," I told her. "Do you need anything? Aspirin?"

"Don't you worry about me," she said. "I have everything I need."

Soon, we pulled into her driveway. I steadied her as we tromped through the thin snow to the back door, asked if she needed me to help her to bed, was told no, waited until the kitchen light went on, and went back to my warm car.

I drove home and didn't even once worry about Cookie.

The next morning I was in the store kitchenette making the first crucial decision of the day—Earl Grey or Irish Breakfast Blend—when the phone rang. Lois snatched it up before I even turned my head.

"Good morning, Children's Bookshelf . . . Yes, she is. One moment please." After a short pause came her call. "Yo, Beth! It's for you."

I abandoned the tea choices and picked up my office phone. "Good morning. This is Beth."

"Oh, Beth," said the faint female voice. "I'm so glad I got hold of you."

It took me a moment to place the voice. "Cookie?" I frowned and sat down. "You sound awful. Don't tell me you went to work today."

"No, no . . ." There was a loud swallow. "I have a horrible upset stomach, and I'm so afraid that I have . . ." Another swallow. "Food poisoning."

"Oh, that's too bad," I said sympathetically. "And food poisoning can be dangerous. Make sure you get enough fluids and . . ." The reason that Cookie Van Doorne was calling me about her health sank in. "Are you saying you think you ate something last night that made you sick?" My mental mom manual was telling me that it usually took twenty-four hours for the nasty effects of food poisoning to make themselves known, but "usually" isn't "always."

"I'm not sure," she said, "but I thought you should know."

"Yes. Thank you. I'll starting making calls right away and—" But I was talking to empty air. Cookie had hung up the phone.

Hoping that Cookie was wrong about the food poisoning, and hoping—selfishly—that if she did have food poisoning, it wasn't because of anything she ate at the PTA event, I dialed a phone number I'd only recently memorized.

"Mary Margaret? It's Beth. We might have a problem."

Mary Margaret told me she'd take care of all the phone calls that suddenly had to be made. "I know just what to do, so don't you worry about a thing. Say, how do you feel?"

In my worry about sickening half of Rynwood, I hadn't once considered that I myself might get sick. "Fine. How about you?"

"Healthy as a horse. Let's hope I stay that way, eh?"

For a long, long time.

The phone tree that Mary Margaret quickly set up worked like a charm. Within a few hours, everyone who'd been at last night's event had been contacted. Some people had been contacted more than once, but better too often than not at all, Mary Margaret reported, and I agreed.

"And now we wait," she said. "I told all my callers to have anyone who got sick call me. That way we can track what's going on."

"Let me know if anyone calls," I told her. "Morning, noon, or night."

"You bet. Now, don't worry, okay? It'll be fine."

We hung up. "Don't worry," I muttered. "I can't believe she said not to worry."

*   *   *

I spent the rest of the day and evening waiting for a
phone call from Mary Margaret. All through dinner, no
phone call. All through evening chores and dog walking,
no phone call. Through bedtime, no phone call. Twice, I
started to pick up the phone to call her but stopped.
She'd said she'd call if she heard anything, and she
would.

The next morning I waited and worried some more.
To alleviate some of that worry, I called Cookie. She
sounded almost like her normal self and thought she'd
be back to work in a day or two. "Must have been one of
those stomach viruses," she said. "Thanks for all you did,
Beth. It meant a lot to me."

"It was nothing," I said, a little itchy at her gratitude.
"Just get better, okay?"

At lunchtime, I couldn't take it any longer and picked
up the phone.

"Hey, Beth," Mary Margaret said. "The only calls we
got were a kid with a sore throat who wasn't even there.
Oh, and Randy Jarvis twisted his knee out shoveling snow."

I heaved a huge sigh of relief. "And I called Cookie a
little bit ago. She said she's feeling much better."

"False alarm, then," Mary Margaret said cheerily.
"Well, all's well that ends well, right?"

"Right," I said. Sometimes things really did work out.

But a few days later Glenn Kettunen stopped by the
store ready to share the unwelcome news. "Say, did you
hear about Cookie? She's in the hospital."

Less than half an hour later, I was in Cookie's room,
accepting her thanks for the flowers I'd brought.

"How sweet," she said weakly, watching as I arranged

the bouquet. "I've never been one for wasting money on fresh flowers, but carnations last a nice long time."

Since "You're welcome" didn't seem to fit, I smiled and drew the guest chair close to the bed. "Is there anything I can get you?" I asked. "Water? Ice?"

"No, thank you." She closed her eyes and laid her head back against the pillow. Her gray hair hung limply against her head, her skin was an odd shade of white, and the lines on her face were drawn long and deep. She looked . . . sick.

I reached out to pat her arm and was surprised at how thin and frail she felt. "If you're too tired to talk, I can come back later."

Her eyes fluttered open. "Momma? Is that you?"

Oh, dear.

I touched her hand and started to say something generically comforting, but her eyes closed, and stayed closed. When I saw that her chest was still rising and falling with reassuring regularity, I sat back in the chair. Out in the hallway, footsteps stepped past, some fast, some slow, some loud, some so soft they could barely be heard. Smells that weren't of home or bookstore wafted in. Voices murmured. Faint beeps beeped.

I hated hospitals.

What felt like ten years later, Cookie spoke. "They've poisoned me."

In a rush it came to me why Cookie and I had never been, and would never be, good friends. Not only did she take life much too seriously, but she was prone to sincerely believing in the worst-case scenario. Sure, I worried about horrible things, but deep down I didn't really believe the worst was going to happen. It was best to be prepared, was more my line of thinking.

"What makes you think so?" I asked. Because, really, how would anyone know? There were a lot of poisons in the world and it was likely that they'd each have a different set of symptoms. Why would anyone slide from thinking plain old flu to the icky thought of being poisoned? Maybe this was just the illness talking. Her comments about the mysterious "they" certainly hinted of medication-induced nightmares.

Cookie's voice rasped out. "Evil walks among us. It's our duty to make things right."

I waited. While I didn't exactly think she was wrong, I also couldn't give a blanket agreement. Finally, I thought of something to say. "Have you tried to make things right?"

With her eyes still closed, she smiled. "Right and wrong," she said in a singsong tone. "Good and evil. They want it all different colors of gray, but we know better, don't we? It's black-and-white, now as it always was."

I shifted in the chair, which had suddenly become uncomfortable. "I think I know what you mean," I said cautiously. "Has someone done something wrong?"

Her lips curved up in a smile. "Oh, yes. So very wrong."

I waited for her to continue. Watched her breaths move in and out. Waited some more. But she was sound asleep.

From the hospital parking lot, I called Gus and told him about Cookie's hazy conviction that she'd been poisoned. "She's very sick," I finished. "I don't know if it's her medication or a fever or what, but she's not exactly her normal self. It's hard to say if this was a real conviction or an illness-induced one, but I thought you should know."

Gus grunted. "Did you tell her doctor?"

"She said she'd run some tests."

"I'll stop by and talk to the doctor and Cookie," Gus said. "Thanks, Beth. You taking care of yourself?"

I assured him I was and ended the call with the vague feeling that I should be doing more.

Over the next few days, I tried to find out how Cookie was doing. I knew the hospital wouldn't tell me anything, and all her bank coworkers knew was that she wasn't at work, so I asked around town.

"Cookie?" Denise, my hairstylist, asked between snips. "Oh, is she in the hospital? That's too bad. I'll have to stop by and see her."

When I stopped by Glenn Kettunen's insurance office, he said, "Cookie? Huh. Didn't know she was still there. I should send flowers, I guess."

Instead of sending Jenna to pick up dinner at the Green Tractor, I went myself and asked Ruthie. "Oh, dear. I'd heard she wasn't feeling good. The poor woman. A hospital is the last place you want to be when you're sick."

Late Wednesday morning, Debra O'Conner knocked on my office door. Once upon a time, Debra-don't-call-me-Debbie had dressed in city-slick clothes, gone to Chicago to get her hair cut, and been on a career path that didn't include Rynwood's local bank as the pinnacle.

A couple of years ago, after I'd made a chance remark I couldn't even remember now, Debra had decided she was perfectly content as a local bank vice president, let her hair grow long, and started cooking dinner for her family every night. I squirmed every time she tried to give me credit for her new happiness; whatever I'd said couldn't possibly have been that profound. I'd happened to say it at a time she was ready to hear it, that was all.

Since that fateful remark, though, we'd become good friends and I smiled as she came into my office and sat in the extra chair. "Morning, Debra. What brings you here?" Then my brain registered the solemn expression on her face. "You have bad news. Your family's all right, aren't they?"

She nodded, then said, "It's Cookie."

My worries and fears of the last days grew and grew until they filled my head and flew out into the room to bounce off the walls and ceiling and floor and come back to me with the strength of ten. "She's doing better, right?" Of course she was. She was so much better that she was headed home and needed someone to bring her a few meals. That's why Debra was here; she was looking for volunteers to help out and—

Debra sighed. "I'm sorry, Beth, but Cookie died this morning."

Chapter 4

"You're not going," Marina said.

I picked a cat hair off my black pants. "Thanks for watching the kids. I should be back in a couple of hours."

"As the coleader of your intervention team, I forbid you to go." Marina crossed her arms and stood in front of her kitchen door, blocking my exit. "You promised you'd take it easy, remember? You gave us administrative power over your activities for six weeks, and if I can read a calendar correctly, which I'm pretty sure I can, six weeks isn't close to over."

I zipped up my coat. "If I'm running longer than two hours, I'll send a text."

"Lois agrees, you know. I called her and she about hit the ceiling when I told her you planned on going. She knows how upset these things make you. She's seen how you get afterward."

Where were my gloves? I patted my coat pockets. Ah. There they were. "It's not about me," I said quietly. "It's about Cookie."

Marina's chin went up, and she opened her mouth to say something, but then she sighed and stepped aside. "Why is it that even when I'm trying to do what's right for you, I get it wrong?"

I frowned. Marina? Being self-critical? If the world was ending, why hadn't I gotten a memo? "Hey," I said. "Is something wrong? Because—"

She opened the door, letting in a whoosh of cold air that swirled around our ankles. "Go on. You don't want to be late."

No, I didn't. But I didn't want to leave this half-finished conversation, either. "You're okay?"

"My deah," she said, slipping into Southern Belle mode, "do Ah look like Ah have a problem?" She did a sideways shuffle and tossed her hair over her shoulder while humming "Zip-a-Dee-Doo-Dah."

It was obvious that something was bothering her, but it was equally obvious that she wasn't going to tell me. So I left.

By the time Cookie's funeral was over, I was thoroughly upset, just as Marina and Lois had predicted. Funerals wrung me inside out and I'd hated every single one I'd attended. But the mere fact of disliking a task didn't mean I could avoid doing it. If that were the case, my windows would never get washed.

Of course, if I was going to be honest with myself, the primary reason I was so upset over Cookie's death was pure, unadulterated guilt. I should have done more. I should have taken her to the urgent care clinic the night of the PTA in Review. If I had, maybe they would have caught what was wrong in time to save her.

When I walked back into Marina's kitchen, postfuneral, she took one look at me and gave me a big hug. "You silly girl," she murmured. "Repeat after me: 'I was wrong and you were right.' Go on, say it."

"I was wrong and you were right," I said. She gave me

an extra-hard squeeze and released me. I wiped my eyes, saying, "But I had to go. I just had to."

"Yes, yes. We need to work on that overdeveloped sense of right and wrong that you have."

"And my guilt complex?"

"Well, duh."

We smiled at each other. We'd been friends for a very long time.

"And now," Marina said, "you go home. Take a nap. I'll bring the kids over in a couple of hours and you will not need to worry about dinner."

"I won't?"

"Nope," she said cheerfully. "Now away with you." She gave me a light shove. "As my grandmother used to say, 'Shoo! Shoo!'"

I zipped up my coat. "You know, for a redhead, you're not so bad."

"That's what all my best friends say. Now go."

So I was smiling as I went.

Two hours later, I heard the kids stomping into the house. Oliver ran up the stairs on all fours and Jenna called for me. "Mom?"

"In here." Yawning, I sat up. The couch springs creaked underneath me.

Jenna appeared in the doorway of the family room. "I'm making dinner, okay?"

Visions of blackened pans, sticky messes, and spattered walls danced through my head. "Oh. That sounds . . . very nice, sweetheart."

"Yeah, Mrs. Neff helped us plan the menu." She gave me a smile full of confidence. "It'll be easy."

"Tell me the kitchen rules," I said.

"Um, make sure nothing boils over, check that there's nothing in the oven before turning it on, clean up spills when they happen, and . . ." Her lower lip stuck out in her effort to remember. Suddenly, her face brightened. "And no using the big knife without you there."

"Maybe I should come in and supervise." I started to get out from underneath the fleece blanket.

"But you're supposed to be taking it easy," Jenna said as Oliver thundered down the stairs and ran into the room.

"Here, Mom." He dropped an armload of books onto my legs. "I couldn't pick, so I brought all of them."

He'd brought down the entire pile that I had on my nightstand. "Oh, honey. That's . . . so thoughtful of you."

My son smiled, a wide happy smile that lit up the room. "Mrs. Neff said we needed to take care of you tonight, and I know how much you like to read, so I thought you could do that while we make dinner."

Fear stabbed at me. My nine-year-old baby boy was capable of many things, but he was still only nine years old.

"I'm making dinner," Jenna interjected. "You get to set the table."

"Yeah, and that's part of making dinner, right?"

Smiling, I lay back against the couch pillows and listened to them wrangle on their way to the kitchen. My children, my loves, my heart, my life. Even if I had to spend half the day tomorrow cleaning up the kitchen, it would be worth it. Tears stung at my eyes for the second time that day, but for a completely different reason.

We had a wonderful dinner of overcooked macaroni and cheese accompanied by a very plain salad of iceberg lettuce covered with far too much dressing. All through the meal, my inside smile was wide and happy and warm.

Once we finished eating, however, things started to change.

Oliver pushed his chair back and jumped up. "I did the dishes last night, so it's your turn, Jenna."

My daughter's face, which up until now had been sunny and clear, darkened. "I did all the cooking."

"Not all," Oliver said, his chin jutting out. "I ripped up the lettuce."

"That's not cooking," Jenna countered. "That's just . . . just doing the lettuce."

"And I put cheese on the salads."

"Too much cheese," she muttered.

"It was not too much!" Oliver said in a near-shout.

"Was, too."

"Was not!"

I was opening my mouth to call a time-out when the front doorbell rang. Before anyone could call dibs on getting the door, a male voice called out, "Anybody home?"

The moment we heard Pete's voice, the mounting tension in the room started to ebb. "In the kitchen," I called. By the time he walked into the room, his cheerful grin in place, any leftover bits of stress and strain had faded away completely.

"It's snowing," he said. "And it's the perfect temperature to build a snowman."

"A snowman?" Oliver's truculent chin slid back to its normal position. "Can we go out, Mom? Can we?"

"I want to build a snowwoman," Jenna said. "I can give her my old goalie stick."

My gaze went from one child to the other. Then it went to the uncleared table. And the unwashed dishes

"We, um, could do them after we come back inside?" Oliver asked. "Mr. Peterson said the temperature is perfect right now. That won't last very long. You don't want us to miss the best snowman-making weather of the winter, do you?"

My eyebrows rose. When had my son learned that little trick?

"Many hands make light work," Pete said easily.

I shook my head. "Pete, sit down. You've been working all day. You don't need to—"

But he ignored me. "Come on, Ollster, you clear the table. Jenna can put the food away, right, Jenna? And I'll fill up the dishwasher."

Jenna pointed. "Mom always makes us wash that pot by hand."

Mom, the ogre.

"And a good thing she does," Pete said. "It'll last a lifetime that way. Come on, time's wasting away while you two mawple about." He clapped his hands lightly and the kids sprang into action.

I watched Oliver speed from table to kitchen counter and back. Watched Jenna spoon the leftover mac and cheese into a plastic container that was a little too small. "'Mawple'?" I asked.

"Combination of 'dawdle' and 'mope,'" he said. "I just made it up. What do you think?" He grinned and headed for the dishwasher.

In less time than it had taken the kids to argue about the chore, the kitchen was clean and we were bundling up into boots, coats, hats, and mittens. Spot, our brown dog, bounced among us barking happy barks and we tumbled out into the snowy night.

The sky was dark with night, but there was plenty of

light from the houses and from the streetlights to illuminate our efforts. Jenna's snow-hockey player took shape quickly, but Oliver's traditional snowman needed all of Pete's strength to lift the middle ball into place.

"Ooof!" Pete grunted. "What'd you make this thing out of, gold? Lead? Boxes of *National Geographic* magazines?"

Jenna ran to the garage and came back with a cracked goalie stick. She propped it up against her freshly made masterpiece. "I like her. She's original, not like the snowmen some other people around here make."

"What's wrong with my snowman?" Oliver, puffy from head to toe in winter gear, stuck his chin out again. "At least mine doesn't—" The end of his sentence was lost forever when a feathery snowball hit him in the chest and exploded.

At that same time, a second snowball hit Jenna on the arm. This one also exploded nicely.

The kids yelled, "Hey!" and turned as one unit to see Pete and me, both grinning, both with our hands cocked back with fresh ammunition.

"Snowball fight!" Jenna shouted, and the game was on.

It ended as snowball fights tend to, with someone getting a big, fat, hard snowball in the face. This time that someone was me.

"Ooof!" I stumbled back, trying to wipe the icy white stuff from my face.

"Sorry, Mom!" Jenna called. "Are you okay?"

"She's fine," Pete said. He stepped close and brushed the snow from my shoulders, my hair, my neck, my face.

"That stuff's cold." I smiled. "Did you get it all?"

"Almost," he said, then leaned in close.

His lips were soft and gentle and warm, warmer than I would have thought possible on such a chill night, but then everything about Pete was warm. His voice warmed me, his laughter warmed me, and his smile did nice warm things to my insides, so it shouldn't have been a surprise that his kiss would warm me down to my toes. Down to, and including, my toes, my toenails . . .

"FWEEEEE!"

And so, it was while kissing Pete Peterson in front of my children for the first time that I learned Jenna knew how to make an earsplitting whistle.

Like mother, like daughter.

On Monday morning Lois, Yvonne, and I were debating the pros and cons of having a midwinter sale when the front doorbells jingled and Gus walked in.

"Chief," Lois said, clicking her heels together and saluting him.

"At ease, men," Gus said. "Beth, do you have a minute?"

"Men?" Lois demanded. "Do I look like a men?"

She did not. Today's chosen ensemble was black pants, black sweater, black shoes, and pink socks with pink sequins. She claimed to be starting a new fashion trend, but I suspected she just wanted an excuse to wear the pink socks her granddaughter had given her for Christmas. The only thing Lois had written on her Christmas gift list was "something pink." Most of her large family had ignored the request, but a few had humored her.

Gus and I ignored her question and headed back to office. He closed the door behind us and we sat. Or I sat and Gus perched on the front edge of the guest chair. Since the chair had arms, and since he was in uniform and wearing his crowded utility belt, there wasn't enough room for all of him to fit between the wooden arms.

"It's about Cookie, isn't it?" I asked.

He nodded. "I've had a preliminary report from the medical examiner and we have cause of death."

There suddenly wasn't enough air in the room. I wanted to rush out of my office and run outside, wanted to breathe deep of the cold, clean January air, wanted to look up into a blue sky spotty with clouds and suck in deep breaths that would wash me clean.

But instead of doing that, I asked, "What was it?"

"An overdose of acetaminophen."

"An . . . overdose?" No. It couldn't be true. I didn't want to know this, not one tiny little bit. "You don't mean . . ." I couldn't say the word "suicide" out loud. Didn't want to let the possibility loose into the room, where it could grow strong enough to escape and get out into the world.

But Gus was shaking his head. "It's actually not that hard to OD on acetaminophen. Tylenol, most people know it by, but it's in a lot of other medications and the lethal dosage is surprisingly low. Cookie had a number of other meds she was taking that included acetaminophen, and if she had a bad headache and had taken a few pills . . . well . . ." He sighed and went on to describe the symptoms of an overdose of acetaminophen.

As he talked about the three phases, about the nausea that can accompany the first phase, about the second phase that starts twenty-four to seventy-two hours after the overdose, the phase that indicates increasing liver damage, about the third and final phase, as he talked about all of that, what I kept hearing was "It's not hard to overdose," over and over again.

When Gus paused, I asked, "So it was an accident? She wasn't really poisoned, right?"

"At this time we have no reason to suspect anything else."

"You're going to do an investigation?"

He nodded. "But I honestly don't expect to find anything. Simple case of accidental overdose."

Simple, but so very sad.

"So if anyone asks"—Gus tilted his head in the direction of the pink-socked Lois—"feel free to tell her what I told you. Probable accidental death, but we're still investigating."

"Thanks for telling me," I said. "It's nice of you to stop by."

"You and Debra O'Conner were her only visitors in the hospital. I figure you both deserve an in-person stop."

He left, and for a long time I sat there, staring at the wall. It was an accident. Cookie had been poisoned, but she'd done it to herself. My heart ached for the pointless tragedy of her death. What a waste and so terribly sad, but there was nothing hidden under the rug this time. No need for anyone to even whisper about murder. No need for nightmares.

I sat there a moment longer, thinking about Cookie, wondering what she'd left undone, wondering what she'd wanted to do but never had, wondering what she'd have done with the rest of her life, if she'd had it given to her.

Then I went back to work.

Chapter 5

At half past noon, I had both kids in the car.

"Mom's kidnapping us," Oliver said, giggling in the backseat.

Jenna tugged her knit hat down over her eyes. "She blindfolded us and everything."

"Yeah, she blindfolded us!" My grinning son yanked his scarf from around his neck and wrapped it around his head. "Think there'll be a ransom? I have thirty-two dollars and eleven cents in my piggy bank. Will that be enough?"

Jenna snorted. "It's not the people who are kidnapped who pay the ransom. It's the people who want them back."

There was a short silence while Oliver thought through the concept. "But if Mom's the one who's doing the kidnapping, who'd want us back bad enough to pay money for us?"

Smiling, I let them play their game. Jenna would be thirteen in June and she'd likely soon grow out of the whimsical nonsense that Oliver reveled in. I hoped not, though. I hoped that they'd both let themselves be silly, at least once in a while, the rest of their lives.

"Where are we going, Mom?" Jenna pushed her blindfold up.

It was the end of the semester for the middle school and the end of a marking period for Tarver Elementary. Both kids had half days through Wednesday, and my intervention instigators were bound and determined that I make the most of their free afternoons.

"We're going to get some lunch," I said.

"You mean at home?" Oliver asked tentatively. "Like peanut butter and jelly?"

Jenna peered through the windshield. "But we're not going home. Or downtown. So we're not going to the Green Tractor or to the Grill or to that fancy new place."

Oliver bounced in his seat. "It's a mystery! Where are we going, Mom?"

"If I told you, it wouldn't be a mystery, now, would it?"

"Keep your blindfold on," Jenna commanded. "I'll give you hints and see if you can guess where we are."

Ten minutes later, when Jenna described a huge parking lot with a really busy road on one side and a really, really big building on the other side, a building that had lots of stores inside, Oliver yanked off his scarf. "The mall! We're going to the mall!"

And so we were. As the owner of a downtown business, I eschewed mall shopping as much as possible, but there were times it just wasn't possible. Today, for instance. Joe, a fellow downtown business owner, had a pizza place named Sabatini's. He'd opened a mall store just before Halloween, and while I'd been meaning to eat there since before Thanksgiving, somehow it just hadn't happened.

With Jenna on my right and Oliver on my left, we scuffed through the dusting of snow that was falling and entered the mall red-cheeked and breathless with cold.

"I know where the new Sabatini's is." Jenna danced ahead. "My friend Alexis told me. It's this way. She says it's really neat. They have a cool basketball game and one of those table shuffleboard things. Oliver, do you want to play?"

My ears shut down while they started to wrangle about rules for a game I'd barely heard of. I loved my children dearly, but that didn't mean I loved to hear every word that come out of their mouths.

Standing a few dozen yards ahead of us was a pair of women, shopping bags in their hands and strained smiles on their faces. Or rather, I knew for a fact that one of them was suffering a little stress, because when she was anxious her mouth always went a little wide, deepening the curves around her lips. Right now the curves were deep as the Grand Canyon and even her red hair, loose today, wasn't hiding the fact.

But I didn't know the young woman Marina was with. A little taller and much slimmer than Marina, light brown hair, long fingers wrapping around the handles of her bags. As far as I knew, I'd never seen her before, and while I was horrible at names, I was pretty good at remembering faces.

Marina's head turned slightly and I raised my arm in a grand wave. The motion caught her attention, but instead of the smile I expected to see, Marina's eyes widened and her mouth opened. She grabbed her companion's wrist and dragged her into the nearest store, a RadioShack, a store that she had heretofore never seen a reason to enter, and vanished among the store displays.

I came to a complete stop. After a dozen paces, the kids realized they'd lost me and ran back.

"Mom, the restaurant's up here," Jenna said. Then she cocked her head. "Are you okay? You're not getting sick or anything, are you?"

Oliver grabbed my hand and looked at it. "At school they say to wash your hands, like, all the time. When's the last time you washed yours? Bet it's been hours!" he said gleefully.

I rubbed his hair. "And now my germs are all over you."

He put his palms to his chest and started fake-coughing. "I'm dying! I'm sure of it. Take me to the hospital, quick!"

"Bet some pizza and bread sticks will take care of it." I took his hand. "If you're still dying after lunch, we'll see about going to the emergency room."

I smiled at Jenna. She smiled back, believing that my smile meant that Mom was fine, that I wasn't sick, that I wasn't hurt, that I was fine and always would be, because that's what Moms are supposed to be like.

Only I wasn't fine, not quite. My best friend was hiding something from me and I had no idea what it was. And worse, I had no idea why.

The waitress served us two pizzas on metal pedestals. Cheese dripped over the edges of the dough and I had to make dire threats of dark punishment to keep both kids from leaning into the cheese with their tongues out.

"Not appropriate behavior," I said sharply. "You're both old enough to know better."

"But, Mom," Oliver pleaded, "it's just *asking* us to eat it that way. Look at it."

"It's tempting you, not asking. It's a test, and you two

are on the edge of failing." I took hold of the triangular pizza server and doled out one piece each.

"Yeah." Jenna grinned at Oliver over her plate. "You wouldn't want your new *girl*friend to see you fail at pizza eating. Ow, quit kicking!"

"Inside voices," I murmured. "And I don't care who started it."

"That's what Coach says." Jenna picked up her piece of sausage, pepperoni, and double cheese. "He says that it's not the player who makes the first illegal hit that gets caught—it's the player who retaliates."

"Your coach is right." I'd been a hockey fan since I'd grown out of my sister's old figure skates and laced on my dad's old hockey skates. I'd been eight at the time. In those days there were no girls' hockey teams, but for years I'd spent winters playing pond hockey until it grew too dark to see the puck. My mother had been marginally horrified that her dainty daughter was out playing a contact sport with boys, but my dad had laughed and convinced her to let me play.

My children chewed contentedly, and it wasn't until I handed out the second pieces of pizza that I went back to the earlier subject. "So, Oliver, what is she like?"

He went still. "Who?"

Jenna opened her mouth, but I quelled her with a look. "Is there a new girl in school?" I asked. Oliver had a penchant for getting a crush on the new girl, and I wasn't aware of any family who'd recently moved into town. There'd been a couple of families who'd moved into the area in August—PTA presidents made it a point to know these things—but that was far too long ago for the New Girl effect.

"She's beautiful," Oliver said, sighing. He put his chin on his hand and ignored the double olive piece of pizza in front of him. "She smiles all the time and has this happy kind of laugh that makes you want to laugh, too."

I shot a look at Jenna. She shrugged.

"What does she look like?" I asked.

Oliver considered. "She's always wearing pretty earrings. She wears shoes that make noise, you know, *tick-tick-tick*, and she makes her hair do really neat things."

My son had a crush on a girly girl? It had been bound to happen at some point, but he was only nine, for heaven's sake. I envisioned a girl wearing purple and pink, a girl who was happy to wear dress shoes, a girl whose mother had the time and patience to learn updos. I'd never learned anything beyond a French braid, and even those tended to look lumpy. "What's her name?"

"Ms. Stephanie," he said dreamily.

Ms.? Wait a minute. . . . "Are you talking about Stephanie Pesch? Your new vice principal?"

He nodded. "Isn't that the prettiest name? Steph-ah-knee." He drew the syllables out long. "Steph-ahhh-kneee."

Jenna rolled her eyes. "I told him she probably doesn't know he exists, but he keeps doing those gaga eyes and making up songs."

I looked at her. "It wasn't all that long ago that you had a crush on someone much older than you. Remember?" Her immediate blush told me that, yes, she did remember, and she'd rather not talk about the weeks she was enamored of Eddie Sweeney, the NHL hockey star who'd done a local hockey-skills clinic.

Oliver was looking interested in the ancient history. Time for a new subject. "So, how is hockey going?" I asked my daughter. "Your team did well over the holidays at that tournament. Are you working on any new drills?"

Jenna took another piece of pizza and didn't answer at first. I waited. She saw me waiting and took a huge bite, a classic delaying tactic since she knew I wouldn't make her talk with her mouth full. I laid my fork down and waited while she chewed. When she swallowed, I asked, "Jenna, what's the matter?"

She looked at her pizza, looked at me, saw what my face looked like—a Mom-combination of patience, endurance, and answer-me-or-there'll-be-trouble—and put her slice down on her plate. "There's a new girl," she muttered.

"And?"

"She's a goalie."

Ah. Goalie was Jenna's position, the only position she'd ever played or wanted to play. She was a very good goalie and her goals-against average was the lowest in her league. "Is she good?" I asked.

"She's from Minnesota." The despair in Jenna's tone said it all.

"I see." And I did. Minnesota was a hockey state. Strong learn-to-skate programs, strong youth programs, strong middle school and high school programs, strong adult programs, and there were ice rinks everywhere. Jenna hadn't even started playing hockey until two years ago, when Rynwood had built an arena. A girl from Minnesota who'd been playing since she could walk would have a definite advantage over Jenna. "Who's playing Saturday morning?" I asked.

"Coach hasn't said yet."

Which could mean anything. "There's nothing wrong

with having two good goalies," I said. "It's good for the team to have . . ." I'd been about to say "a backup goalie" but stopped just in time. Jenna would think I'd be assuming she'd be backup. " . . . to have two goalies. Just like some football teams have two quarterbacks." Didn't they? I scrambled to think of one, but couldn't. Pete was a much bigger football fan than I was. If Jenna called me out, I'd tell her to ask Pete next time he came over.

But she didn't question me at all. What she did was start to pick at her third piece of pizza. The girl who usually scarfed down four pieces in the blink of an eye was letting good pizza get cold.

And Oliver, who'd moved up to three pieces, was picking at the remains of his second.

Good job, Beth. Take the kids out for a lunch treat and ruin both their appetites. Excellent. If my children had anything to do with the voting, I would not be winning the Mother of the Year Award this year.

Again.

For the twelfth year in a row.

I sighed and lifted my own piece of pizza to take a bite. As I did, I caught sight of a flash of red hair. Marina was at the door of the restaurant with that young woman at her side.

I lifted my hand in a come-sit-with-us wave.

Marina's gaze passed through me. She turned and walked out of the restaurant quickly, her companion tagging along after her.

Chapter 6

Tuesday afternoon's outing with the kids went a little better, as it involved more doing and less talking. I splurged for admission to a water park and we spent the afternoon and part of the evening running and splashing and sliding. Dinner was sub sandwiches on the way home and we fell into bed exhausted but happy.

Wednesday's fun was more low-key: I picked the kids up at their schools and drove them home. After first getting promises of dish-doing, I let the youngsters each pick what they most wanted for lunch. Jenna wanted a three-cheese grilled sandwich and tomato soup; Oliver wanted macaroni and cheese. By the time we'd cooked, eaten, and cleaned up, their father was in the driveway, having left work early to spend some extra time with his children.

I gave both kids a hug and a kiss and waved at them from the kitchen window as Richard backed out of the driveway. Then I went back to the store.

"What are you doing here?" Lois asked. Her attire was a simple cable-knit sweater over brown tweed pants. The only eye-catching thing about the ensemble was a bracelet of ancient pull tabs from soda cans. That morning she'd said everything she wore came from the seventies. I'd desperately wanted to ask about her underwear, but the phone had rung and the moment had passed.

Now I pulled off my gloves and shoved them into my coat pockets. "I work here, remember? Matter of fact, if I recall correctly, the owner of the store and I share the same name."

"You're supposed to be spending time with your children this afternoon, not working."

"Richard took the kids and they won't be back home until tomorrow after school." My former husband lived in a three-bedroom condo and kept the kids overnight on Wednesdays and his weekends. From all accounts, they spent a lot of time playing video games and watching television while Richard fussed with paperwork from his office, but there wasn't much I could do about that.

Lois grunted. "Then why didn't you stay home and take a nap or something? I told you we had the store covered."

Before I could come up with a good response, the bells on the front door jingled and a tall, wide, bald man walked in. Saved by the bells. "Aha!" He pointed a long Ghost of Christmas Past finger at me. "There she is!"

"Hello, Glenn." I eyed the insurance man warily. Glenn Kettunen was funny, smart, and interesting. He also couldn't keep a secret if the lives of ten thousand people depended on it. "What's up?"

He sidled close. "I hear you have the inside scoop on what happened to Cookie Van Doorne. Tell all to your Uncle Glenn, dearie."

"What makes you think I know anything?"

He spread his hands, palms up. "Come on, Beth. Everybody knows you took Cookie home that night, that you went to see her in the hospital, and that Gus came in here to talk to you the other morning. Patient man that I am"—he crossed one ankle over the other, stuck his hands in his pockets, looked at the ceiling, and hummed for three seconds before breaking the pose—"I've waited two days for you to seek me out. Now here I am, still waiting." He drummed his fingers on the glass counter.

There was a petty part of me that wanted to let him wait until doomsday, but I relented and said, "It was an accidental overdose."

"Overdose of what?" Glenn asked. "Heroin? Crack?" He rubbed his hands. "Meth? Come on, you gotta tell me."

"Acetaminophen," I said. "Gus said it's actually fairly easy to overdose on it. It's in a lot of other medications and if you're susceptible you can OD and not even know what you're doing."

Glenn's face had gone still. "Plain old acetaminophen? I take that stuff all the time."

"It's perfectly safe," I reassured him, "as long as you don't take too much. If you have any other meds, check to see if it's in there. I'm sure you're fine." But my last words were said to his back because he was already rushing out the door.

Lois cackled. "Did you see the look on his face?" She slapped her thigh. "Never seen ol' Glenn look so scared."

Great. Now I'd started a panic.

And a very small part of me, way deep down inside, smiled.

That night was the regular January PTA meeting, the second meeting to have Claudia's indelible stamp on it. During the November meeting, Claudia had insisted on adding "refreshments" to the agenda. "Food will add to the PTA camaraderie," she'd stated. "We'll get to know each other better."

Treasurer Randy Jarvis, his mouth half-full of corn chips, had agreed. Secretary Summer Lang had shot me an apologetic look. "I like the idea."

I didn't. I thought it added even more burden to the already busy PTA members and had the potential to add pounds to my hips, but I'd been outvoted three to one on the topic of having coffee and some sort of dessert snack after every meeting.

In December I'd had the will to stay away from the Christmas cookies. Tonight, however, Carol Casassa had brought dark, gooey brownies. With walnuts.

There they were, on the far side of the classroom we commandeered for the meeting, on the table Claudia had persuaded Harry, Tarver's janitor, to set up for us. The table sat directly underneath the cabinet that Claudia had coerced the classroom's teacher to let us have Harry install. The cabinet was small, but large enough to hold coffee supplies, napkins, and the multitude of other items that went along with having refreshments. The only thing that didn't fit in the cabinet was the coffeemaker itself, but Claudia had convinced the school to let us store it in the kitchen.

I called the meeting to order. All went smoothly until we came to the only agenda item of any real importance. "Storybook Sale Proceeds."

Just under a year ago, the PTA had paired Tarver Elementary students with residents of Sunny Rest Assisted Living. The end product was a paperbound book telling the life stories of the residents as seen through the eyes of the children. Sales had done much better than expected. and for the first time ever, the Tarver PTA had serious money.

But, as everyone except me had probably anticipated, not all was rosy. Half of the PTA wanted to spend the money on sports-oriented projects. The other half wanted to spend the money on fine arts projects. The two viewpoints had split our group apart with name-calling and other conduct unbecoming to PTA members and I was past fed up with the entire mess.

I fingered the gavel's handle and looked out at the group. It was like a church wedding with a twist: pro-sports on that side, pro–fine arts on the other. Marina sat on the artsy side, Tina Heller on the sports. Nick Casassa and his wife, Carol, sat on different sides. "As most of you know," I began, "last fall we had two committees draw up two different plans for disbursement of the storybook monies. Each of you should have a copy in front of you."

There was a rustling and all the heads went down.

"If you were on a committee," I went on, "you'll notice one thing—"

"Half our stuff is gone!" Tina said. "Where's my suggestion for a zip line? And what about the climbing wall?"

"Where's the line item for purchasing instruments?" Carol asked. "How can we build a strong music program without instruments?"

I'd known there would be objections, which was why I'd met with the rest of the PTA board an hour earlier to review this pared-down list. There had been grumblings, of course, but they'd seen the necessity.

"What both committees handed in was a wish list," I said. "Even if we spent every dime of the storybook money, the PTA couldn't afford half the total items." T my left, I could feel Claudia stir, so I kept talking. "We have to be realistic. We have to be wise and we have to think of what will most benefit the children of Tarver, the children of today and the children of the future."

"Exactly," Claudia said into the pause I'd created when I stopped to draw in a breath. "That's why—"

I gave up on getting a full breath and kept going. "That's why I approached the Tarver Foundation with this." I tapped the paper of short-listed projects. "The two top projects are new playground equipment and the hiring of a part-time music teacher for a minimum of five years. The next projects are an irrigated soccer field and the creation of a summer arts camp."

The original lists had gone on and on. Accessible playground equipment. Hiring a full-time art teacher. A disc golf course on school property. A swimming pool. Having weekly dance instruction. Bus trips to Milwaukee and Chicago for everything from attending professional sporting events to attending ballets. The estimated dollar amounts had made my eyes bug out and I'd almost crunched both lists into cat toys and e-mailed the committees to start over again.

But I'd walked away from the fantasy lists, then gone back to them a few hours later with a fresh viewpoint. I'd told both committees they wouldn't get everything they asked for, and had told them so more than once. I'd been on the fine arts committee myself and had had to rein them in from pie in the sky.

Now I put down the list and looked at the audience. "Yesterday I had an appointment with the Tarver Foundation and I have some good news. The foundation has agreed to match our funds. If we choose, we can fund all our of these projects."

There was a short moment of pregnant silence, and then the room filled with applause and cheers and shouts of joy. I heard "Atta girl!" and "Bet even Erica couldn't have done that," which made my head swell with pride until I heard Claudia mutter to Randy that "If it's that easy to get money, why haven't we done it before?"

When the noise started to subside, Rachel Helmstetter waved for recognition. "Not to rain on anyone's parade, but you said '*some* good news.' Does that mean there's also some bad?"

"Not bad bad," I said. "Not exactly, anyway."

The energy in the room whooshed out so fast I thought my ears might pop. What had been a happy band of PTA smiling members was now a glum group presenting me with a wall of stony silence.

"What does that mean?" Claudia asked.

"There are some strings."

Simultaneously, the audience slid down in their chairs six inches.

"Not huge strings," I hastened to add. "Just . . . foundation strings. They're not horrible—really they're not. We just have to be held accountable, and that seems reasonable to me. If the board votes to accept their offer, that is." I nodded down at the other three board members.

"What do you mean, 'accountable'?" Randy asked. As treasurer, he would be the one stuck with the bulk of the paperwork, and he knew it.

I checked my notes from yesterday's meeting and outlined the basics of what the foundation wanted. Estimated costs, receipts, time sheets, weekly progress reports, monthly progress reports, quarterly progress reports, anticipated outcomes, estimated completio

dates, actual completion dates, actual outcome, and un-
intended outcomes. All done on the computer, please, in
the latest version of Excel.

Randy's face remained placid. When I was done, he
shrugged. "We can do all that."

Claudia slapped the table with her open palm. "We
can, but why should we have to? Don't they trust us?
We're the PTA, for crying out loud! Do they really think
we're going to cheat them?"

I tried to soothe her. "Starting this year, the foundation has tightened up their grant disbursement policies.
We're no different than any other group that—"

"No different?" Claudia fairly shrieked. "Of course
we're different! We're the PTA! We're parents of the future parents. We're here to do what's best for our kids.
How dare they question our honesty? If they're going to
call us thieves, why don't they do it to our faces instead
of through you?"

I let her talk. Interrupting Claudia in midrant would
take more energy than I wanted to expend.

"Honestly, Beth, what were you thinking?" she went
on. "You handled this all wrong. You should have shown
them that we're doing them a favor by giving them a
chance to fund our projects, not gone to them all wishy-
washy and pretty-please-give-us-your-spare-change."

My eyebrows went up. Letting her talk was one thing.
Letting her launch a personal attack was something else.

"And you shouldn't have gone in the first place."
Claudia gave the table a thump with her fist. "If anyone
was going to present anything to the foundation, it
should have been the entire PTA board and it should
have been after the entire membership voted on it."

I flashed back to the meeting I'd had yesterday morn-

ing with the board of the Tarver Foundation. The very
citified and straitlaced businesswomen and men who
wielded the power behind the foundation's extremely
deep pockets. The financially conservative people who
didn't waste their time on projects they didn't deem wor-
thy. The extremely proper people who didn't care for
hyperbole or exaggeration or any shade of gray. Pictur-
ing Claudia in front of that prim group brought the
phrase "bull in a china shop" to mind. No way would the
board have handed the PTA money after Claudia got
done with her demands, and demands they would have
been.

But she was right about one thing. I should have
waited until the membership voted. And, if the situation
had been as she described, I would have.

"My appointment with the foundation," I said, making sure I was speaking loudly enough to be heard even
by the father half-asleep in the back row, "was strictly for
fact-finding. My only intention was to get information on
applying for funding."

Claudia glared at me. "Then what's the deal with you
walking away with approval for doing this?" She flicked
at the list.

A shameful thought sparked. I could say it was my
superior negotiating skills, my instant rapport with the
foundation's board, and my magnetic personality that
coaxed the money out of them. The spark flashed, then
died. "It was luck."

In the front row, Marina put her head in her hands.
After I'd told her what had happened yesterday, she'd
told me to play it up for all it was worth. "That'll teach
that Claudia Wolff," she'd said with satisfaction.

But I couldn't do it. "Sheer luck," I said. "In December they had a reorganization of the foundation's priorities. At the top of the pyramid is the advancement of Rynwood's youth. The board liked all these projects and they answer to no one but themselves." And the ghost of former Tarver principal Agnes Mephisto, I thought, whose inherited money was the foundation's nest egg. "They're ready to approve the funding if we agree to their terms."

Claudia pounded. "*If* we agree," she said. "If you ask me, that's a big if. Why should we agree to their restrictions? Why should we do all that extra work?" Out in the audience, at least one person grunted. Claudia, naturally, assumed it was a supportive grunt and warmed to her new theme. "Hours and hours of extra time, and what's the gain? To answer to some faceless board?"

She wasn't the one who'd be doing the work, it would be Randy and me, but I decided not to pursue that particular point. "The foundation's board isn't holding us back from doing anything," I said. "They just want accountability."

Claudia waved off my words. "That's what they say now. What will they want next week? Next month?" She shook her head. "I vote to reject the foundation's offer."

Since no one had made a motion, her vote was out of order. I started to say so, but she ran roughshod over my mild statement.

"I see that most of you agree with me," she said, smiling, "and I appreciate your support."

What I'd seen was Tina Heller, Claudia's best friend, nodding like a bobblehead. How one person's assent could be construed as "most," I wasn't sure, but Claudia had managed to do so. How nice to be able to see the world as you wanted it to be, instead of how it really was.

"We should reject their offer." She crossed her arms. "We have plenty of money of our own to do what really needs doing. And first thing is to redo the soccer field. We could write a check to do that right now. The contractors could get started as soon as the snow melts and—"

"Over my dead body!" Summer stood up so fast her chair hit the wall with a *thunk*.

I winced at the phrase. There had been too many dead bodies in the recent past. One had been in this very building. But no one else seemed to notice the poor word choice. Marina had a small grin on her face as she watched the action at the front of the room, Carol's face was starting to get red, and there was more than one glance at the door. Judging the distance for escape purposes, I assumed.

Summer's cheeks were flushed. She leaned on the table, looking around Randy Jarvis and staring Claudia down. "We are not—I repeat, not—going to continue to ignore the artistic needs of our children. Keep on going the way we're going and the next generation will grow into a bunch of ignorant adults who don't know a sculpture from a sonata."

Tina turned around and looked at Nick Casassa. "What's a sonata?" she whispered.

Nick had been on the sports committee with Tina, Claudia, and Whitney Heer. Nick's wife, Carol, had been on the fine arts committee. At Tina's question, Nick shrugged. Carol rolled her eyes.

"Who cares about sonatas?" Claudia flared back. "What's more fun, listening to boring music written by some guy dead for three hundred years, or being outside in the fresh air learning sportsmanship and fair play?"

"Sportsmanship?" Summer snorted. "You mean like in the fall when you tried to bribe the referee?"

Claudia jumped to her feet. "I didn't bribe anybody! I was just being nice to him. Nobody likes refs. I thought it would be a nice gesture to give him that gift certificate, that's all."

"Right before the championship game?" Summer asked. "You really expect anyone to believe that?"

The room erupted. With no great expectations that my hopes would come true, I waited a moment for people to sit down and stop shouting. It didn't happen, of course, so I slowly but steadily banged the gavel on the table until there was silence.

"Thank you," I said. "Summer, is there a motion on the floor at this time?" She shook her head. "Thank you. Now. We have ten days to accept the Tarver Foundation's offer. Everyone, please go home and think about this. Consider what we'll lose if we reject their money. Consider what we'll lose if we accept. Decide which option is best for the children. And not just our children, but all the children of Tarver, today's and tomorrow's."

I looked around the room, meeting the gaze of every person who would look at me. "We have ten days," I said again. "I move that we hold a special meeting next Wednesday evening for a vote on the issue."

"Second," Randy said.

"All in favor?" I asked. The board members said, "Aye," in grudging unison. "Those opposed? The 'ayes' have it. We're adjourned." I banged the gavel and the meeting was over.

I stood and tried to get around the table, but Summer was faster. "Can you believe her?" She tossed her head at Claudia, who was already in a huddle with a small group of like-minded friends. "Just assuming we'd all go for the sports stuff. I mean, jeez, all you need to play soccer is a ball. Why do we need to spend thousands and thousands of dollars on—"

"Hang on a minute, okay?" I sidled around her and trotted across the room. "Marina? Hey, Marina, wait up a minute."

But she was already moving away from me. "Sorry, Beth," she said, zipping up her coat. "I have to get home right away. I have to . . . to . . . help Zach with his homework. He's having a hard time with . . . with his math homework. Word problems, you know?" She picked up her purse. "I'll see you later."

I stared after her. For all she said I was a horrible liar, she wasn't much better. One, the kids were on half days and the likelihood of homework was slim to none. Two, if Zach had math homework, Marina's DH would help their son. Marina could hold her own in many subjects, but her math skills were more the practical type, like how to split four pieces of pizza among three people, or calculating how many loads of laundry were left in a jug of detergent.

What was going on? She'd done a duck and cover at the mall not once, but twice. Then, when I'd called her, she'd evaded my questions with "Oh, you were at the mall, too? Nice day, wasn't it?"

I shied away from the reality of what was happening, but kept coming back to the sore point. True-blue Marina, my bosom buddy, my best friend forever and ever, my cheerleader, confidante, propper-upper, and architect of my improvements, was avoiding me.

The hurt swelled and started to go deep. What had I done that was making Marina treat me as if I had a contagious disease? What had I said? Whatever it was, I'd take it back. I'd undo it, I'd make it all better. A life without Marina as a companion would be drab and gray. Annoying as she could sometimes be, she knew how to make life sparkle with fun.

I stood there, looking at the vacant doorway, feeling my future turn into a series of dreary days, one after another.

"Stop it," I muttered to myself. I'd figure out whatever was wrong with our friendship and fix it. If it was unfixable, well, I'd learn to live with it. In the meantime, there was no one here from the intervention squad, and since the best cure I'd ever found for the blues was to help somebody, what was I doing standing there like a stump?

I turned. At the refreshment table, Whitney was waiting for the snackers and coffee drinkers to finish. She'd given birth to a beautiful baby boy in the middle of December and this was her first night out on the town. During the meeting I'd seen her texting at least half a dozen times, asking her husband, no doubt, about the status of their child.

Perfect. I walked to Whitney's side. "Hey, Mom."

She blinked, looked left and right, then focused on me. "It's still weird, being called 'Mom.' I mean, my mom is the *real* 'Mom.' How can we both be moms?" Her expression was puzzled, yet radiant.

I knew exactly what she meant and exactly how she felt. "One of the happiest moments of my life was the first time Jenna called me Mommy."

"Oh . . ." Whitney's breath caught. "I'll melt. I swear, I'll just melt."

"I'll do the cleanup tonight," I said. "You go home to your baby."

"Really? Are you sure? I mean, I told Claudia I'd stay, and I don't want to back out on a promise." But she was already halfway into her coat and fishing for her car keys.

"Go on," I said, laughing.

"Thanks, Beth." Whitney gave me a quick, hard hug. "You're the best." She backed away, grinning broadly. "The absolute best!"

By this time, the room was mostly empty. Claudia and Tina were still there, talking about what color to paint Tina's living room, and Carol and Nick Casassa were still there, talking to Rachel.

"Anyone still eating?" I asked, gesturing at the food-stuffs. Claudia and Tina ignored me; the others shook their heads. Soon everything was done except washing the lemonade jug and cleaning out the coffeepot, a task I'd never cared for, as my skin had an odd attraction to coffee grounds. The wet gritty stuff stuck to my hands with the power of a covalent bond and spread to my arms, clothes, and face in my efforts to get it off.

Well, maybe this time would be different.

I trudged down the hall to the kitchen, jug under one arm and holding the coffeemaker as far away from my body as possible. The leftover coffee went down the drain and I pulled open the little drawer where the coffee grounds hid out. Sure enough, one side of the filter was folded down.

Different, I told myself. This time will be different.

I carried the drawer to the garbage can and tipped it upside down.

Nothing.

I tapped the drawer on the side of the can.

Nothing. Once again, I'd been foiled by the incredible surface tension of coffee grounds. No wonder I drank tea.

I gave the thing one almighty hard tap and *ka-blam!* Wet grounds scattered across the lip of the garbage can, all over my hands, across the front of my shirt, and up against the bright white kitchen wall.

The mess was tremendous.

For a long moment I looked at it. Then I sighed and started the cleanup.

Half a roll of paper towels later, everything was as I'd found it. Everything, that is, except a part of the wall that was very hard to reach. For some reason, the countertop ended three inches shy of the wall, creating a gap destined to collect dust, dirt, and stray coffee grounds.

I dampened a couple of paper towels, knelt down, and wiped down the wall. The towels came out thick with coffee grounds and other unknown gunk. I tossed them into the garbage and did it all over again. This time the towels weren't as gunky, but they still weren't what anyone except a teenaged boy would call clean.

Once again I went into the fray. Last time, I promised myself, and stretched my arm as deep into the gap as possible. I even squeezed my elbow back there. After all, as my father had often told me, if you're not going to do a job right, why do it at all? It had been a way of life for Dad, and now here I was, on my hands and knees, cleaning what probably hadn't been cleaned in—

The far edge of the paper towel touched something that rolled. It was a plastic-sounding roll.

A spice jar, I figured. Easy enough to see that happening. Pepper, maybe, falling on its side, rolling toward the wall, and dropping over the edge. Too much trouble to retrieve, so it had been abandoned.

Poor pepper, I thought, and extended my arm a little more. Almost . . . a little farther . . . *Ha! Got you!*

I scooted it out into the light and picked it up. Peered at it. Not a spice jar at all. It was a small pill bottle for an over-the-counter medication. I picked it up and immediately recognized the label. Acetaminophen.

That was weird. Or maybe not. Almost everybody had a bottle of the stuff in their house. Maybe one of the kitchen staff got regular headaches and had carried it in her purse.

I shook the bottle. No rattle.

Huh. More weirdness. Something was in there. I could feel the weight of it shifting around. I fussed with the childproof cap, wishing Jenna was there to open it for me, and finally figured out how to pop off the top.

As I'd suspected, there were no pills inside. But there was something.

I leaned the bottle this way and that, trying to get the contents into the light. There, at the bottom, was . . .

From my kneeling position, I sat down hard on the floor. Pulled in some deep breaths. Maybe I'd been wrong, maybe I was too tired to see properly, maybe I was hallucinating from lack of sleep. It was possible. Likely, even.

I looked into the bottom of the bottle and saw exactly what I'd seen the first time.

Powder. White powder with little bits of reddish orange scattered throughout. Powered acetaminophen. It didn't take much of a mental leap to land on a conclusion I really didn't want to face.

Cookie hadn't accidentally overdosed on acetaminophen. Someone had sprinkled the bitter stuff into her coffee.

She'd been poisoned.

She'd been murdered.

Chapter 7

I made sure the other PTA members had left; then while still in the kitchen, still staring at the bottle, I called Gus and told him what I'd found.

"All right," he said calmly. "I'm on my way. Is anyone else in the building?"

"Harry," I said. "He came back to make sure the school was locked up."

"That's fine. Harry's a good man. I'll be there in ten minutes."

I thumbed off my cell and looked at Harry. He was the school janitor, the security guard, and the fixer of all things, but above all, a quiet and usually unnoticed presence. I'd known Harry for years but didn't know anything about him.

"Chief Eiseley will be here in a few minutes," I said.

A great conservator of words, Harry just nodded. Sadly, Harry was also a fan of Chicago's NHL team, the Blackhawks, instead of being the Minnesota Wild fan that he should be, but we'd learned to discuss hockey without coming to blows.

"That girl of yours," he said. "she's a good goalie."

I beamed. "Thank you." My smile faded as I remembered that she now had competition for the starting spot. I said as much to Harry.

"A test for her," he said. "If she keeps on, it'll happen again. Better if she learns now how to deal with it."

He was right. And if I was smart, I'd remember to pass on his advice to Jenna. Matter of fact, it was such good advice that I wondered how much experience he had in giving it out. "Do you have any children, Harry?" He didn't wear a wedding band, but not all men did, especially men who, in the course of any given day, could come in contact with everything from thick mud to live wires to leaking pipes.

Instead of answering, he reached into his back pocket and pulled out his wallet. With a flick of the wrist, he flipped it open and held it out for me to see.

I blinked. Blinked again. It was a family photo. A smiling Harry sat shoulder to shoulder with a happy-looking woman. Grouped around them were two young men and three young women. "Your family?" I asked.

"Old picture, though." He studied it. "Need a new one that has the grandbabies."

Harry had grandchildren? My mouth flopped open and shut a few times before I could get my vocal cords working. "How many?" I asked.

"Two." He paused. "For now. Two more on the way."

I looked again at the picture. "You look very happy. You all do."

He shrugged. "We get along most days."

"Do they live around here?"

"Oldest son." Harry pointed at the photo. "He's out in Seattle, doing computer stuff for that big company out there."

"Microsoft?" I asked faintly.

"That's the one. Oldest girl, she's career army, about to move up to captain, she says. Next son, he's teaching history at that college in Indiana. South Bend."

"Notre Dame?"

"Yuh-huh. Next daughter, she's not too far away, over in Milwaukee. She and her husband, doctor and doctor." He chuckled quietly. "Busy folks, those two, always cutting up somebody and putting them back together."

"Surgeons?"

He nodded. "Our youngest girl, she was in the Peace Corps. Now she's in Washington, doing flunky work for some senator." He tucked his wallet back into his pocket. "She's talking about going to law school. My bride and I, we're not so sure that'd be the best thing for her, but she'll do what she'll do."

"Kids tend to do that." I stared at him. How could I not have known any of this? How could I not have known that after decades of marriage, Harry still loved his wife deeply enough to call her his bride? Why on earth hadn't he ever mentioned the many accomplishments of his children?

"Beth?" Gus walked into the kitchen. "Are you okay? You look a little strange."

"It's been . . . a strange evening," I said.

"Where's the bottle?" he asked.

I gestured to where it was standing like the cheese all alone on the stainless-steel countertop. "I was cleaning up something I'd spilled and found it down there." I showed him the small gap. "My fingerprints are all over it. I'm really sorry, but I didn't know what it was when I picked it up, so I couldn't help . . ." With great effort, I made myself stop babbling like an idiot.

Gus took a pair of bright purple gloves from his pocket, pulled them on, and studied the bottle and its contents. For a long moment no one said anything. Harry and I watched Gus as he screwed the bottle's top back on. Police work in action. Gus reached into an inside coat pocket for a paper bag. An evidence bag, I'm sure he would have called it, but to me it looked remarkably like a brown lunch bag.

After using a black marking pen to make some notations, Gus dropped the pill bottle into the bag and extracted a small stapler from his coat pocket to secure it.

He turned to face us, and his expression was as grim as I'd ever seen it. The Gus I'd known for years was a kind man given to buying more cookies from Girl Scouts than was good for anyone's cholesterol. Right now, however, he looked every inch the hard, weatherworn, experienced police chief that he was.

"I don't have to tell either of you how important this evidence could be." He held the brown bag with his index finger and thumb.

"Sorry about the fingerprints," I said again. "I wouldn't have touched it if I'd known what it was."

"Not your fault. But I will ask you to come down to the station tomorrow. We'll need to fingerprint you for elimination purposes. This could be critical information," Gus said, tapping the bag, "or it could be nothing. We won't know for a while. Beth, Harry, I'm asking both of you to keep quiet."

Harry, the man who had never told anyone about the many accomplishments of his children, wasn't the one Gus was concerned about. It was the fact that I told Marina pretty much everything and that Marina told everybody everything.

But things were different now. "I promise," I told Gus.

*   *   *

The short drive home was quiet and dark, which matched the quiet and dark of the empty house. First thing I did after walking in the door was turn on every light in the kitchen. Maybe light would chase away the sadness that was settling in on my shoulder.

I picked up the phone and dialed.

"You're late," Richard pointed out.

My former husband had a knack for stating the obvious. "Yes," I said, and left it at that. If I explained, he'd start lecturing me about getting involved in things I had no business being involved in, I'd get my back up about him lecturing me about anything at all, and we'd devolve to a level of acute politeness that would take weeks to thaw. "Is Oliver still up?" I asked.

"I was about to send him to brush his teeth," Richard said.

"This won't take long."

Richard sighed and put down the phone. A moment later I heard my son's voice. "Hi, Mom."

Maybe someday I'd hear those two words and not melt into warm mush. But I hoped not. "Hi, Ollster. What did you do tonight?" I asked.

"I played with that new video game Dad gave us for Christmas."

Wonderful. "Anything else?" I asked.

"I made up a new song."

Oliver's songs were usually composed of roughly two notes and two sentences, but they were my favorite songs in the world. "Can I hear it?"

"It's not quite done yet, but it goes like this." He hummed a dah-di-dah sequence, then sang, "Miss Stephanie is pretty as can be. Miss Stephanie has a smile for me. Miss Stephanie is . . ." He stopped. "That's all I have right now."

"You can finish it tomorrow," I said. And maybe tomorrow would be the right time to talk to him about how cute little Mia Helmstetter was looking this year. I sent him a good-night kiss. "What's your sister doing?"

"Nothing. After supper she shut herself up in her room and hasn't come out."

That didn't sound good. "Knock on her door, please, and tell her I want to say good night."

I heard his *tap-tap* on the door. "Jenna, Mom wants to talk to you." There was a pause. "Mom? She says she's asleep."

Riiight. "Okay, sweetheart. Tell her I love her and to sleep tight."

"And don't let the bedbugs bite."

"Not a single chomp."

He giggled. "Night, Mom."

After he hung up, I pulled out the phone book and flipped it open. "Coach Doan?" I asked. "This is Beth Kennedy, Jenna's mother."

His voice was cautious. "I thought I might hear from you. How's she taking it?"

Bingo! "Well, that's the thing. She's staying with her dad tonight, so I don't know what's going on."

It didn't take long for him to give me the story I'd already anticipated. "Of course I understand," I reassured him. "And I'll do my best to make sure Jenna does."

"She's a good kid," Coach said. "It'll be fine in the end."

Fine? Easy for him to say. I wasn't so sure it would be that simple to find the words to console a young girl who was no longer the starting goalie for her hockey team.

Fatigue was starting to tug at my eyes. It was only nine o'clock, but I was ready for bed. I took Spot out for a short walk and brought George the cat upstairs with me. Five minutes later I had my teeth brushed and my pajamas on. Just as I was crawling under the covers, the phone rang.

Jenna. Maybe she'd felt the need to talk to her mother about the goalie situation. Maybe it was Marina, ready to talk. Maybe it was my mother, ready to move from northern Michigan to Florida.

All that flashed through my head in the time it took my hand to pick up the phone.

"Hello?"

"Hey. How are you?"

Smiling, I finished my crawl into bed. "Pete, did you know you're the only person I really wanted to talk to right now?"

"I was hoping so," he said.

We talked about his day; then I told him about Oliver's crush on his vice principal and about Jenna's displacement from starting goalie. But I didn't tell him about Marina, and I didn't tell him about what I'd found in the school kitchen. One would have been a betrayal of a deep friendship; the other would have been a betrayal of the promise I'd made to Gus. Pete wouldn't talk; as a forensic cleaner he knew better than most how to keep things to himself, but still.

As Pete gave me comforting reassurances about Oliver and said that Jenna would learn how to deal with her new hockey reality, I felt the muscles at the back of my neck start to relax.

"You really think it's going to be okay?" I asked.

"Everything's going to be just fine. Sleep tight, sweetheart."

When he hung up, I held the phone to my chest for a moment, keeping him close. He was right. Everything would be okay. There was no reason to worry and get all worked up about things that wouldn't happen. Oliver would be fine. Jenna would be fine. Marina and I would find a way back to normal, and . . .

And Cookie was dead. Poisoned by someone who'd been at the PTA in Review night.

I put the phone away and cuddled up to my comfortable cat, but even his loud purrs couldn't quiet the thoughts that were racing through my head.

Cookie had been poisoned.

She'd been poisoned by someone during the PTA in Review night.

Cookie had been murdered.

By someone I knew.

At some point sleep swept over me, but it was a long time coming.

Chapter 8

The next morning I presented myself at the police station bright and early. But it was my second stop. First, I'd knocked on the back door of the antiques store until Alice Barnhart let me in.

"It's not even eight o'clock," she said, wiping flour from her hands onto her flour-covered apron.

"I know, and I'm sorry for barging in like this when you're not open, but there are people out there in desperate need of your cookies."

"These are the only ones out of the oven." She dropped half a dozen freshly baked M&M cookies into a white bag. "People? You, for instance?"

"Me and everybody else in this town," I said. "Everybody in the state, if they knew about your cookies. You could franchise and make money hand over fist."

"And you could do the same thing with your bookstore."

I squinched my face. "That sounds horrible."

"For you and me both," she said cheerfully. "Big money means big headaches. I'm much happier with the money I have and my only headache being getting Alan to the doctor once a year."

I thanked her for the early sale and she shooed me off.

"Don't worry about it. Now get out of here and let me start the next batch."

A cold biting wind pushed me down the sidewalk. Light snow swirled around my ankles and dusted the evergreen shrubs with white. With my head down against the blustery weather, I cradled the cookies like a swaddled infant and hurried into the police station.

"And what to my wondering eyes should appear," said Gus, "but a children's bookstore owner and a kind offering for a morning snack?"

"Doesn't scan." I handed over the bag.

"That's why I'm a cop and not a poet." He reached in for a cookie. "Hey, these are still warm. How'd you manage that? Alice isn't open for another hour."

"My methods are top secret."

He led me down the hall not to his office, but to the small lab-type area where the fingerprinting was done. I was mildly disappointed not to have the pads of my fingers stuck on a pad of ink.

"Haven't done that for years," he said, rolling my thumb across the glass of what looked like a small copy machine. "Besides, I always got more ink on me than on the people I was fingerprinting." He studied a small screen and nodded. "One down. If I get the rest done without a redo, do I get another cookie?"

"Maybe I should check with Winnie first."

He smiled. "My wife trusts me implicitly."

In most ways, I was sure that Winnie did. In others, I was certain she absolutely did not. After the fingerprinting—which seemed a misnomer to me, since there were no prints, only digital images—we adjourned to Gus's office, where he waved me to the visitor's chair, which Winnie had refinished so recently that it still smelled faintly of polyurethane.

Gus sat behind his desk, pulled out a drawer, and propped his feet up. He smiled his not-quite-a-smile, the one that meant I wasn't going to like what was coming. "You want the good news or the bad news?"

I slid down in the chair. "Bad." Always best to hear the bad and get it over with.

"Wrong answer," Gus said. "Because the bad news won't make sense unless you hear the good news first."

"Then why did you give me a choice?"

"Just to see how far you'd slide down in that chair. Remember the time you almost fell onto the floor?"

"No. What's the good news?"

"I talked to the sheriff's office this morning, and they won't be taking over the investigation into Cookie Van Doorne's death."

"Okay." Most times murder investigations went straight to the much larger county sheriff's office with its experienced staff and deeper technological capabilities. "Why?"

"That's the bad news." Gus looked at me straight on and I prepared myself for a blow. "They're not convinced Cookie was murdered."

I shot up out of the chair. "They *what*? That's nuts! Cookie would no more have committed suicide than"—I scrambled for an analogy—"than I would have turned down the corners of a first-edition *Secret Garden* instead of using a bookmark. She hadn't shown any signs of depression, and someone said she left a knitting project half-finished."

Wise man that he was, Gus didn't tell me to calm down, but let me rant and rave as long as my breath held out. When I was done and settled back in the chair, he asked, "Were you good friends with Cookie?"

I slid back into a slouch. Didn't say anything. His next question was as inevitable as it was unwelcome.

"So," he said, "if you didn't know her all that well, how can you say with any credibility that she wouldn't have committed suicide? And before you get all up in arms, I'm just whistling in the dark. Convince me. You know I'll listen."

I thought back to the previous year when I'd kind of sort of not on purpose proved that a death from two decades earlier hadn't been the suicide so many people had thought it was. It had been murder, but people had seen a reason for suicide and leapt to the wrong conclusion.

"Last May," I said. "Remember when—"

"Yes. But that was the opposite situation."

"I'm just saying that you never know what's in someone's head. How can anyone really know anything about someone else's motivations?" Because I wasn't even sure about my own motivations most of the time. How could I guess at the whys and wherefores of someone I'd hardly known?

"You do realize you're not convincing me of anything," Gus said.

"It doesn't make sense," I said stubbornly. "I've heard that pills are the most common form of suicide in women, but that doesn't prove anything. And why on earth would she do it at a PTA meeting?"

Gus shrugged. "Maybe she was hoping someone would stop her. Maybe it was an impulse. Maybe she was driven to it by having to listen to May Werner for an hour." He looked at me. "That last one was a joke. It would probably take two hours."

"Was there an autopsy?" I asked. "Was she sick, otherwise?"

He opened a folder on his desk and flipped through papers. "No sign of substantial heart disease, no sign of any cancer, no sign of anything except an overdose of acetaminophen."

I let my head drop back and stared at the stained ceiling tiles. "Are you ever going to spend some money on updating this place?"

"Not on my budget. Beth, have you realized that a suicide would be a lot easier to deal with, considering where that pill bottle was found?"

Of course I'd considered it. I'd considered it half the night. Why did he think my eyes were so bleary and why I was too tired to keep my head up? "What is convenient shouldn't be a consideration," I said heavily. "What matters is the truth."

"You know what might happen."

I knew. If Cookie's death wasn't suicide, it was murder. If it was murder, it was committed by someone I knew, even someone I liked. Perhaps someone I trusted and considered a friend.

"Maybe I'm leaping to the wrong conclusion." I slid down a little farther in the chair.

"But you don't think so," Gus said.

"No." We sat in silence a moment. "Do you?" I asked.

He shut the folder. "There will be an investigation and I will keep an open mind to all possibilities. But there's something you can do for me," Gus said. "Let me know if you hear anything."

"What I hear right now is the wind howling at your window."

"Listen carefully if you hear anyone talking about Cookie. Pay attention to anyone who is acting out of character. Watch to see if relationships change. You listen," he said, "and you pay attention. That's two major skills for law enforcement officers."

"Last I checked, I was a children's bookstore owner, not a detective."

He let his feet drop to the floor and put his elbows on the desk. "Beth. Do you think Cookie was murdered?"

I closed my eyes. Relived the car ride from school to her house. Remembered the phone call. Went through the visit at the hospital and—

"What?" Gus leaned forward. "You've remembered something."

"At the hospital, when I visited her. I'm not sure how I could have forgotten. It was when she said she was being poisoned."

"What else did she say?" His voice was calm but held an underlying edge. "Keep your eyes closed. Go back to the hospital room and remember what she said. She was lying in the bed and . . ."

"She said that evil walks around with us. She said it's our duty to make things right." My eyelids snapped open. "I didn't take her seriously. You know how she exaggerated, how she took everything so seriously." My lower lip trembled. "Why didn't I take her seriously? If I had . . ."

"If you had," Gus said, "nothing would have changed. By the time she was admitted to the hospital, the damage had been done. There was nothing you could have done to change what was going to happen."

He was wrong, of course. I could have stayed at the hospital. I could have gone back for another visit. I could have held her hand. I could have believed her.

Gus reached for another cookie. "How's Pete doing these days? I hear you're seeing a lot of each other."

"I haven't seen him for a few days," I said as heat rushed around in my head.

Gus grinned. "Your ears are turning pink."

I snatched the bag of cookies from underneath his outstretched hand. "You've already had two. Any more and Winnie gets a phone call." I picked up my purse, stood, and headed for the door.

"Beth?"

I turned. Warily. "What?"

"My opinion, for what it's worth. Pete's a good man."

The warmth of a spring thaw coursed through my skin and down into my bones. I swallowed once, then twice, but still couldn't get my voice to work properly. So I went back, tipped the rest of the cookies out onto his desk, and left.

My walk back to the store wasn't far, but the wind made it feel like a twenty-mile trek. How the wind could have been in my face both walking to and walking from the police station, I wasn't sure, but my bright red nose attested to the situation's reality.

With my head down, all I saw were the brick pavers that made up most of the downtown sidewalks. I didn't see the mishmash of architecture that somehow made the Rynwood storefronts into one lovely whole, I didn't see Alan Barnhart out sweeping the bricks in front of the antiques store until I almost ran into him, and I didn't see or hear the SUV roaring past me until the slush it sprayed out splattered all over my pant legs.

I also didn't see that Lois and Flossie were in the middle of an argument. If I'd been paying attention, I would have seen through the storefront window that they were arguing fiercely. As it was, I didn't get a clue until I walked in, jingling the front doorbells.

They both flicked me a quick glance, but their voices continued.

"How could anyone think *The Little Princess* is a better book?" Flossie asked fiercely. "That Sara is the definition of insipid."

Lois glared at her. "She's kind and considerate, which is more than I can say about some people around here. And I'd rather have my characters be kind and considerate than be like that brat Mary Lennox."

I could see Flossie's chin go up and her mouth start to open. Quicker than speech, I made my thumb and middle finger into a circle, put them in my mouth, and blew an earsplitting whistle.

When the echo faded, I gave them both hard looks. "I don't know what's going on here, but I want it to stop. Now and forevermore."

Lois's face had a mulish expression. Flossie looked abashed. "I'm sorry, Beth," she said. "We shouldn't have been arguing in the store, even if it's empty. It won't happen again, I promise."

"Yeah, me, too. Sorry, Beth." Lois bumped Flossie's arm. "Next time we'll go out back in the alley, okay? Say, have you ever read *The Lost Prince*? Now, there's a classic."

I didn't know what was more odd, two grown women arguing about children's books written a century earlier, or the fact that Lois and Flossie were arguing at all. Before I'd hired Flossie, I'd talked at length with Lois, Yvonne, and Paoze and they'd all been happy at the idea of working with her. What had changed in the last three months?

"Flossie?" I asked. "Would you mind going to the grocery store and getting some milk for the tea? We're almost out."

When she was out the door, I turned on Lois. "All right, what were you two really fighting about? And don't tell me it was about Frances Hodgson Burnett's books."

"What makes you think anything is wrong?" Her mulish expression was still there.

"Sara Crewe and Mary Lennox?" I asked dryly. "Come on."

"Anyone who doesn't like Sara Crewe needs some serious counseling. There's nothing wrong that can't be fixed by making a certain person write a comparison paper between *The Secret Garden* and *The Little Princess*. Mary Lennox. As if." She huffed and stomped off.

Midstomp, she turned around and pointed at me. "And quit worrying about this kind of stuff. It's not on your recovery agenda and we're only halfway in." She returned to her former program of stomping and made her way to the graphic novel section.

"They'll be okay," a soft voice said.

I hadn't noticed Yvonne coming into the store, but there she was, standing at my left shoulder. "When did you get here?"

She smiled. "At the insipid remark."

"What were they really fighting about?" People fought about everything from the origin of the universe to the best way to wash a floor, but if you took away the argument from the other day, I'd never seen Lois and Flossie speak a cross word to each other, not even during the week before Christmas.

Yvonne straightened a stack of bookmarks. "I really don't know."

Which could be interpreted two ways. Either she didn't know or she didn't know for absolutely sure but could guess and wasn't going to tell me. And judging from how diligently she was straightening the bookmarks, I was pretty sure it was that second one.

"Well," I said, "maybe Paoze knows."

Yvonne tilted her head to one side and surveyed the bookmarks from a slightly different angle. She made a tiny adjustment. "Maybe."

And if he did know, he'd be the employee most likely to spill the beans.

I retreated to my office. Not even ten o'clock in the morning and I was already tired. Lois was right. I should stop worrying about this kind of stuff. If coworkers couldn't work together, one of them would have to go. After all, I'd fired people before. Well, person. I'd fired one person and I'd hated doing it, but if that's what it took to keep the store running smoothly, that's what would have to be done.

And then I'd have to hire a new employee.

Ick.

I leaned back into my creaky wooden chair and rubbed my eyes.

Had I done the right thing in hiring Flossie? What had seemed so right was now turning sour in a big way. I wondered how to fix what was wrong. But since I didn't know what was wrong, figuring out how to fix it would be hard.

Then I wondered how to fix Jenna's problem. But there was little I could do about that, other than comfort and support her. Same with Oliver and his crush on Miss Stephanie.

Then I got to wondering about Cookie and bitter white power and coffee.

And then I spent a long time wondering about the line between what could be done—and what should be done.

Chapter 9

That evening when we stopped at Marina's to pick up Oliver, Jenna ran ahead of me, then turned around. "Do we have time for me to play Zach's new video game?"

"You're not playing the shoot-everything-in-sight game," I said.

"I *know*, Mom. But he has that new football game, too. Can we play?"

Dinner was already in the car in the form of nice tidy white containers, and the only thing I'd have to do was warm it up in the microwave. The ready-made meals were the one thing I was truly going to miss when my rest period was over.

But although dinner was waiting for us, Oliver's homework was undoubtedly not done, and Spot needed a nice long walk. "You can play until halftime," I said. Then, seeing the imminent protest, I added, "A full game takes at least an hour, and it's already almost half past five. Do you really want to wait until seven to eat?"

"We could have a snack," she said in a wheedling tone. "Please?"

"You can play until halftime. And if I hear any whining when I pull the plug, there won't be any video games for a week."

She kicked at a piece of snow. "Okay," she muttered, then ran ahead into the house, her long hair fluttering behind her.

I stopped on Marina's back deck and looked up at the darkening sky, trying to focus on the wonders of the universe.

It's a wonderful world, I told myself. *Don't let what happened to Cookie drag you down. Look at the stars, those tiny pinpricks of light, and think about all the fantastical things that could be out there.*

Marina's back door opened. "What are you doing out there?" she asked.

"Looking at the stars," I said dreamily.

"Most people look at stars when it's not three hundred degrees below zero. Get in here, silly, before you freeze to death."

Hearing Marina call me silly lifted my spirits. Maybe she hadn't been feeling well yesterday when she'd run off on me. Maybe everything was fine and I'd been, once again, taking things too personally.

I knocked the snow off my boots and entered the warmth of her cozy kitchen. Before I'd even hung my coat on the back of my normal chair, Marina had swooped in with a mug of tea.

"Sit, sit, sit," she said. "We have lots to talk about and not enough time to do it in. Put what I assume are your freezing cold hands around that mug and listen to what I have to tell you."

A small knot somewhere in my middle relaxed and disappeared as if it had never been. Finally, I'd find out who she'd been with in the mall. I'd find out why she'd acted so oddly, and I'd find out what the heck was going on.

"Gladly," I said, smiling at her. "I've been waiting for this."

"You have?" She gave me a puzzled look. "What Ah mean," she said, sliding into Southern belle mode, "is of *course* you have, mah deah." She dropped into the chair opposite me. "Ah am the imparter of all local news and Ah do have news, why, yes, Ah do."

The mug suddenly didn't feel as warm as it had a few seconds ago. "You want to talk about local news?"

"That's the best news of all." She blew the steam off her mug. "Much better than news about things that are happening in countries we've barely heard of. I mean, does anybody actually know where Nauru is? Geography for four hundred, Alex."

I knew Nauru was in the South Pacific, but I also knew she was trying to get me off track. "Seems to me we should be discussing something other than news, local or otherwise."

"What I want to know is if you've heard what I've heard."

Suddenly, what I wanted to do more than anything else was to go home and crawl into bed. The world wouldn't end if I did absolutely nothing until the next day. It might even be better off if I stopped poking a stick at it. What had ever made me think that it was my job to fix everything?

"Beth?" Marina asked. "Are you okay?"

I opened my eyes. Somewhere in the midst of my reverie I'd closed them. She'd asked me a question; what had it been? Oh, yes. "Until you tell me what you've heard, there's no way I can know if it's what I've heard."

"Well, then." Marina glanced toward her living room, whence came kid cheers and groans. She leaned forward and lowered her voice. "I had to call the bank this afternoon and I got talking with Ashley—you know, the one who always worked next to Cookie? Well, she said that Gus came in and talked to her."

Uh-oh. "About what? The weather? How he didn't get what he wanted for Christmas? That he wants to retire?"

Marina sat up straight. "Gus is retiring? He can't do that! That'd be like Auntie May turning into a nice little old lady."

There were times when I truly did not want to know how Marina's thought processes worked. "How are those two things the same?"

"Because neither one bears thinking about. Life without Auntie May to spice it up just wouldn't be the same. Just like life wouldn't be the same if Gus wasn't our chief of police."

That almost made sense. "What was Gus talking to Ashley about?"

"He's not retiring?"

"I was joking. As far as I know, he's going to stay chief until the next millennium."

Marina blew out a breath that fluffed up her red bangs. "Whew. You had me worried. Anyway, Gus was asking Ashley all sorts of questions. Like if Cookie had arguments with bank customers, or if she'd ever said anything about feeling threatened by anyone."

I didn't say anything but sipped more tea. It was lukewarm.

"Don't you see?" Marina asked. "That means Gus is thinking that Cookie was murdered, that he doesn't think she took that acetaminophen accidentally. Or even on purpose."

"Or it could mean that he's following procedure."

"What procedure?"

"Police ones. I'm sure there are things that have to be done when anyone dies unexpectedly."

Marina sat back and studied me. "You've talked to Gus, haven't you? You know something and you're holding out on me."

There was no way I could to lie to her. She'd pick up the faintest whiff of prevarication in a single sentence. "I promised Gus."

"Promised him what?"

"That I wouldn't talk about . . . about the investigation."

She pounced on my hesitation like a cat on an untied shoelace. "You know something, don't you?"

"I know lots of things. I know where Nauru is and I know—"

"And what I know is you're not telling me something." She fixed me with a steely glare. "You're breaking rule number one of the best friend code."

I glared right back at her. "Okay, then, who were you with in the mall the other day?"

Marina's ruddy cheeks faded to a sickly white. "No one," she said in a hoarse whisper. "I don't know what you're talking about. I came alone and left alone and there's nothing else to talk about." She stood up. "And I just remembered. I need to run to the store for some lettuce for tonight's dinner."

I looked at her kitchen counter. An unopened bag of romaine hearts sat right next to her favorite salad bowl. A shiver of sorrow rippled through me, because she was lying to me. Flat-out lying. "Are we going to talk about this later?" I asked softly.

"There's nothing to talk about. Good. I'll see you later, okay?"

She grabbed her purse off the counter and went out into the cold January night just like that, no hat, no boots, no gloves, no coat.

Even though I didn't have to cook dinner, there was still a pile of dishes to wash. More than once I'd been tempted to go to paper plates and plastic utensils, but every time I started to open that particular cabinet door, my mother's voice started reverberating inside my head.

"Elizabeth Ann Emmerling, don't you start taking the easy way out. That's not how I was raised, that's not how your father was raised, and that's not how we're raising you."

At the time, she'd been lecturing me about not moving the dining table chairs before I vacuumed, but somehow her words had sunk deep into my brain and become part of my psyche. I wasn't so sure that my own children were being raised quite the same way, because never once had my mother left her Christmas decorations up until the end of January, and never once had my mother tossed the entire household's dirty clothes into the bathtub and shut the shower curtain so the new minister wouldn't see how we really lived.

Then again, Mom hadn't been a single mother and business owner.

I pushed away Mom's oft-expressed opinion my single mother status was my own fault, and took the large bowl Jenna was handing me to dry.

"Why can't we put this in the dishwasher?" she asked.

"Because this was your great-grandmother Chittenden's bowl. It was made before dishwashers were invented, so it wasn't designed to take the heat of a dishwasher. If we put it in the dishwasher, that pretty yellow color would fade and the material would weaken and chip or even break."

"Then why don't we use it to hold, like, apples and oranges or something, and buy a new bowl to use for mashed potatoes?"

"Because . . ." I stopped. What I'd been about to say was *because that's the bowl Grandma Chittenden always used for mashed potatoes.* I thought a moment, then said, "Actually, Jenna, that's a good question. I do it because I really like the idea that we're using the same bowl for the same thing that my grandmother, your great-grand-mother, did."

Oliver, who was putting away the silverware, looked up at the ceiling. "Do you think maybe she knows when we use her bowl?"

I smiled. "It's a nice thought, isn't it? Maybe she does. It's kind of a nice way to remember our ancestors, isn't it? Using something the same way they did."

My son was sold, but Jenna looked unconvinced and somewhat troubled. "Who are you going to give the bowl to? I mean, if you give it to me someday, do I have to use it for mashed potatoes?"

I wanted to laugh, but my children's faces were so serious that I didn't dare. "Whoever gets the bowl can use it for anything she or he would like."

"A dog dish?" Oliver asked, bouncing up on his toes and grinning.

Jenna looked at the simple bowl that was so precious to me. "I think it would make a good place to put extra hockey pucks."

"Anything." I stowed the bowl away in the cabinet.

Just a piece of glass, but every time I touched it, I felt the love of my grandmother. Someday it would break, and though of course I knew that nothing lasted forever, I'd cry over the loss. Then I'd find some other way to feel my grandmother's love and forget all about the bowl. Almost. "Okay, kiddos, you two can finish this up. I need to take a look at today's mail."

I walked into the small room off the kitchen. George was curled up in the desk chair. He squawked when I picked him up, but started purring when I sat down and put him on my lap.

"You're a big faker," I told him. "I'm pretty sure you make that horrible squawking sound just so I feel sorry for you and let you stay on my lap and get black cat hair all over my pants."

He kept purring, which I took as confirmation of my new theory.

Cats.

The mail was the typical mix. Junk mail, catalogs full of things that I didn't need and couldn't afford, bills, and a letter. A handwritten letter.

"That's not typical," I told George. "Do you know how not typical it is?"

George yawned. Apparently, he didn't care. And he didn't care even when I told him the last time I'd received anything handwritten outside of Christmas cards, birthday cards, and the occasional wedding invitation was in 1997, when my college roommate had sent me a letter announcing that she was pregnant with twins.

I studied the envelope. Standard number ten, common flag stamp, no return address. I didn't recognize the handwriting, and the postmark . . . I squinted. The city name was a long one, but it was so smudged, I couldn't make out most of the letters. The state letters were also smudged, but I was pretty sure they were *AK*.

Weird. Why on earth would anyone in Alaska be sending me a letter?

I slit open the envelope and pulled out the single piece of paper it contained. Tri-folded, plain white copy paper. I unfolded it and began to read.

Dear Beth, if you're reading this, I'm dead.

My vision tunneled until all I saw was that single sentence, then a smaller and even tighter circle until all I saw were two words. *I'm dead.* There was no air to breathe, no life in the world, no nothing save that single stark phrase.

I'm dead.

My breath eventually came back and my vision gradually widened enough for me to look at the bottom of the page for the name. Cookie Van Doorne.

I put the letter down. If I didn't read it, I wouldn't have to know what Cookie had wanted to tell me. There was little to no chance that what she'd written was something I wanted to know. Did I have to read it? Was I obligated to read it?

Well, yes. I was.

I picked up the letter.

Dear Beth,
    If you're reading this, I'm dead. For a few weeks now, I've suspected someone has been trying to kill me. I even talked to a police officer, but I could tell he thought I'm a batty old lady with cobwebs in her head who has nothing better to do than be scared of things that go bump in the night. In his defense, though, I have no proof. A car that came close to

*running me over on a rainy night and noises in the
backyard aren't things that show up on those investigation shows.*

*If my death looks like something other than mur-
der, please find out what really happened. My health
is good and taking my own life would be a sin.
Please help the police. Everybody knows how smart
you are. There will be clues and I'm depending on
you to figure out what happened.*

Please, Beth, please help me rest in peace.
Sincerely,
Cookie Van Doorne

I picked up the phone and dialed the number for Gus
and Winnie's house. Maybe this could wait until tomorrow, but I'd feel better if I could tell him now. The phone
clicked and I opened my mouth to say hello, but the
machine clicked in. "Hi," said a tinny version of Winnie's voice. "You have reached the Eiseley household . . ." With Cookie's letter in my hand, I waited out
the message, then left one of my own, asking Gus to call
me tonight, otherwise I'd stop by his office the next
morning.

"Mom?"

I jumped. "Jenna! You startled me."

"Sorry." She stood in the doorway, looking at me
looking at the letter. "Um, are you okay? You look a
little funny."

I put on a smile, folded up the letter, and slid it into
my purse. "I'm fine, sweetie. Are you two done with the
dishes? Then what do you say to a rousing game of triple
solitaire?"

*   *   *

After one too many card games, I sent the kids upstairs to brush their teeth and get into their pajamas.

"But, Mom," Jenna said, "it's Thursday night. That's almost like a Friday night, so we should get to stay up a little longer."

"And you have. It's ten minutes past when I should have sent you upstairs. Now go before I have to send the flying monkeys after you."

Oliver giggled. "I could be one of those." He made screeching noises and ran up the stairs flapping his arms.

Jenna rolled her eyes. "He's so embarrassing sometimes."

I laughed. "At least he didn't do it in public."

A look of horror flashed across her face. "He won't, will he? Make him promise not to, Mom. I'd die, just die, if he did that in front of my friends. I'd have to change schools."

I laughed again. "Most of your friends have younger siblings, too. I'm sure they'd say the same thing. Maybe you could start a new school. The Rynwood School for Humiliated Older Siblings."

Jenna grinned. "We could call it RSHOS. Riss-hoss." She said it again. "Yeah, I like it. Our hockey team would be the Mustangs, and—"

"Lights out in half an hour." I pointed toward the stairs. "Do you want to spend the time fantasizing about your new school or do you want to spend it reading *The Red Machine*?" The book about the rise of the Soviet hockey dynasty was a gift from her aunt Darlene, and it had been her bedtime companion since Christmas.

She headed up, but her mutterings trailed down the stairs. "Riss-hoss. We'd make it an all-girl school. No stinky boys. And no guy teachers. Just us girls. What do we need boys for, anyway? All they do is make trouble."

I wanted to call up after her that girls could make plenty of trouble, too, but she knew that already. At least she should.

By the time I'd tidied up the family room, I'd heard Oliver come out of the bathroom and pad down the hall into his bedroom. I went up and found him buttoning his pajamas and humming a little song. It sounded a lot like the dah-di-dah song he'd sung for me the previous night.

"Is that your song about Ms. Stephanie?" I asked.

He nodded. "I need more words that rhyme with 'be' and 'me.' Can you think of any?"

I could think of quite a few, but I didn't want to encourage the writing of a paean to a woman decades older than my son. "We can look in the rhyming dictionary on Sunday when you get back from your dad's." And, with any luck, he would have forgotten about the whole thing by then.

"Okay." He jumped into bed and pulled the covers up to his chin. "Or maybe I could take the dictionary with me?"

"Sorry, Ollster. I need it this weekend." For something, I'd make sure of it.

"Oh." His face fell. "Maybe I can get Dad to help me come up with some rhymes."

"Never hurts to ask," I said. "I was talking to Mrs. Helmstetter the other day. She said Mia is learning how to play the flute."

"Maybe I could teach her the Ms. Stephanie song." Oliver hummed his song. "Mom?"

"What, honey?" I sat on the bed and snuggled him close to me. My little boy was getting so big.

"Do you think Ms. Stephanie will wait for me to grow up? I'm too young now, but we could get married when I'm older, can't we?"

Oh, dear. I kissed the top of his head. "Sweetheart, Ms. Stephanie already has a boyfriend." At least I was pretty sure she did. Just after New Year's, I'd seen her walking out of a downtown restaurant hand in hand with a man who was smiling down at her with infatuation written all over his face.

Oliver hummed a verse of his song. "Okay, but when they break up, you know, like you and Dad did, then I can marry her, right?"

My bedtime talk with Jenna didn't go any better. I knocked on the door of her room, then went in.

I'd expected to see her sitting up against three pillows, legs drawn up, book resting on her knees. Instead, she was lying on her side with her back to me. I sensed more than heard the sniffles.

I sat down on the edge of the bed and put my hand on her shoulder. Didn't say anything.

She sniffed. Sniffed again. "Mom?" she asked. "Do you think I'm a good goalie?"

Instantly, I gathered her up into my arms. "Sweetie, you're a wonderful goalie."

"Then why isn't Coach playing me?"

Her pain seared me inside and out. My daughter, my heart, my life, my love. I caressed her hair. "Because he knows you're good, and it's only fair to let the new girl have a chance to play."

"I don't want to be fair," she whispered. "I just want to play."

"That's because you're a goalie. A very good one." I

rattled on about her drive and her ambition. About her constant work to improve, about the biographies she'd read about professional goalies. About how this was a test, and how she'd come through in the end.

But though I talked on and on, I could tell it wasn't helping. My darling Jenna had reached the age when Mom couldn't fix everything.

I ran out of words and simply sat there, holding her, loving her, doing my best to send her all the strength and courage I had. She could have it all, if she needed it. She could have everything.

Finally, I felt her relax into sleep. With an ease that came from years of motherhood, I slowly extracted my arm from around her shoulders, pulled the covers up, and stood over her, watching. Could there possibly be a more beautiful sight than a sleeping child?

I stooped to kiss her forehead and left.

My own bedtime came not too much later. I plumped up pillows and read a few chapters of a new Krista Davis mystery before turning off the light, but though I was tired, sleep didn't come easily.

Oliver. What could I do to help my son?

Jenna. What could I do to help my daughter?

And then there was Cookie. What could I do? What should I do?

George jumped up onto the bed. He found my feet, walked up my legs, and settled onto my chest. His rumbling purr was comforting, but I didn't find sleep for a very long time.

Please help me rest in peace.

Chapter 10

The next morning I dropped Jenna off at the middle school. I sent her off with an air kiss from the front seat and an admonition to be nice to their father's new friend.

"He's not going to marry her, is he?"

It didn't require the use of the rearview mirror to know Jenna was scowling. "He hasn't said anything to me about it," I said. Not that he would. If Richard remarried I'd learn about it via a phone call from his mother asking what size dress she should buy for Jenna.

"Just be nice," I said. "It goes a long way."

But from the look of Jenna's scuffing steps up the sidewalk, the poor woman wasn't going to get a lot of nice from my daughter. Horrible person that I am, the thought made me smile a little.

After Oliver hopped out of the car and headed for Tarver's before-school activity room as he tried to work out another line for the Ms. Stephanie song, I headed for the bookstore's copy machine. After that, the Rynwood Police Department.

"Sorry I didn't call you back last night," Gus said. "But we had tickets to that show everybody's talking about and didn't get back until late. What's up?"

I handed him the letter. The original, not one of the copies I'd made. He read through it once, twice, then three times. "You got this yesterday?"

I nodded.

"Interesting," he said. "Wonder who she talked to. I never saw an incident report." He drummed his fingers on the desk and I could tell he was lining up his staff and considering them one by one. All the Rynwood officers were very nice people, and I didn't want to know who got the dressing-down.

"You got this yesterday." Gus tapped the letter.

"Yup."

"And you didn't get much sleep last night, did you?" He smiled.

I put my hands under my legs to keep from touching the dark circles I'd tried to hide. Clearly, the cover-up I'd used wasn't doing the job as well as the packaging had claimed.

"So what do you think?" Gus asked.

"About what? The weather? It's January, so complaining about the cold and the snow is pointless. If you're asking about the rise in the Dow Jones, I can't explain it. And if you want to know what I think about postmodern art, I'll have to get back to you."

Gus paid no attention to my ramblings. He knew a stalling tactic when he heard it. He picked up the letter and read it one more time. "You realize this letter isn't proof of anything except Cookie's state of mind."

"She says she'd never take her own life," I protested.

"No, it says taking her own life would be a sin. Doesn't mean she didn't decide to be a sinner after she wrote the letter. And before you get all worked up, like I said yesterday, I'll be investigating." He leaned back in his chair.

"Clues, she said. Do you have any idea what she's talking about?"

"Nope."

"She also says everybody knows how smart you are."

I made a rude noise in the back of my throat. "No one would think that if they knew what I did the other day."

"Yeah?" Gus half smiled. "What's that?"

"Promise you won't tell?" At his nod, I went on with the story. "The other day I needed to fax an order to a distributor, and I couldn't find the fax number. So I looked up their phone number on my computer contacts list and called them."

"Doesn't sound dumb so far."

"I called and asked for their fax number, then wrote the number down."

"Still not dumb."

"I wrote the fax number down on a memo pad the distributor had sent me. A memo pad that had their phone and fax numbers on it."

Gus threw his head back and laughed. "Can I take that promise back?"

"Not a chance."

He wiped his eyes and let his laughter fade. "So," he said, sighing, "more circumstantial evidence that Cookie was murdered, but no hard evidence. What do you think?"

"That I really, really wish she hadn't sent me that letter."

He nodded and fingered the envelope. "Alaska. Wonder what that's all about."

I had no idea, and said so. "Why is it that the older I get, the more I realize I don't know anything?"

"Some people might call that wisdom."

"And some people use an apostrophe to denote a plural, but that doesn't make them right." I got up to go. "Anyway, I thought you should see the letter."

"Thanks, Beth. You'll call if you come across anything?"

I nodded and headed for the door.

"You're smarter than you think," Gus said.

In a low voice I said, "Remember the fax number," and left with Gus's laughter trailing after me.

When I unlocked the store, the darkness inside felt harsh and heavy. I flicked on every light switch and immediately felt better. So much easier to look on the bright side of life when the stuffed Winnie-the-Pooh bears were happily lit with sparkling halogen rays.

"Good morning to you, too," I said to the short row of rag Madeline dolls.

I turned on my computer and made up a mug of tea.

My hand reached out for a pad of paper to start the day's To Do list, but my fingers stopped just before my fingers wrapped around the pen.

First things first.

I opened e-mail and was momentarily distracted by the distressing number of incoming messages. "I'll deal with you later," I told the e-mails, and started typing.

Dear Ms. Neff, I wrote. *The president of the Tarver Elementary PTA wishes to meet with you at your earliest convenience. While the president understands your schedule is filled with the demands of the day, she would like to impress upon you the urgency of this request. Please consider this a priority.*

Sincerely, Elizabeth Ann Kennedy, President, Ezekiel G. Tarver PTA.

I read over the e-mail, thought a little more, then added *P.S. Marina, please talk to me. I know there's something wrong and I want to help. If I've done something to hurt you, I didn't mean it; if I've—*

"Stop it," I said out loud, and deleted the entire postscript. Then, before I could think about it too much, I clicked the SEND button.

I imagined it flying thought the wires, zooming from downtown Rynwood over the treelined streets to Marina's house. Saw it arrive on the laptop she kept in the kitchen. Watched as it pinged onto her screen.

It was after nine o'clock. Right now she'd be having her day care kids playing some energetic game in the basement. When she finally saw the e-mail, would she answer? If she did, what would she say?

I wrapped my hands around my mug, but the tea had cooled to room temperature. No comfort there. I pushed back my chair and offered up a thank-you to whoever invented the microwave. If it wasn't for that wonderful appliance, half of my tea would be dumped down the drain.

My e-mail pinged. I blinked. Marina had answered already.

I swallowed a mouthful of lukewarm tea. Swallowed another, just to remind myself just how much I disliked tea at that temperature, then opened the e-mail.

We're headed to the hill as soon as I get their boots on.

That was all she'd written. Not exactly an invitation, but not anything close to a go-away-forever, either.

Lois popped her head through the open door. "What's up for today, boss?"

"Looks like I'm going sledding."

*   *   *

The sky was so low and gray, it made me wonder if the cloud cover was stuck to the upper layers of the atmosphere. Maybe we'd never see the sun again and—

"Look out!"

The soprano shriek startled me into awareness. With a quick hop, I jumped out of the way of the kid sliding past on the saucer.

"You came." Marina, red-cheeked and red-nosed, gave me a quick glance, then went back to studying the sledders. "That Joshua is going to age me before my time. Joshua!" she called. "Don't you dare go any higher than halfway up!"

A small boy in a blue snowsuit looked over his shoulder. "But, Mrs. Neff—"

"If you don't do what I tell you, we're going back to the house."

His shoulders drooped with what was obviously a heavy sigh, but he turned his tub sled around. "Banzai!" he yelled as he took a running jump and landed face-first on the sled.

I winced, but the kid whooped with delight all the way down the hill. "Where are Noah and Kendra?" I asked.

Marina pointed to the far side of the hill where a red snowsuit and a yellow snowsuit were falling down and getting back up again. "They both got snowboards for Christmas."

"I didn't know they made snowboards for four-year-olds."

"They shouldn't," she said. "And no one should ever have bought a pet rock, either, but they did."

After that, the conversation languished. I watched the kids; Marina watched the kids. We stepped aside for an incoming sledder. We watched the kids. Time ticked away. My toes lost all feeling.

"So," I finally said. "I have a proposal."

"About what?" Marina kept her gaze fastened on the snowsuits, which were now sitting down and tossing snow up into the air.

Not all of what had kept me awake last night had been Cookie's letter. "About how we deal with whatever it is you don't want to talk about." I watched her closely, but her expression didn't change. Which in itself was a sign of strangeness, since on an average day, Marina's face was constantly on the move.

I plunged ahead. "Something is bothering you. Before I present my proposal, there's one thing to clear up. Have I done something to upset you? Is this my fault?"

Slowly, she shook her head.

I waited her to say something. She didn't. "Then here's what I suggest. I truly wish you'd talk to me about whatever this is, but I respect your feelings and assume there's a good reason you're keeping this to yourself."

She made a small nod.

"Okay. Do you think you'll ever talk to me about this thing?"

For a long time, we stood there. Tectonic plates shifted, continents collided. When the sea level had risen and fallen again, Marina said, "Yes. Someday."

A spring that had been coiled up tight inside my tummy relaxed. "Good," I said. "Do you think we can pin down a date?"

"Beth—"

The raw pain in her voice tightened the muscles back up again. "Just tell me this. You're not sick, are you? No one in your family's sick?"

For the first time, she looked straight at me. "Is that what you think this has all been about? That I've been diagnosed with ... with something awful and I didn't want to tell you?"

I swallowed. "Maybe."

She thumped me on the shoulder with her mittened hand. "Silly old you. Of course I'd tell you something like that. I mean, really, Beth. Of all the things to think. Puh-leese."

"What was I supposed to think? You haven't given me much to go on here."

"I know," she said. "And I'm sorry. I just ..." She looked away. "Just can't right now."

A compromise was in order. "Okay. So there's something going on in your life that's troubling you, and though talking to your best friend would undoubtedly help, you can't or won't do so."

She nodded.

"Then I'll wait," I said. "You're my best friend, and I'll help you in any way I can. If that means standing back from this, then I will."

Marina made a choking noise, the weird snort she made when she was trying not to cry. I usually heard that noise when we were watching sappy movies and every so often when we were talking about our families, but this was the first time I'd heard it out in public.

"But I won't wait forever," I warned her. "If you haven't told me by ..." By when? Clearly, this was a Big Thing for Marina, so I had to give her time. But too much time and this divide would widen until it might split us apart. I thought fast, then made up my mind. "If you haven't told me by Mother's Day, I'm going to camp on your back deck until you start talking."

She wiped at her eyes with the back of her mitten. "Mother's Day. I'll tell you by then, I promise."

I marked the date in my head with a big fat red felt pen. "I'll hold you to that."

"I know," she said, and thumped me on the shoulder again.

A glow of happiness warmed me. Marina and I were all right. One thing in the world was straightened out, only three point two billion things to fix. The glow faded and I reached into my pocket. "Read this," I said, and handed over Cookie's letter.

Marina's eyes opened wide as she read. "You've got to be kidding me. A letter from the dead? That woman watched too many soap operas. You're not taking this seriously, are you?" She folded up the letter and studied my face. "You are taking it seriously. Oh, jeez . . ."

She pulled her phone out of her pocket. "We have a problem," she said to whoever was on the other end. "Emergency meeting at the sledding hill. Right now. Do what you can."

I frowned as she turned back around. "Don't tell me," I said.

She grinned. "Yep. We're having an emergency meeting of your intervention team."

Far too short a time later, Lois and Ruthie arrived at the sledding hill. Marina nodded at me. "Show them."

"Do I have to?"

She glared. "Yes."

Sighing, I handed the letter to Ruthie, who read it silently and passed it to Lois, who asked, "Has Darlene heard about this?"

"I sure have," my sister's tinny voice said from the cell

phone Marina was holding out into the middle of our small circle. "Was this woman nuts, or what?"

"But," I said "that doesn't mean Cookie wasn't right. Just because she . . . she . . ."

"Had a few screws loose?" Lois asked.

"Just because she had a different way of looking at life," I said firmly, "doesn't mean she didn't have a point. And, yes, I've shown this letter to Gus. He said he'll keep it in mind as he's looking into her death."

"Then that's all taken care of," Ruthie said, "and you don't have to do a thing."

"She'd better not," Darlene said. "I'll tell Mom if you do, Beth."

It wasn't as much of a threat now as it had been thirty years ago, but it still carried some steel.

"And look at her," Lois said. "You can tell she hasn't been sleeping right. See those circles under her eyes? She's starting to look like she did last fall. When did you get that letter?"

"Last night."

Ruthie clucked at me. "Girl, you need to lay off this thing. Request of a dead woman or not, you have to take care of yourself first; otherwise you're not good to anyone else. Think of your children, sweetie."

I was. I did. I was never *not* thinking of them. But still . . .

"Let Gus take care of it this time," Marina said. "I know you've figured out things ahead of him before, but let him do this one. Heck, with what he's learned from you, he'll track her down lickety-split."

"Track what her down?" I asked.

"The killer, of course."

I frowned. "How do you know it's a woman?"

"Everybody knows poisoning is a woman's crime. No fuss, no muss, no nasty loud guns that make a big mess. Men like to make a statement. Women just want to get the job done. A woman killed Cookie. I'm sure of it."

I wasn't so sure her logic sequenced properly, and it sounded pretty sexist to me, but I kept quiet.

"Let it go," Ruthie said. "You've done your job by showing the letter to Gus. Let him take over."

"I can't." I looked around at my friends, at the women who cared enough about me to do the hard thing of intervening. "Cookie asked me to help her. How can I turn my back on a request to help her rest in peace?"

The trio shuffled their feet and didn't say anything. They studied the snow, their boots, one another, then finally looked back at me.

"Don't stop me," I said. "*Help* me."

"Beth's right."

I'd heard approaching footsteps, but hadn't realized they were Pete's until he spoke.

Marina glared at him. "What kind of interventionist are you if you let her do too much?"

He smiled, shrugging. "Not a very good one, I guess. But how can we keep her from doing what she thinks is right?"

Dear Pete. I made a mental note to bake a big batch of his favorite cookies.

"I say we help her." He put his arm around my shoulders. "She's smart and she knows what she's doing."

Clearly, I hadn't told Pete the fax number story.

"Is that Pete?" Darlene asked. "Pete, if she's so smart, ask her why she ruined the starter on Dad's car by trying to turn on the engine when it was already on."

"Hey," I said. "That's not fair and you know it. Dad said that starter was already going bad and—"

Lois made the time-out sign. "Chill, sisters. We need to concentrate because my toes are about to fall off from frostbite. If that happens I'll have to get rid of all my flip-flops and I just bought a pretty purple pair with sparkles all over."

"What do you say, ladies?" Pete asked. "The faster we figure out what really happened to Cookie, the better it will be for Beth. Are we in?"

Marina smooshed her mouth with her mittens, then said, "I am."

"And me, I guess," Darlene said.

Ruthie nodded. "Me, too."

Lois flung her fuzzy yellow scarf around her neck. "I can see I'm the only one with any sense. I just hope this doesn't turn out bad. Remember what almost happened last fall."

And suddenly I was back in that alley, crouched in the dark, waiting for—

"Don't worry," Pete said, giving me a one-armed hug. "Last fall was a one-off. And this time it'll be different because we'll be helping you."

My smile was genuine, but my gaze was looking back in time. Maybe instead of the alley, I'd park in the city lot for the next few weeks.

Chapter 11

After I closed down the store on Saturday, I went home to walk Spot, then headed for Marina's house. My two were with their father, and Marina's DH and Zach, their only at-home child, were at a comic book convention in Minneapolis.

"He's going to turn into an engineer," Marina said glumly. "I just know it."

"Most mothers would be excited at having a child enter such a potentially lucrative career."

"Yeah, well, most mothers aren't married to an engineer. I know what they're really like. Zach's already starting to read science fiction."

"Cheer up," I said. "Even if you lose one child to the engineering profession, you have three that didn't see the attraction."

"That's true. My genes rule, don't they?" She held her hand up for a high five. Cheered, she got up from the kitchen table. "This calls for a celebration. How about guacamole and bits of toasted pita bread?"

Marina's adult snacks were usually more of the brownie, coffee cake, or cookie variety. "Did you make a New Year's resolution you didn't tell me about?"

"Variety is the spice of life. And Zach has decided

that for something that's green and is supposed to be good for you, guacamole isn't so bad. Next week I'm going to sneak some tomatoes into it and see what happens."

"Here's to the manipulation of our children." I held up a guac-loaded chip.

"May it last forevermore." Marina grinned and we touched chips.

After we made a happy dent in the food, Marina said, "So, now what? If I'm going to help you help Cookie, I suppose we should be doing something. Let me guess." She closed her eyes and put her hands to her forehead. "We're going to make a list."

"Do you have any better ideas?"

"Eat more guacamole?"

"We can eat and make a list at the same time, you know."

"Multitasking!" she crowed. "See, you are smart. Say, can we triple-task? Because I wouldn't mind adding a little dissing of Claudia Wolff into the mix. Did you see how she wanted to tear into you at the last meeting?"

"Two things are as much as my brain can handle, thanks." I extracted a pad of paper from my purse. "And no making fun of my list making. If you'll recall, it was one of my Saturday lists that helped you remember your mother-in-law's birthday."

"And she was so happy to receive a subscription to *Cosmopolitan*, you wouldn't believe it." Marina popped a piece of pita into her mouth. "So what list is this?"

The previous night I'd thought about what would help figure out this puzzle and had come to a very obvious conclusion. "We need to figure out who was in the kitchen the night of the PTA in Review."

Marina stopped, a piece of pita half-dunked. "Everyone was in the kitchen that night."

Which was exactly the problem. "I know. We had so many breaks that half the PTA was in and out of the kitchen cutting and serving and making coffee and taking money."

Marina brightened. "Claudia was there. I'm sure of it."

"No, she wasn't. She was out in the gym."

"She was?"

"I was on the stage, remember? She was sitting in the front row." With her arms crossed, staring daggers at me the whole time. "I think she got up once, and that was to get something to eat, not to go help in the kitchen."

"Well, darn."

Marina had been trying to make Claudia a suspect in everything from littering to arson to murder for years. As frosty as the relationship was between Claudia and me, it was eternal friendship compared to what went on between Marina and Claudia.

"So who was in the kitchen?" I looked at the blank sheet of paper, considered a few titles, then wrote *Kitchen Candidates*.

Marina peered at my handwriting. "It'd look cool if you spelled candidate with a *K*."

"No, it wouldn't." I started writing names.

Marina rolled her eyes. "Once again, your overgrown sense of right has twisted your brain. What's the point of putting your name down when we all know you didn't do anything wrong?"

"Because it's a complete list. And your name's going down, too."

"Hey, you can't do that!"

"I just did. You were in there more often than I was."

"Fine." She slumped down in her chair. "Then you'd better put Alan Barnhart down."

"Alan?" I blinked. "He's not in the PTA. What was he doing in the kitchen?"

"He saw we were shorthanded back there and said he'd be glad to help out." She watched me write his name. "So Alan becomes a suspect because he was being a nice guy?"

I didn't like it, either. "We're trying to figure out who was in the kitchen and who might have put that acetaminophen into Cookie's coffee. We have to look at everybody. We can't eliminate people just because we like them."

"We can't?"

I wrote another name. "Isabel Olsen. She was cutting up brownies, wasn't she?"

"Kirk was back there, too." Marina smirked. "He must have spent twenty bucks on Rice Krispies squares. He was scarfing them down like there's no tomorrow. Maybe that's why he got a membership at that fancy gym." She laughed. "He'd be better off paying for hair implants. That receding hairline ages him faster than those extra pounds."

"Who else?"

Marina twisted up her face into think mode. "I think what's her name, the new vice principal, was there for quite a while."

My pen paused. "Stephanie Pesch?"

"Yeah. Why, what's the matter?"

"Oliver's making up songs about her."

"Crush time? The boy has good taste. She's pretty hot. I mean, for a thirtysomething blond with a great body and long legs, she does okay."

I tapped the list. "Anyone else?"

"Can't think of anyone."

We stared at the short list.

In a low, quiet voice, Marina said, "I don't think I like doing this."

I didn't, either. "I'll call Gus. He'll know what to do next."

But when I dialed the police department, I was told that all available officers had been called out to the expressway to a multicar accident. I left a voice mail asking him to call me.

"Now what?" Marina asked.

I tucked the list away in my purse and reached for a pita piece. "Eat more guacamole."

And stay as busy as possible, because if I didn't, I'd think far too much about the names on that extremely short list.

All Saturday evening, I expected Gus to call, but the phone never rang. When I walked into the choir room Sunday morning, I looked around. "Where's Gus?" I asked the director.

"Hmm?" Kay was sitting on her stool, studying the morning's offertory anthem and frowning.

"Gus. He's usually here by now."

"Not today." She stood and tapped the music stand with her thin baton. "Ladies and gentlemen," she said loudly. "Time for warm-ups. Let's start with oooo's in the key of C." She nodded at the pianist and raised her hands for the cue.

"Kay, where's Gus?"

"Sick." She lowered her hands in a firm downbeat and

the room filled with oooo's in various octaves. Time to get to work.

After the service, I tracked Winnie down. I found her in a Sunday school classroom, putting away craft supplies. "I hear your husband is sick."

"First time in years," she said cheerfully. "He's got that nasty flu that's going around, and he's being a horrible patient. He wasn't feeling very chipper when the call came in about that accident on the highway, but did he leave it for someone else to take care of? Of course not. Instead of staying inside where it's nice and warm, he went out in that cold and wind and snow for hours on end. I tell him he's going to be in bed even longer if he doesn't rest, but there you are, what husband ever listens to his wife?"

"A smart one."

"Now there's an oxymoron for you," she said, and we both laughed.

"Do you think husbands say mean things about their wives when they're not around?" I asked.

"Honey, the battle between the sexes has been going on for thousands of years. The best we can do is to find a way to get a giggle out of it. So what do you need with Gus?"

I hesitated. "It can wait."

"Is it police business? Because that nice Officer Zimmerman is going to be in charge while Gus is out sick. You go talk to him if you need something."

I thanked her, but walked away knowing that I wouldn't. I couldn't talk to anyone except Gus. He was the one running the investigation, and since it had barely started, he probably hadn't done any paperwork or told anyone else about any of it. And Gus had at least some small measure of confidence in the things I told him. I didn't want to hand over my little list to another officer and have it tossed in the trash.

No, I'd have to wait until Gus came back to work. And, really, what difference would a few days make?

I zipped up my coat, pulled on my gloves, and went out into the cold.

Monday morning, I wandered around the store aimlessly, alphabetizing the cart of sale books and studying the Valentine's display in the front window.

"Move away from that window," Lois said menacingly. "Last week you said it was fine. Don't you dare go changing your mind now. I invested too much time in it."

"The display is fine," I said vaguely. Red hearts, white hearts, and red ribbons twined around stacks of all the red, white, and pink books Lois had been able to dig up. Since Christmas, we'd been collecting the titles of children's favorite books, and each of the hearts had the title of one of those books written on it. The great big heart in the middle of the display said *I love to read*. It was a great display, and I said so.

"Then what is your problem?" Lois asked. "You've been mooning about all morning. Wait a minute. . . ." She tapped her nose. "It's that thing with Cookie, isn't it? Gus is out sick and you can't stand nothing being done. You want to go out and play Nancy Drew, don't you?"

"Trixie Belden," I muttered.

"Go on." Lois waved me away. "You're not getting anything done here—that's for sure. As much as you're contributing to this store, you might as well be in Alaska."

"Alaska?" I blinked.

"Hawaii, if you want somewhere warm."

I looked across the store. It was empty except for me, Lois and Flossie. January in small-town Wisconsin.

"We need to finish checking the stock for the home-schoolers," I said. "And . . ." And there must be something else that needed doing, but I couldn't think what.

"Flossie and I will do that," Lois said, grinning. "Right, Flossie?"

A startled Flossie looked up from the greeting cards she was sorting. "I'll what?"

"Help out," Lois said.

"Ah. Yes. Whatever Beth thinks is best."

I glanced from one to the other. "You're sure?"

Lois had already gathered up my coat and purse. "Here. Put these on and git. We have work to do."

"Well . . ."

She pointed to the front door with a firm index finger.

I went, and was heartened by the fact that Flossie and Lois seemed to be getting along better. Maybe the recent arguments were over. Maybe I didn't need to worry about the situation at all.

But just as the door shut, I heard Lois say, "Well, if you don't understand, maybe you should go back to that grocery store."

I stood there a moment, thinking about going back inside, then thinking about what would happen if I did—which would be nothing, because neither of them would tell me what was going on—and headed down the street.

Courtesy of a dusting of new snow, my shoes made little noise on the sidewalk. I was Stealth Beth, sneaking up on evildoers with my weapon of choice, my trusty purse,

which would give any serious bad guy a nasty whack upside the head.

As if. The likelihood of me being able to have the
courage to act that sensibly in the face of danger was
remote. Still, it was fun to think about, so I was smiling
as I opened the door of Made in the Midwest.

"You're looking perky this morning." Mary Margaret
wagged her eyebrows. "On a Monday, no less. Did you
have a good weekend?"

"The cold air makes my cheeks turn red, that's all."
There was no reason at all for me to tell Mary Margaret
about the lovely Saturday evening Pete and I had spent
together. Some things are best kept close to the heart. "I
have a question for you."

She made her hand into a pistol shape and fired it
over my head. "Shoot."

"Back a couple of weeks ago, at the PTA in Review,
do you remember whose idea it was that refreshments
be served at every break?"

"Huh." She scratched her forehead. "I sure don't. It
was a last-minute thought. I remember that part. At the
committee meeting someone said we could maybe raise
more money that way, and if we all brought a little something it wouldn't be much work . . ." She stared at the
ceiling, then shrugged. "Nope. Sorry. Why do you want to
know, anyway?"

If I'd been smart, I would have figured out an answer
to that before walking into her store. "Um, since it did
make a nice amount of money, I'd like to give credit to
the person who came up with it." Ta-da! Beth pulls a fast
and believable answer out of thin air!

"I'll think on it," Mary Margaret said. Then she
frowned. "You sure that's the reason? Because your ears

are turning a little red. From what I hear, that means . . . Well, you know."

Okay, maybe not so believable. But at least it was fast. "My ears turn red from the cold pretty easily. You'll let me know if you remember? Maybe you could ask some of the other committee members."

"Not a problem." She nudged my elbow, smiling slyly. "Anything to help recognize a good idea."

I made my escape, ears and face burning bright.

With my back to the wind, I pulled my cell phone from my purse and made a quick phone call, ending with "Ten minutes? Perfect. I'll be waiting."

Now that I had a destination, moving was easy. I pushed open the door of the antiques store and welcomed the burst of warmth that enveloped me. "Is or is not central heating the best thing ever invented?" I asked.

Alan, who was standing behind the front counter, considered the question. "Indoor plumbing is pretty good."

"But what good is indoor plumbing without a warm house to keep it in?" I unzipped my coat and let the heat soak in. "Those pipes freeze up and you might as well get out the outhouse."

He laughed. "What can I do you for this morning, Beth?"

"I'd like to hog one of your tables for a little while."

"Stay as long as you'd like." He swept his arm out, palm up, indicating the completely empty store. "You can see how busy we are."

"Cold days are hard on retail."

"No doubt about it," he agreed. "And I've already done

inventory. Alice says she's going to make me do it all over again if I don't stop complaining."

"And I will," Alice said, bustling in from the kitchen with a tray of warm, fresh cookies. "Morning, Beth. You looking for some of these?" She brandished dozens of oatmeal raisin.

"If I eat that many I'll explode right here in your store."

"Then take six. That shouldn't do much more than give you a happy little tummyache." She put the tray in the glass case and pulled off her silver oven mitts. "Or are you looking for these?" She jiggled the tray labeled AMAZINGLY AWESOME. "I know these are your favorites."

"I'll take four." Weak, that's what I was. Weak. I'd walked in intending to buy two coffees and one cookie, yet here I was, succumbing to weakness.

"That's my girl." Alice beamed. "You're getting to be nothing but skin and bones. And are you getting enough sleep? Seems like those circles under your eyes are a little darker than last time I saw you."

"Cookies will help."

"Of course they will. Cookies help pretty much everything. A bag? Oh, you're staying. How nice. And two coffees. You pick a table and I'll bring everything—"

Crash!

"Alan!" Alice shrieked. I was twenty years younger and tens of pounds lighter than Alice, but she still reached Alan first.

"Honey, are you okay? What happened? What broke? You're bleeding! We need to get to the hospital right this minute," she said breathlessly. "We need to get you to the emergency room. You'll need stitches. I'm sure of it."

"What you need to do is calm down," Alan said. "It's

just a scratch. That plate slipped, that's all. It slipped and I caught at it and it broke in my hand. There's no need to make a federal case out of it. Look, the bleeding has stopped already." He held out his hand.

It hadn't completely stopped, but it had already moved from the flowing stage to the ooze level. His wife looked unconvinced. "I think he's right, Alice," I said. "A good wash, some triple ointment, and a sticky bandage is all he needs."

"Are you sure?" Lines appeared around her mouth. "Alan . . ."

"I'm fine," he said shortly. "I'm a grown man, Alice. I know how to take care of myself."

She watched him go with a troubled look on her face. There was more going on here than a small cut. I was about to ask a gently probing question when the front door opened and a blast of fresh air rushed into the room.

"What's with the sour looks?" Debra asked.

Dressed in a long floppy sweater, ankle-length skirt and fuzzy boots, slim, blond Debra bore little resemblance to the woman whose closet had once been filled with severely tailored suits in colors that ranged from black to gray to navy blue. This was a kinder, gentler Debra, and I much preferred this version.

She flopped into the wire-backed chair next to me. "Alice, I am dying for a cup of coffee."

Alice woke up from her pensive pose. "Mugs or china?"

When she'd settled us in with mugs and the best cookies in the world, she said, "I'm going to check on Alan. If you need anything, I'm just a yell away."

Debra blew across the top of her coffee. "What's that

all about?" she asked, nodding at Alice's back. I gave the short version and she nodded. "Hope he's had a tetanus booster lately. You know how Alice can be."

"It really was just a scratch."

She nibbled at her first cookie. "And these really are awesome cookies." She sighed. "Cookie Van Doorne. That's why we're here, right? What do you want to know?"

"I drove her home from the PTA in Review," I said. "I'd known her for years, but that was the first time I had an extended one-on-one conversation with her."

Debra took another bite. "And?" she asked through the crumbs. "How did that go?"

I added enough cream to my coffee to turn it a lovely shade of brown. Coffee was okay, every once in a while, but I couldn't drink it down without cream, or at least milk. "I realized that I didn't know her very well."

Debra nodded. "That's Cookie. She was one of those women who was acquaintances with everyone, but not close friends with anyone."

"No best friend?"

She made a face. "Cookie was also one of those women whose best friend changed every couple of years. Weird, if you ask me. You know when I met my best friend? Kindergarten. She chased after me with a garter snake. I ran away shrieking, but somehow we ended up the best of friends." She went on to say that though her friend now lived in California, they e-mailed almost daily and visited every year.

I wondered how anyone could switch friends as if they were replacing a pillow. That's not what a best friend was—a best friend was someone who would always, always be in your life.

Then I remembered that my own best friend was keeping something important from me. As Debra talked about a long-ago road trip with her friend, I wondered if my friendship with Marina was changing into a shape I didn't recognize.

Mother's Day couldn't come soon enough.

"Was there anyone who didn't like Cookie?" I asked.

My question interrupted Debra's story. She sighed. "Right. Cookie." She sipped at her coffee. "I'm sorry. What was the question?"

I didn't want to think about Marina. Debra didn't want to talk about Cookie. Outstanding. I pushed an Amazingly Awesome toward her. "Was there anyone who didn't get along with Cookie?"

This time Debra bit, chewed, and swallowed before she answered. "There's a big difference between not getting along with someone and being her enemy." She looked at me carefully. "And why are you asking, anyway?"

Once again, if I'd been as smart as some people claimed I was, I would have prepared an answer for this obvious question. Since I wasn't all that smart, I said, "Well, um . . ."

Debra sighed. "So it wasn't an accident. Poisoned, then, right? And what you really want to know is if I know anyone who might have killed her."

"Gus is out sick," I said.

Which didn't make any sense, really, but she nodded. "All of the other tellers got along with her well enough. But they were all coworker friends, not real friends. She didn't mix with any of them outside of the bank."

"How about bank customers?"

Debra's hand stopped with her coffee mug halfway to

her mouth. "I can't believe I forgot about this." The mug went down with a crash. "I should tell the police, I suppose. Do you think it can wait until Gus is back?"

"Tell me," I said.

"Well, maybe he knows already." Her startled look started to fade. "It's no secret. Everyone in the bank heard it. I could hear them from my office and came out myself to calm things down."

"Cookie had an argument with someone?"

Debra nodded. "And how. It was one of those screaming-at-the-top-of-your-lungs things. Stephanie almost went over the counter at Cookie, and I thought I was going to have to call the police."

The small kernel of worry that, with the birth of my children, had taken up permanent residence in my stomach doubled in size. "Stephanie?"

"Sure," Debra said. "You know her. Stephanie Pesch, the new vice principal at Tarver."

Chapter 12

When I left the antiques store the cold bit at me with teeth so sharp they would have gone through multiple layers of Gore-Tex, fleece, down, and wool.

Then again . . . I looked at myself. Or, since I was so preoccupied, I could have forgotten to zip up my coat and put on my gloves. In three seconds, I was back to thinking about what Debra had told me, and not liking it all over again.

"Beth? Hey, Beth!" A woman jumped down from a large brown box truck parked on a side street. "I have a package for you. It was addressed to your house, but I figured I could drop it off downtown. Do you want it now?"

"It's not books, is it? Because if it is . . ." I looked at the long length of sidewalk between me and the store's front door.

She laughed. "It isn't heavy. Hang on." She popped back into the truck and popped right back out again, a box balanced on one hand and her digital doohickey in the other. "Sign here . . . and this is all yours. Have a good day!" The truck rumbled away.

It was a nice box: tidy, with no smashed corners, a neat strip of packaging tape keeping it closed, and a simple handwritten label. The shipping label said it had come from Chicago, which didn't make any sense because I recognized the handwriting. This, too, had come from a dead woman.

"Cookie, what are you doing?" I asked the air quietly. Luckily, no one answered.

I tucked the box under my arm and headed to the store.

"What do you have there?" Lois asked, nodding at my square companion.

"A box," I said.

Her mouth opened for a quick retort, but the phone rang. She glared at me and spun around to pick up the phone.

Flossie, busy with straightening an endcap of small stuffed animals that unstraightened itself whenever your back was turned, gave me a smile as I went past and said merely, "Good morning, Beth. Hope you stayed warm out there."

"Morning, Flossie. Not really, but spring is only two months away."

Once inside the relative safety of my office, I shut the door and, for the first time ever, wished I had a lock on it. Not so much to keep people out, but to keep whatever was inside the box in.

Cookie's box. Cookie's letter had said there would be clues. Maybe this was one of them. So why did it feel like a box that Pandora might have sent me? At least Pandora's had hope flitting out of the bottom. I didn't anticipate Cookie's containing anything so positive.

Evil walks among us, she'd said. It's our duty to make things right, she'd said.

Maybe things were black-and-white to her, but I

could rarely see things so clearly. I wasn't comfortable judging people. If I judged others, that surely meant others were judging me, and the thought made me squirm.

What else had Cookie said? That the punishment doesn't always match the crime. That shouldn't we be trying to make sure life is as fair as we can make it?

We'd had that part of our talk in my car, and if I remembered correctly, I'd been too busy trying to skate out from underneath her attempts to pin me down to really think about what she was saying.

"Yes," I said out loud, looking at the box. "We should be trying to make life as fair as possible." *And,* I thought, *I'm sorry I didn't say so when I had the chance.* When Jenna and then Oliver were born, I'd vowed that I'd never miss a chance to tell them how much I loved them. I'd tried hard to keep that vow, but how many chances had I missed with other people? Okay, not that I was ever going to tell Cookie Van Doorne that I loved her, but still. "Sorry, Cookie," I said quietly. "I should have listened to you. Everyone deserves that."

"What did you say?" Lois called through the door. "Do you want some tea?"

"Later, thanks."

Ignoring all of the warnings my dad had ever given me about using the right tool for the job, I used a pair of scissors to open the box. There were box cutters galore in the workroom, but I'd have to run the Lois gauntlet twice to get there and back, and I didn't feel up to it.

I slit the tape without incident. Put the scissors back in the drawer. Shut the drawer. Looked at the box. Opened one outside flap. Opened the other outside flap. Looked at the interior flaps. Thought about Lois's offer of tea. Tea would be good right now. I could brew a mug, wander through the store, think about changes in lighting, consider new shelving, brew another mug—

"Stop that," I said.

There will be clues, Cookie's letter had said. I'm depending on you, she'd said.

Well.

If Gus had been hale and healthy, I would have taken the whole kit and caboodle over to the police station and we could have opened it together. But he was sick, and from what Winnie had said, he'd been hit hard.

My hand reached out before my brain knew what it was doing. One flap, then the other flap opened up. Out came the bubble wrap, and inside . . .

I frowned. Inside was a jumble of completely unrelated items that looked as if they'd come from a garage sale. Or were bound for one.

Even without touching anything, I could see a doll in the shape of an infant. A Christmas ornament. A white paper bag so flat that nothing could possibly be inside it. A ceramic figurine of a football player. A framed high school graduation photo that, from the clothing and hairstyle, looked about fifteen years old. A brochure for . . . I couldn't quite make it out, so I took a pen from the mug on my desk and lifted it. A brochure for an African safari.

I released the brochure, and it settled back into place among its neighbors. If these were clues, I was in trouble. The trouble with people having the mistaken assumption that you're smart is that people expect you to do smart things.

"Beth?" Lois pounded on my door. As I slapped the box flaps shut, she turned the doorknob and burst in. "We have a problem. The computer up front is doing the blue screen thing again, the credit card machine won't work, and Mrs. Tolliver wants to buy a full hardcover set of Harry Potter books for her grandson, and you know how—"

"I'll be right there."

Lois ran to take care of the wealthy, generous, and difficult Mrs. Tolliver. I shoved the box under my desk and hurried after her.

A few minutes later, Mrs. Tolliver's purchases were wrapped and bagged. She signed the ancient carbon credit card slip I'd unearthed from the back of a drawer and handed it back to me.

"Computers," she sniffed. "We're too dependent on them. Is there really so much advantage in using these beasts?" Her well-rounded chin gestured at the computer screen.

"I often wonder the same thing," I said. Especially whenever the annual bill for software support came around, whenever a new computer had to be purchased, and whenever someone spilled tea on a keyboard.

"Really," Mrs. Tolliver said in a tone that meant she didn't believe a word of what I'd said. She picked up the bright yellow plastic bag I was holding out and turned to leave, but my right hand wouldn't let go.

"The white bag," I whispered.

"Is there a problem?" Mrs. Tolliver asked icily.

I blinked. "No. Sorry." I released the bag's handles. By rights my face should have been burning with embarrassment, but not this time. Odd. "Have a nice day, Mrs. Tolliver. Stay warm out there."

Before the jingling bells attached to the front door stopped ringing, I had my coat on and my purse in my hand. "Lois, Flossie, I'll be back in a little bit."

"Where are you going?" Lois asked. "You're supposed to be taking it easy, and here you are, running out into that sharp cold twice this morning. How are you supposed to ever get—"

I was out and away. I didn't like leaving so abruptly, but I had to do this before my courage left me. What I really wanted to do was go back to the quiet of my office and sip a hot mug of tea while I reread *Emily of New Moon*.

"Later," I promised myself. "You do this thing and that can be your reward."

My pep talk got me down the street and through the same front door I'd gone through earlier that day.

"Didn't get enough, did you?" Alice asked, smiling. "What do you need this time? Coconut? Oatmeal raisin? Those are almost like health food, you know."

Her plump face beamed at me over the glass display case. "Actually, I need to talk to Alan a minute."

"I sent him home," she said. "You saw that cut he had. On a cold day like this, we're not going to sell any furniture, so I shooed him off home to put his feet up."

I sagged. Now I'd have to gird up my bravery a second time. I hated when I had to do that. Girding once was hard enough.

"What did you want to talk to him about?" Alice put her arms on the case and leaned forward comfortably. "Maybe I can help. If not, I can have him call you."

On the other hand, talking to Alice might be better. They were one of those hand-in-hand couples who told each other everything. Alice would know why Alan had been at the PTA in Review and she'd know if Alan had known Cookie. And if she knew those things, the answers might go a long way to explaining why one of her white cookie bags had been in that box.

"Did you and Alan," I asked, "know Cookie Van Doorne?"

"That woman." Alice pushed herself away from the glass case, her face flaming hot, and stood as tall as a rounded five-foot-two-inch-tall woman could. "Not to speak ill of the dead, but I can't think of a woman I liked less. She was always looking for the worst in people. It's only people who are bad themselves that see bad in others. She had her own skeletons—I'm sure of it—and if Alan hadn't said no, I would have found them. I would have . . ." Her shoulders slumped.

I watched as the fury drained out of her, leaving her limp and wounded and empty.

"She's dead now," Alice said flatly. "And I can't say I'm sorry. Not without being a liar, and I won't let her do that to me. I know I should regret anyone's death, but I can't, not this time."

"What happened?" I'd never heard anything bad about Alan in all the years I'd lived in Rynwood. He and Alice were both retired teachers. They'd opened the antiques store/cookie bakery because they weren't the kind of people to ride off into the sunset in an RV or to sit around and do nothing. "Did she do something to Alan?"

Alice's face went red again. "*Do* something? He was the best history teacher Rynwood High School ever had and she tried her best to get him fired!"

I frowned. "Why would she do that?"

Alice cast her eyes to the ceiling. "Her son. Her precious can't-do-anything-wrong son. Back about twenty years ago, Alan caught him cheating on a final exam and flunked him for that marking period. Cookie threw a fit, said Alan hadn't liked her son since the time he cut across our backyard on his minibike right after we'd paid good money to have it leveled with good black dirt and spent all weekend raking it flat and rolling it and seeding it.

"The kid," she went on, "was a rotten, selfish brat, but Alan would never have flunked him if he hadn't really cheated."

She was right. Alan was right up there next to Gus in the honorable department. Which was why I'd found it hard to even write his name on the suspect list. Still, you never knew about people. "That was a long time ago," I said, putting on a smile. "Don't tell me you've held a grudge all these years."

Alice snorted. "Wasn't me with the grudge. It was that Cookie creature. When Alan wouldn't change that grade, she went to the principal. When the principal supported Alan, she went to the school superintendent. When the superintendent supported both the principal and Alan, she started writing letters to the editor, saying that a certain male history teacher was abusing his position, that he had no business being so harsh on today's youth, that what children needed was a guiding hand, not a hand holding a whip."

Alice slapped the glass case with the flat of her hand, sending a sharp echo through the room. "A little more paddling is what that kid needed, if you ask me. She'd spared the rod and spoiled the child and now what is he doing? Moving from job to job, last I heard."

I vaguely remembered Cookie's son from the funeral. Dark suit, downcast eyes, and a wife and two sons who looked much the same.

"But Alan wasn't fired," I said.

"Not for want of her trying." Though the red in Alice's face had faded, her expression was still a far cry from her normal affable smile. "And that was just the first phase."

"First phase of what?"

"Of her attempts to ruin Alan's life." She looked at me sourly. "You seem surprised. Obviously you didn't know Cookie like we did."

I'd hardly known Cookie at all, it seemed. "What did she do?"

"It was soon after we retired from teaching when we opened this place." She waved at the cookies, the china, the collectibles, the chintz-covered furniture, the carousel horses, and the brass cash register. "She probably planned it the second she heard we were opening an antiques store."

"Planned what?"

Alice's face hardened. "Whispers. Nothing but whispers."

"I don't understand," I said.

"We couldn't prove a thing," Alice went on, "but it was slander, sure enough. Where else could it have come from?"

I didn't say anything. I didn't want to think Cookie had been the kind of person to willfully hurt someone, didn't want to think that she'd tried to have Alan fired. I liked to think the best of people, even my sister Kathy.

"It started the first summer we opened," Alice said. "Whispers, like I said, that the antiques we had such high prices on were really cheap reproductions from China. From China!" Her red face had returned in full force. "As if we'd want to sell reproductions, as if Alan, a *history* teacher, would sell a reproduction as real!"

Of course, although I wanted to believe the best of people, every so often they disappointed. I was sure more than one antiques dealer in the world had tried to do what the whispers claimed. Not Alan, though. He'd

once run after me to return a tiny handful of change I'd
absentmindedly left at the cookie counter. "What did
you do?" I asked.

"Alan took care of it." Alice smiled broadly. "He took
care of everything. He hired three different experts to
authenticate everything in the store. Cost us a fortune
and put us in a great big financial hole, but he was right,
we had to do it to save the store."

"It obviously worked."

"We publicized the results in the paper for three
weeks running and posted a guarantee sign in the window so big that you could hardly see the antiques. The
whole thing had me so scared, but Alan said he'd take
care of it, that he'd take care of her." Alice blew out a
breath. "Goodness, I didn't mean to carry on so. It was
over and done with years ago and I'm a silly old woman
to bring it all back up again. Here, take a bag of peanut
butters back to your nice store to share. How's Flossie
doing? It was such a good thing, for her to start working
there."

Alice pressed a white bag into my hands. "Now, you
won't tell Alan that I got all hot and bothered about that
Van Doorne woman, will you? He wouldn't want me
sharing our dirty laundry with you. But you won't tell,
will you? Ah, that's a good girl."

I walked back to the store with my head down, thinking dreary thoughts about the things Alice had told me.

He took care of everything, she'd said.

He'd take care of *her*, she'd said.

I didn't want to think that Alan had carried his promise to the ultimate conclusion. Didn't want to think that
one of the nicest business owners in all of Rynwood
could have . . . could have . . .

"Morning, Beth," someone called.

I waved to a shape on the opposite sidewalk and kept on going.

This was the problem with investigating something as horrible as murder: you learned too much. I didn't want to know that Cookie had tried to get Alan fired, didn't want to know that she'd probably started a slanderous campaign to ruin a new store, didn't want to know that Alice and Alan hated Cookie so much.

So much for crossing Alan off the suspect list. He might even have moved up a line or two.

I shivered in the chill air. It had been cold for a week, but the morning's forecast had predicted that an even harsher cold spell was on its way.

I believed it.

That evening Ruthie sent us home with a big box of fried chicken. When she'd called at noon to let me know what we'd be having for dinner, I protested at the fried part.

"You'll eat it and you'll like it," Ruthie had growled.

That wasn't the point, and I said so.

"Fine," she'd said. "If you're so concerned with healthy eating, how about I send over some tossed salads instead of biscuits and mashed potatoes? And I'll put in a nice big serving of steamed squash."

I'd been content with that compromise and showered Ruthie with so many thanks that she'd growled again and hung up on me. At the dinner table, my children didn't show nearly the same appreciation.

"Where're the mashed potatoes?" Jenna asked when I'd laid the food out on the table. No serving bowls tonight and I hoped my mother hadn't figured out how to install a secret webcam in the ceiling light fixture. After all, she'd stayed with us for a week at Christmas and had been left alone in the house more than once.

"We're having salad instead." I went to the refrigerator for dressing. Jenna took the bottle of ranch and promptly covered her nice green romaine lettuce with a thick layer of white.

"I really like the Green Tractor biscuits." Oliver looked hopefully at the plastic bag still on the counter. "Didn't Mrs. Ruthie put in some biscuits for me?" I opened the bag, took out a foam container, and put a spoonful of squash on his plate. The hope fell off his face. Landed splat on the floor, probably, where I'd have to sweep it up later.

We ate in a silence punctuated only by food-related noises. Oliver concentrated on pushing his squash around so that I'd think he'd actually eaten some of it. Jenna concentrated on eating every single molecule of white meat off her chicken breast.

I concentrated on not concentrating on anything. There were so many things I didn't want to think about. Alan. Stephanie Pesch. Cookie. If Cookie had been the vindictive woman Alice had described her to be, was I still obligated to help Gus find her killer? Of course I was, and I was ashamed of myself for even having that thought because no one deserved to be murdered and—

"May I be excused?" Jenna was already halfway out of her chair.

"Me, too." Oliver gave a piece a squash a final push and jumped up.

I looked at my beloved children. They deserved better than this. "No," I said. "You're both going to sit down and finish eating."

Jenna's chin went up. Oliver's lower lip pushed out. "But, Mom—"

"Sit," I commanded.

"I'm full." Jenna patted her stomach.

"Me, too." Oliver thumped his midsection.

I gave them the full-out Mom Look. First Oliver, then Jenna dropped into their respective chairs. "Thank you," I said. "Now. Oliver, eat two more bites of squash and you can be done. Jenna, your salad seems to have reached the saturation point. Would you like some greens that are less soggy?" At her nod, I whisked the old bowl away and got her a new one. To this serving, she applied a slightly less liberal amount of dressing.

I asked how their days had gone, heard about a science experiment for smells, a pop quiz in math, and eventually our dinner eased into something approaching normalcy.

When their plates were acceptably empty, I said, "There are cookies from Mrs. Barnhart for later. Now, be off with you!" I waved them away.

Jenna shot up from her chair but didn't immediately disappear. "Don't we have to do dishes?"

"Not tonight, sweetheart." There weren't many to do, and the only other chore was taking Spot out just before bedtime. Just this once, I'd let the kids off the hook. "Tomorrow, and all the other nights of your life, yes, but not tonight."

"Cool." She sprang for the basement door. "I'm going to practice." The words were tossed over her shoulder as she clattered down the stairs.

Oliver went after her. "I'll throw pucks at you, if you want."

There were some conversations that just couldn't be repeated without a long and detailed backstory.

By the time I'd put the silverware in the dishwasher

and taken the garbage out, Oliver was back upstairs. He climbed onto the stool at the kitchen island—a much smaller climb than it had been for him six months ago—and sat with his elbows on the counter and his chin in his hands.

"What's up, Ollster?" I asked.

"Bored."

"I thought you were helping Jenna practice."

"She's not using any pucks."

That was odd. I was about to suggest that he play a game on the Christmas computer when I stopped myself. "How about getting out a jigsaw puzzle?" I asked. "We can set it up on the table in the family room."

Oliver brightened. "We haven't done a puzzle in a long time."

As I recalled, we'd done half a dozen over the holidays, but a month to a nine-year-old was clearly much different from a month to a fortysomething. "Go pick one out. I'll ask Jenna if she wants to join us."

"She wants to practice," Oliver said, but he slid off the stool and headed down the hall.

When my former husband and I had purchased this house, we'd envisioned the unfinished basement as a future rec room for the kids. A pool table. A Ping-Pong table. Floor space for amateur gymnastics and spontaneous dancing. A large-screen TV with surround sound for movie-watching. Finished cabinetry with shelves filled with games and books and music.

I eased down the bare wooden steps to the concrete floor and watched my daughter. Against the far wall was a hockey goal. Painted on the floor in front of the net was the crease, made up of a red goal line and a red half circle filled with blue paint.

Nearby, her goalie equipment was laid out on cheap metal shelves I'd picked up at a garage sale. Her downstairs practicing was typically Oliver throwing pucks at her when she was in full gear or she did drill after endless drill with her stick and a puck, working on handling skills.

Tonight she wasn't doing either one of those things. Tonight she was standing close to the wall, stick in hand, watching her shadow. She practiced elbow jab after elbow jab. Hook after hook. Hip check after hip check.

I watched, not saying anything. But then she picked up her stick and started to aim its blade at her shadowy opponent.

"Jenna!" I called sharply. "Spearing. That can be a five-minute major."

She flipped her stick around like a baton. "I wasn't spearing. I was just . . . trying a new way to block a shot."

I came down the rest of the steps and crossed the room. What she'd just practiced could hurt someone badly, which was why it could carry such a heavy penalty. "And what's with all the elbowing and hooking?"

"It's just . . . just . . ." She struggled to find an answer I'd believe, but I'd been a hockey fan for thirty-five years. No way would I believe anything except the truth—that'd she been practicing illegal moves, ones that could take out other players. And I could guess who that other player was.

"Hurting that new girl will get you kicked off the team," I told her. Although how, exactly, one goalie could hurt another goalie, even in a team scrimmage, I couldn't quite imagine, but Jenna was nothing if not resourceful.

"I don't want to hurt her," Jenna protested. "I just . . ."

She just wanted her to go away. I sighed. "Let's sit down a minute."

Jenna flopped into a white plastic chair that, in summer, lived outside on the back deck. Instead of looking at me, she fiddled with the knob of cloth tape she'd put on the end of her goalie stick.

"Youthful indiscretions can easily lead to regrets," I said, "and regrets are one of mankind's great wastes of time."

Jenna didn't say anything but continued to pick at the black tape. Which wasn't a huge surprise, since I hadn't said anything worth responding to. Or certainly anything that, at age twelve, she'd understand.

I tried again. "There's only one way to be truly successful."

"What's that?"

"To do your best."

She successfully pulled off one end of the tape. "But what if my best isn't good enough? What if I work really, really hard and play really, really hard and I still end up as second-string goalie?" Her voice quavered.

My daughter, my love, my life. I wanted to gather her up into my arms and hold her tight, but there were things that had to be said. "Do you think playing dirty will make you a better player?"

Squirming, she said, "Nooo."

"Then the only other thing to do is to work and play hard." I hesitated. I didn't want to go on, but she was twelve, almost thirteen. It was time to tell her. "And, sweetheart, it may be that the new girl is better than you, no matter how hard you work."

Tears glistened in her eyes and spilled down her cheeks. "Do *you* think she's better than me?"

I gathered her up into my arms and held her tight to my heart. "Not a chance," I said, kissing the top of her head. "Not a chance."

Chapter 13

The next morning was one of those crisp, clear winter days when it seems that the top of the world has blown off. It feels as if you're looking straight up into what might be heaven, and, if only our eyes were made a little differently, we might see the pearly gates and welcoming angels.

"Silly," I murmured to myself. One of these days I'd tell the wrong person about the odd turns my mind sometimes took and I'd find myself shut up in a nice, quiet room for a long, long time.

But even that thought made me smile on this day of blue skies, a beautiful morning made for walking to the bank to get more change for the cash register. Who cared if people laughed at me? Let them see the real me, fanciful warts and all.

I tipped my head back and stared up and up and up, trying to see nothing except blue, because if I could eliminate the tall edges of the brick downtown buildings and see only sky, surely that would be good luck. And with a bit of good luck, Jenna would work through this goalie thing and Oliver would move on to his next crush and—

"Hey, watch where you're going."

My head came down with a jerk. "Sorry," I muttered,

and stepped to one side of the sidewalk instead of saun-
tering down the middle. A man I didn't recognize
brushed past me. Stifling the urge to stick my tongue out
at him, I went back to looking at the endless sky.

But it wasn't the same. The sky was still gorgeous,
high, and deep, but my ebullient mood was gone. What
had been an adventure of walking to the bank to get
change for the cash register was now just an errand to
get over with as quickly as possible.

Sometimes being an adult wasn't any fun at all.

"What are you smiling at?" A very large man blocked
my path.

"Morning, Glenn. It's a beautiful day, isn't it?"

"It is, Beth," Glenn Kettunen said, "and I'm glad
someone else is noticing. Days like this are a gift and—"

"Yo! Beth!"

Glenn and I turned. On the other side of the street, a
pair of golden retriever–esque dogs was racing down the
sidewalk, side by side and in step, almost as if they were
harnessed. In hot pursuit were Mary Margaret and Lou.

Last fall, when Mary Margaret discovered that her
husband had got himself a couple of dogs, she'd made
noises that made me think the dogs weren't going to be
a permanent presence in the Spezza household. Now
here she was, chasing after them as if her life depended
on it.

"Beth!" Mary Margaret called again. "It was—" Her
words were lost to me as a pickup truck rumbled past.

"What did you say?" I started a slow trot after her,
then a faster trot, then an all-out run. We were a fast,
small, and very unusual parade, two dogs, two out-of-
shape fiftysomethings, and one fortysomething bringing
up the rear. I was catching amused glances from many a

person inside a warm storefront, but that was something I'd almost grown accustomed to. "Mary Margaret! What did you say?"

She whipped around and ran backward, cupping her hands around her mouth. "I remembered whose idea it was that refreshments be served at every break! Isabel Olsen!" Then, in one less than graceful step, she turned back around and kept on running.

So. Isabel Olsen had originally requested the multiple refreshment breaks at the PTA in Review. Quiet, shy, please-don't-say-boo Isabel. Not that she wasn't smart and didn't have a lot of ideas, but Isabel was the last person I'd guess for pushing a new and somewhat radical idea through a committee.

Isabel. Mother of Neal and Avery, wife to Kirk, who was also in the PTA and had also been in the kitchen that night.

But . . . Isabel? What possible reason could she have had to kill Cookie?

I watched my feet move along the sidewalk and thought drearily about all the things we didn't know about people we'd known for years. Isabel had been a regular at the bookstore since her first pregnancy. I knew what her children liked to eat, read, and play with, but I didn't know much about Isabel herself. I didn't know if her parents were still alive. I didn't even know if she was from Rynwood and I didn't—

"Beth."

Two large male feet stood in front of me. I looked up, then farther up, to the extremely handsome face of Evan Garrett. Not so very long ago, the sight of him would have sent my pulse rate up twenty points. But that was before I realized that what I'd felt for him was infatuation rather than love. You'd have thought that I'd know the difference at my age, but no.

"Hi, Evan. Nice day."

"For a run?" He smiled.

I was determined not to blush. Of course, in this cold, my nose and cheeks were probably bright red anyway.

"How was your Christmas?" Evan asked.

"Fine. Yours?"

"The girls came over Christmas afternoon and we had a nice dinner at the country club."

Evan and his ex-wife had married young and raised two daughters who were now adults. I'd never actually met them, but I'd seen their pictures in Evan's condo. "Sounds nice."

"It was. And you're seeing Pete Peterson, I hear."

I smiled, a wide, happy kind of smile. "Yes, we've been dating for a few months. How about you? Are you seeing anyone?"

"No one seriously."

He gave me that crooked smile that used to make me melt into a pathetic little puddle. Today there was no melting, and not only because the temperature was twelve degrees below freezing. "You'll find someone," I said.

"I thought I had."

His light blue gaze met mine with an intensity that should have made my spine tingle. A movie-star hand-some and shockingly wealthy man was sending me an invitation that might as well have been engraved and slid into a deckle-edged envelope.

But there was no sizzle. No tingle. No emotion at all except a vague sense of sadness. "The truth is . . ."

Evan waited, but I didn't say thing else. Couldn't, really, because my brain had zigged off into a completely different direction and I forgot where I was and who I was with.

"Beth?"

I blinked. "Oh. Sorry about that, Evan. I just remembered something. Have a good day, okay?" And off I went, in the opposite direction of both the bank and my bookstore.

I had to wait a few minutes, but eventually I was allowed back through the maze that was the *Rynwood Gazette* offices and into the inner sanctum of Jean McKenna, editor. Not only was Jean an extraordinary editor, but once upon a time, she'd been my boss. Yes, shy and retiring Beth had once graduated from journalism school. Why I'd ever thought that might be a good fit, I wasn't sure, but all's well that ends well. My current career as a mother of two and owner of one bookstore suited me down to the bone.

Jean looked up at me over her reading glasses. "And what's your question today?" She kept typing into her computer as she talked, a skill I envied deeply. If I tried to do that, I'd end up typing what I was saying, or saying what I was trying to type.

I moved a stack of newspaper inserts from the guest chair to the floor and sat. "Maybe I just wanted to stop and say hello."

"Possible." She flicked a glance at the screen and frowned. "Unlikely, though. Hang on a sec and I'll be done." Her fingers whacked at the letters on the keyboard. She'd learned to type more than forty years ago and had never quite learned that you didn't have to thump a computer keyboard as hard as a manual typewriter.

"And it's done." She pushed herself back from the desk and shoved her glasses on top of her short gray hair.

"Shocking scandal in city hall?" I asked.

"We had elections in November, remember?" She sighed. "Half the council is new, and so far they're all getting along. Nothing more boring than a board meeting where everyone agrees with each other."

"It won't last," I said comfortingly. "It never does."

She brightened. "You are a ray of sunshine and I hereby give you permission to stop by and bug me any time you please."

"I already do that."

"Oh, yeah." She grinned at me. "So. What's up in your world? Is that Pete treating you right? You know, I never knew what you saw in that Evan Garrett, anyway. Rich, sure, and easy on the eyes, but he wasn't good enough for you."

"Some people would say it was the other way around."

"And some people are idiots, but we still let them vote and have drivers' licenses."

"If there were laws against being stupid," I said, "we'd all be spending time in jail." Jean looked thoughtful, so I hurried on. "Back when I was working here, right after I got married, you always told me to write the truth."

Jean nodded. "Now, there's another guy who wasn't good enough for you. That ex-husband of yours never saw through that bumbling act you used to put on all the time. You don't do it nearly so much these days."

I sat up straight. "I don't bumble."

She made a rude noise in the back of her throat. "Right. And I don't need a haircut," she said, pushing her too-long bangs out of her eyes. "You were talking about truth. Generally or specifically?"

"I'm looking for the truth about Cookie Van Doorne."

Jean made a "huh" kind of noise and gave me a long look. "Do you know something I don't know?"

"Doubt it."

"See, you're doing it again. That bumbling thing." She looked up at the ceiling. "Cookie Van Doorne. I never knew her real name," she mused. "Must have been something horrible to want to stay a Cookie all your life."

"It can be hard to shake a nickname," I said, thinking about a boy I'd known in grade school who was still called Ants because he'd once sat on a hill of the little creatures and ended up with ants . . . well, in his pants.

But Jean wasn't paying any attention to me. "The truth is, I don't know much about Cookie."

"Oh." So much for that bright idea. "Well, thanks for trying. I'll—"

"Get that hound dog look off your face. Just because I don't know anything doesn't mean I can't help. There's someone else here in town that knows everything about everybody. I'm surprised you didn't go see her first."

A feeling of impending doom descended upon me. I slid down in the chair. "Please tell me you're not going to say what I think you're going to say."

Jean chuckled. "You want the truth, don't you? Go talk to Auntie May."

Right after lunch, I once again donned boots, coat, and gloves and headed into the wild world that lived outside the safety of the bookstore.

"I'm off," I said, waving to Lois and Yvonne.

Lois waved back. "Good luck storming the castle."

I smiled at the reference to one of my favorite movies

of all time. My smile went even wider when Yvonne asked in a puzzled voice, "What castle? I thought she was going to Sunny Rest."

Lois shook her head sadly. "So young, yet so out of touch with the finer things in life. Lucky for you, I happen to own the twenty-fifth-anniversary edition of *The Princess Bride.* Do you want butter or extra butter on your popcorn when you come over to watch it? How about tonight?"

The door closed on Yvonne's response. On the other hand, the wild world might be safer than my bookstore when Lois was feeling Lois-y.

A few blocks later, I walked into Sunny Rest Assisted Living. "You look half-frozen!" exclaimed the receptionist.

"Another lovely day in Wisconsin," I said, smiling. Or at least I tried to smile. My cheeks were so numb from cold I wasn't sure what they were doing. "Do you happen to know where Auntie May is?"

The receptionist scrunched up her face. "You sure you want to do that? She's been on a tear today. She's made two aides cry since lunchtime."

It was more of a need than a want. I took off my gloves and unzipped my coat, welcoming the warmth that was starting to spread through me. "What do you think it would take to make Auntie May cry?"

She looked at me sourly. "Losing a big pot in the weekly poker game."

I laughed. "I'm surprised she can get a game together these days. She's won money from everybody in the building." The games were played with pennies, but still.

"You know Auntie May. She's a pretty good persuader." The receptionist told me to look in the sunroom. "I walked past a few minutes ago and she was in there trying to get up a euchre game."

The wide carpeted hallway absorbed the sound of my feet. Sunny Rest was a comfortable facility, run and staffed by dedicated people who did their best to make the building a home for its residents, a fiendishly difficult job. So many regulations to adhere to, so many details to deal with, so many—

"I hear you're looking for me."

The purple wheelchair was planted in the middle of the hallway. Somehow I'd managed to walk right up to Auntie May without being aware of her presence.

"You awake in there?" Auntie May snapped her fingers under my nose. "I suppose you want to talk about Cookie, eh?" At my nod, she pointed her chin in the direction of the sunroom. "In there. It's empty. Everybody ran off when I wanted to play euchre. Bunch of cowardly, spineless jellyfish. So what if I win all the time? It's the playing that's fun." Her wheelchair rolled to a stop next to large windows that let in so much light they made me squint.

I dragged a chair around so my back was to the glass and sat down. "Jean McKenna said I should talk to you about Cookie."

"Can't believe you went to Jean first. You should have come to me days ago. I been waiting for you, you know." She sniffed.

Was it possible that I'd hurt Auntie May's feelings? There were entire socioeconomic groups in Rynwood that fully believed she didn't have feelings and that her heart had shrunk to the size of a pea. I looked at her closely. "I'm sorry if I hurt your feelings," I said.

She snorted. "Feelings, schmeelings. Got no time for that kind of crap, and you shouldn't, either, not if you're going to . . . ah . . . ah-*chooo*!"

I pulled back fast, but tiny sneeze droplets spewed all across my hands. Ick.

"Darn cold," Auntie May said, rubbing at her nose with the tissue that was in her hand. "Doctor says I gotta be careful it don't turn into pneumonia, so he's not wanting me to go on the casino trips."

Ah. May lived for the days the facility bus shuttled interested residents to the closest casino. No wonder she was making everyone's life miserable. I got up, used the hand sanitizer sitting on a nearby table, and came back, rubbing my hands.

"Pansy stuff," Auntie May said, sneering at the liquid. "In my day we got used to germs."

I deeply wanted to ask her why she had a cold if she was so tough, but that wasn't an argument for today. Or probably any day. Auntie May had a tendency to win every battle she fought. The day I figured out how she did that, I'd take notes and write a how-to book that would make me millions.

"Cookie Van Doorne," I said. "What can you tell me?"

Auntie May cackled and rubbed her palms together. "Hope you don't got anywhere to go, Bethie. We could be here awhile."

There was little I wanted to do less than sit and listen to May Werner dish out gossip, but I couldn't think of any other way to get the information. For a very short moment, I wondered if I could teach Auntie May how to use e-mail and Facebook, but as soon as I visualized the number of e-mails she'd send me every day and the types of things Auntie May was likely to "share" on Facebook, I banished the idea from my brain.

Auntie May squinted a look at me. "What's in that pretty little head of yours, missy?"

Nothing, absolutely nothing. "Do you know what Cookie's real name was?"

"Cookie," she said promptly.

"You're joking."

"Does this look like it's joking?" She pointed to her lined features, wrinkles crisscrossing wrinkles that crisscrossed wrinkles. "Cookie's parents had a slew of kids and she came last in the bunch. She didn't even have a name for a long time, just Baby. Cookie was her first word, and it turned into her real name."

I gaped at Auntie May. "She didn't have a name for a year? How can that be? I had to give the hospital my children's names before we went home."

May shrugged her bony shoulders. "Things were different back then. We got away with all sorts of stuff you'd get tossed in jail for these days. Like the time Jimmy Stynes got into the —"

I did not want to hear about Jimmy Stynes, who I'd always known as a very nice man who'd died in his sleep at the ripe old age of ninety-five. "What else do you know about Cookie?"

Auntie May harrumphed, made a snarky comment about kids these days, then said, "Cookie was a big tattletale as a kid. One of those creepy little kids who always pops up in places they shouldn't be."

By great effort, I held my tongue and did not compare Cookie to Auntie May. "And as an adult?" I asked.

May nodded. "Same thing. Only she got sneakier about it."

Was "sneakier" a word? I debated the question and reached no conclusion. I'd have to look it up later. "What do you mean?"

Auntie May settled back in her chair. "You want recent stuff or old stuff?"

I didn't want any of it. "Anything involving people in the PTA." I listened to what I'd said. "Anything involving anyone in the PTA or from Tarver Elementary," I amended.

"Hmm." May rubbed her chin. "Okay, okay. I got something. No, I got two somethings." She cackled. I winced. "First one." She rolled her chair closer to mine. "Isabel Klein."

"You mean Isabel Olsen?"

"How many Isabels you think are running around this town?" The front wheels of her chair bumped up against my boots. "When Isabel was a girl, she wanted a puppy for her birthday. Her mom—that's Kim—drove up north to look at this litter of puppies. Border collies, sheepdogs, Labs, something like that." Auntie May flicked the detail away as unimportant. "This place was out on some back road, one of those places where if there are two cars on the road at the same time, it's a traffic jam."

I nodded. I'd grown up on a road like that.

"Anyway, Kim was driving down the street and some kid rode his bike straight in front of her. Oh, he wasn't killed, don't look like that. Broke his leg, I think. And it wasn't Kim's fault at all, but Cookie had never liked Kim."

May stopped, and for a moment I wondered if she was going to express some sympathy—empathy, even—for Kim or the boy or for Cookie.

"Never did get the goods on the Cookie-Kim story,"

she said regretfully. "Anyway, Cookie heard about the accident before most everyone else and got to spin it the way she wanted. By the time Kim got home, Cookie had got the story around town that Kim was a driving menace, that maybe she'd been drinking, that she should be in jail for what she did to that kid on the bike."

"That's . . . that's . . ." I couldn't think exactly what it was.

"After that, Kim didn't do well. She got all depressed, ended up losing her job, would have lost her house if her brother hadn't helped out. She's better now, but she's not the same."

The nasty little story made me want to go wash my face. "Are Isabel and her mom close?"

May smashed her thumb and index finger together. "Like this. Kim's husband took off when Isabel was still in diapers. Kim raised that girl best she could, but she's not one of those real capable women and Izzy grew up taking care of Kim as much as Kim took care of her. Close as sisters, those two."

"What's the other story?" Maybe this would be a nicer one.

Auntie May grinned. "Stephanie Pesch. She's hated Cookie for years. Years!"

I looked at my lap, then back up at Auntie May. If I left now, I wouldn't hear what she had to say about the object of Oliver's crush. I sighed. "Why did Stephanie have a problem with Cookie?"

"Cookie had a daughter, Deanna."

I frowned. "Her son was at the funeral, but there wasn't a daughter." Although she'd had two children, I remembered.

Auntie May's cackle grated on my ears. "Deanna. She

hadn't talked to her mother in years. Guess her funeral wasn't a good enough reason to come back to Rynwood."

The impossibility of not attending my mother's funeral rattled around in my head for a while, then rattled on out. "What does Stephanie have to do with that?"

"Stephie and Deanna were best friends from the time they were little kids. Hardly had any other friends, they were so close. Up out of high school, Deanna fell in love with this Darren. Love at first sight."

May clasped her hands and batted her eyes at me, then snorted. "Like that really exists. Anyway, Cookie didn't like Darren, didn't think he was good enough for Deanna. He went up north on a hunting trip, and when he came back, Cookie made sure to tell him Deanna had been seeing someone else when he was gone."

She shook her head sorrowfully, but I was sure the emotion didn't go deeper than the hair on her chin.

"He went off mad. Wouldn't believe Deanna, so he probably wasn't good enough for her, but that didn't keep Deanna from blowing up at her mother. She packed up and moved to Hawaii to get as far away from her mother as she could. Voilà!" Auntie May kissed her fingertips and flared out her hand. "Instant hatred! Stephie's best friend was gone forever and it was all Cookie's fault."

Another nasty little tale. "Did Cookie have any redeeming qualities?" I asked.

Auntie May shrugged. "Nice girls don't hit my radar."

I thanked May for her time, answered her questions about Pete as obliquely as possible, and headed back to the store.

Could Isabel really have poisoned Cookie? Could Stephanie? Maybe they both disliked Cookie immensely, but the disliking was a long way from murder. Then I wondered if poisoning someone would even feel like murder. Could you convince yourself that poisoning was a solution to a problem, and not a cold-blooded murder?

I watched as my boots made their way down the sidewalk.

I hoped not. I truly hoped not.

When I got back, the store rang with the silence of suspended arguments. I looked from Lois to Paoze, then glanced at my watch. Flossie must have just left for the day.

"What's up?" I asked.

"Nothing," Lois said. "What makes you think there's something wrong?"

Her outfit of the day bore a striking resemblance to what female ice skaters might have worn in the early 1900s. Long brown skirt, long button-up sweater over a white shirt with a lace collar, beret worn at a jaunty angle. Instead of skates she wore leather boots that were so old, she must have dug them out of the back of Auntie May's closet.

"What makes me think so?" I sniffed the air. "Seems to me there is a lingering, yet distinct, odor of unfinished arguments in this room."

"It's these boots," Lois muttered. "I couldn't get all the mildew off them."

"Paoze, do you have a minute?" I motioned him to the back of the store. "You're the tallest one here, and there's a spiderweb in my office that's ripe for the picking."

The gentlemanly young man nodded. "Of course, Mrs. Kennedy." He rolled up the sleeves of his pristinely white shirt and headed back.

When he got there, he looked around and said, "I do not see a web, Mrs. Kennedy. Could it have fallen down?"

I shut my office door quietly. "There isn't a spiderweb, Paoze. I want to ask you something, and I don't want Lois to know."

He went still. "Have I done something that is wrong? I am sorry, Mrs. Kennedy. Please let me—"

"Don't be silly." I waved him to the guest chair and sat in my own. "It's Lois. Or, more specifically, Lois and Flossie."

Sitting with a straight spine, he put his hands in his lap. "I am not certain what you are asking."

I rolled my eyes. "Please. Every time I walk into the room, they switch whatever argument they're having into a fight about books. I prefer L. M. Montgomery's Emily books over the Anne books myself, but there's no way I'd yell at someone over it. And they were working fine together all last fall and even through the holidays. Something happened and neither one of them will tell me what it is."

Paoze looked at his hands. "I am very sorry, Mrs. Kennedy, but I cannot help you."

I studied him. I would have preferred to watch his face, but with his head down, all I could see was the top of his head, and the perfectly combed black hair wasn't much of an indicator of anything except exceptional personal hygiene.

It was obvious that he knew what was going on between Lois and Flossie, but it was just as obvious that he didn't want to tell me. Which meant he'd been told something in confidence, and I didn't want to force him to break a promise. I sighed. "Tell Lois you smashed a big hairy spider. That should perk her up a little."

Paoze stood, opened the door, then hesitated. "Mrs. Kennedy?"

"Yes?"

But he was looking at his hands again. "Nothing. I am sorry to trouble you."

This time, since I was sitting and he was standing, I could see his face. "Paoze," I said, "if there's something troubling you, you can talk to me. Doesn't matter what it is. I'll listen. It can be about the store, or school, or your family, or about the horrible play-off season the Green Bay Packers had. I'm here, okay? And you know I can keep a secret."

"Yes, Mrs. Kennedy." He spoke so quietly that if I hadn't seen his lips move, I might have imagined I heard anything. "Thank you, Mrs. Kennedy."

He left, but I stared after him for a very long time.

Chapter 14

I drove to work the next morning with the express intention of dragging Cookie's box out from under my desk. No matter how much the thought of the task creeped me out, it was past time. Cookie had had the box sent to me for a reason, and the least I could do was examine its contents.

Well, actually, the least I could do was leave the box where it was, perhaps use it for a footstool, and forget where it had come from, but thanks to the sense of obligation instilled in me by my mother, that was unlikely to happen.

I'm depending on you.

"But I'm just a children's bookstore owner," I told the box. "Wouldn't it be best if I handed you over to the police? Gus is still out sick, but surely this can wait a few days. What's the hurry?"

Please help me rest in peace.

And that was the kicker. She'd asked for my help and there was no turning away from that fact. With a grunt, I picked up the box and put it on my desk. My tiny and cowardly little mind had long ago shut away the memory of what I'd seen when I first opened the box, so viewing the odd jumble of items was a fresh surprise.

A baby doll?

A Christmas ornament?

I leaned on the desk and stared. "What were you thinking, Cookie?" I murmured. "Maybe to you this looked like a boxful of clues, but to me it looks like—"

"Like a fine morning to play hooky." Lois walked into my office, followed closely by Pete. "We have plans for you," she said, "and whatever is in that box isn't part of them."

I flapped the box closed and did my best to shove it casually back under the desk. "My plans today include confirming author programming through May, memorize the new security code, putting together the boxes for tomorrow's school deliveries, and looking at the inventory numbers."

Given an uninterrupted thirty minutes, my plans also would have included combing through Cookie's box with the suspects in mind. I could have told this to Lois and Pete since they'd agreed to help with this amateur-hour investigation, but it would have felt like a betrayal of Cookie.

Lois shook her head. "Bzz! You're not doing any of that."

My eyes thinned and my mouth started to open.

"At least not this morning," she added quickly. "Right, Pete?"

He looked at her, at me, then back at her. "Sometimes people feel better if they get their work done first and play later."

Lois snorted. "This one will just keep finding work to do and never get around to playing."

I wanted to protest, and even started to, but stopped. She was pretty much right. Okay, she *was* right. Which was why I'd agreed to these six weeks of enforced relative inactivity. "What do you have in mind?" I asked.

Pete picked up my coat and held it out. "If I told you, it wouldn't be a surprise, now, would it?"

Lois smiled that smile, the one that always made me a little nervous. Usually she had that expression on her face right before she hit Paoze with a tall tale along the lines of fetching a left-handed shelf from the hardware store. "Excellent. She hates surprises."

Half an hour later, Pete and I were in the Agnes Mephisto Memorial Ice Arena. Not only were we inside the arena, but we were both on the ice. Wearing skates. And skating. Sort of. Pete was skating smoothly and easily; I was hanging on to the boards and trying to remember the last time I'd been on the ice.

"You're doing fine." Pete skated a little ahead of me and flipped around so he was skating backward.

I scowled at him. "You do that backward as well as you do it forward."

"Backward is my second favorite direction."

"I'm thinking all my directions are going to be down in a minute."

"You're doing fine," he repeated. "All you have to do is loosen up. Here." He held his hands out to me.

"Not a chance." I held the wall with a death-defying grip.

"You're wearing knee pads and wrist guards, and there's no one here to see you. What's going to happen?"

I risked a glance at the stands and ice. Vacant and empty. Still. "Bones break easily when you're old," I said darkly.

His voice was soft and warm. "Beth, do you really think I'd let you hurt yourself?"

A ripple of something I couldn't quite identify went though me. Pete wouldn't let me fall. He'd catch me before I came even close to hitting the ice. I knew this with as much certainty as I knew that the new security code to the store was . . . was . . .

"Rats," I muttered.

"What's that?" Pete asked.

I shook my head. Took one hand off the wall. Didn't immediately collapse onto the ice. Took my other hand off.

"There you go." Pete took my mittened hands in his bare ones. "Not so bad, is it?"

"It's not bad at all," I said breathlessly. "Do I look as awkward as I feel?"

"You look beautiful," Pete said. "Now, long, even strokes with your blades. Right, left, that's it." His smile made him downright handsome. "You've got it!"

And I did. All that ancient muscle memory from winters spent skating on the frozen lake was coming back. Once upon a time I'd loved to go out under the full moon and skate with my brother until Mom called us in. It had been too long since I'd skated. Why had I ever stopped?

Pete released one of my hands and flipped around again so we were skating side by side. "Nice, isn't it?"

The rhythm was coming back to me. Right, left, right, left. I gave him a quick glance. My strides were more or less even, but they had nowhere near the grace and ease of his. Clearly, this wasn't his first rodeo. "I didn't know you skated. You never said."

"There's a lot you don't know about me," he said, smiling.

"Are you going to share?"

He squeezed my hand. "All you have to do is ask."

Another ripple went through me, but this time I knew what it was.

Happiness.

Less than eight hours later, that happiness was but a fond memory.

"I say we tell the Tarver Foundation to take a hike." Claudia crossed her arms and stared straight ahead.

"That's just dumb," Summer said. "If we want to do all these projects, we need their money."

"We don't need it that bad," Claudia snapped. "We still have book money coming in, and we have our regular fund-raisers, too. All we have to do it save until we have enough."

"Save?" Summer made a disbelieving noise. "The book money is slowing down and it will take us years to have enough bake sales and dances and school carnivals to make up the rest of that money. It's nuts to even consider rejecting their offer."

Yes, it was another PTA meeting that was going nowhere positive. The few people out in the audience looked as bored as I felt. It was probably time for me to intervene, but I'd held out hope that Claudia and Summer could put down their hammers and tongs and come to some sort of solution.

As Summer and Claudia bickered, I spun the gavel in a circle, where it stops no one knows. Like spin the bottle, only not nearly so much fun. Not that I'd know. I'd never been at a party where kids played the game. Did today's youth even know what it was? So many questions in my head and so few answers. Maybe Pete would know.

"What are you smiling at?" Claudia asked.

After a long pause, I realized she was talking to me. "I think it's time for a vote."

"Excuse me?"

Pointedly, I looked at the wall clock. "We've been discussing this for almost an hour, and as far as I can tell, we're no closer to a conclusion. So" — I spun the gavel again — "I move that we accept the Tarver Foundation's offer to match our funds." I sensed Claudia's mouth opening, so I plunged ahead. "And that we accept their matching offer contingent on the foundation accepting that we submit monthly progress reports instead of weekly ones."

"Second," Randy said.

I smiled at the gavel. While I wasn't manipulative enough to have primed Randy to make the second, I was manipulative enough to have asked him (last week) what he objected to most about the foundation's accountability requests. And since I'd also talked to a representative of the Tarver Foundation that afternoon, I was quite confident they'd accept our mild counteroffer. "All in favor, say aye."

Three voices said, "Aye."

"Opposed, say nay."

"Nay!" Claudia glared at me. "I'm telling you right now that this is a mistake. Please have the secretary put in the minutes that I say you'll all live to regret this vote."

"So noted," I said, nodding at Summer. "This meeting is adjourned." I gave the gavel a happy bang. The PTA and the Tarver Foundation would be funding four sorely needed projects. New playground equipment, a part-time music teacher, irrigating the soccer field, and starting up a summer arts day camp. Each one was a large undertaking, and the thought of the work ahead made me sway a little, but the results would be well worth it.

"It's a mistake." Claudia planted herself in front of me.

"Yes, you said. Excuse me a minute." I eeled around her and steamed straight for Isabel Olsen. Surely, by the time I reached her, I would have come up with an appropriate question. Something a little less than "Are you a cold-blooded killer?" and a little more than "Say, did you hear about Cookie?"

"Hey, Beth, do you have a minute?" Travis Heer, Whitney's husband, tapped me on the shoulder. "What do you think about collecting box tops?"

I slowed. "Sure, but can you wait a second? I need to talk to . . ." I looked in Isabel's direction, but she'd already reached the doorway and was gone. Rats. I stifled a sigh and smiled at the young father. "I'm all yours. Box tops, you said?"

"Yeah." He launched into a long and detailed explanation of the virtues of box tops. How no other PTA in the area was collecting them, how we could make out like bandits if we put together a collection system, how all the things we could do with the cash we earned would be great. "We could do more of those things on the lists, right?" He was practically bouncing as he talked. "Sports stuff, arts stuff, who cares what kind of stuff as long as it's for the kids, right? I mean, as long as we can get kids active in something, it's all good, right?"

I beamed at him. "That's exactly right. I'll put it on next month's agenda. Are you willing to get up and talk about it? Because I'm warning you, if you do, you're going to get nominated to do all the work of setting up the collection system."

"Figured as much." He grinned. "But I'm good with that. For the kids, you know?"

There was nothing like youth and the energy that went with it. "Travis, you are a treasure. Would you like to run for PTA president?"

He backed away, laughing. "What, when you're doing such a good job?"

Clearly, he thought I was joking. He was wrong. I made a mental note to add him to my short list of potential replacements. Erica, my PTA presidential predecessor, had told me finding a new president was one of my most important jobs. I'd laughed, but she'd been serious.

"If you care about this group, and I know you do, start thinking about it now," she'd said. So I did, and still was. Travis, I thought. The first male president of the Tarver Elementary PTA. We could do a lot worse.

I looked around the room. Claudia and Tina were clustered in a corner, heads together, sending the occasional ocular dagger in my direction. Carol and Nick Casassa were zipping up their coats and arguing about where they should go over spring break. It sounded as if Carol wanted to take the kids skiing and Nick wanted to go to Arizona to catch the last Milwaukee Brewers spring training game.

When there was a pause in their friendly sparring, I jumped in. "Have you seen Marina?"

Carol pulled on her mittens. "She scooted out after the meeting so fast I wondered if she'd left something in the oven." She laughed. "If it was those brownies she makes, they won't be fit for man nor beast. Not even boy beasts."

"You talking about me?" Nick puffed up his chest. "I have standards. Lots of them."

"Oh, sure." Carol lightly bumped his chest with her wool-covered fist. "Like you won't eat anything that has a sell-by date more than five years old."

Nick grinned. "Like I said. Standards."

They left. Claudia and Tina had already gone. I put on my coat and gathered my things.

"Done here, Mrs. Kennedy?" Harry stood in the doorway.

"Yes, Harry. Thanks for staying."

"Just doing my job."

I walked out of the room and he shut and locked the classroom door. "Well," I said, "you're doing it in an outstanding fashion."

"Thank you, Mrs. Kennedy. You drive safe home, okay?"

"Yes. Thanks. Have a good night, Harry." I walked out into the cold, started the car, turned on the headlights, and drove out of the parking lot.

But I didn't head for home.

I stood there, hands in my coat pockets, hat on my head, and toes warm in my boots, watching the snow falling on Cookie Van Doorne's dark house. My house was dark, too, since the kids were with their father, and the thought of that emptiness had somehow sent me here.

Cookie's house was a simple Cape Cod. I studied the windows and pictured a living room toward the street, dining room and kitchen behind, three bedrooms upstairs. Half bath down, full bath up. Nothing fancy, nothing to set it apart from the other houses on the street, nothing to tell you who had lived behind its walls.

The curtains were drawn across and the shades were pulled down. It could have been a house whose owners had gone away for a vacation or down to Florida for the winter, but it wasn't, and I felt the house knew it, too. Its owner had been murdered. By someone I knew.

It was not a comfortable thought, so I tried not to think it again. But since that's a lot like trying not to think about how tired you are when you have insomnia, I kept circling back to the list of names Marina and I had drawn up.

Mine. Hers.

Alan Barnhart.

Isabel Olsen.

Kirk Olsen.

Stephanie Pesch.

It was too short, that list. There must be more names to put on it. There must be someone we missed, someone we hadn't considered. Maybe someone had snuck into the kitchen when everyone else was listening to Auntie May try to get in her dig at Walter Trommler.

I sighed. No, it had to be someone who'd worked in the kitchen. Someone had put the acetaminophen into a foam cup, filled it with coffee, and handed it to Cookie.

The snow fell.

My toes started to get cold.

More snow fell.

Cookie's house sat there, quiet and somehow accusing.

Why haven't you found her killer? it asked. *Why aren't you doing something to help Cookie instead of standing in the snow, staring at me?*

It was a very good question. Too bad I didn't have an answer for it. "Sorry," I muttered. "This is hard for me, okay? These people are my friends and Cookie was, well, you know how she was."

"What did you say?"

I shrieked. Jumped. Twisted in the air and landed two feet away from where I'd started. Breathed hard and couldn't talk.

"Sorry," the woman said in a laughter-filled voice. "I didn't mean to scare you. I thought you were talking to me."

"Just"—I panted—"talking . . . to myself."

The woman planted her snow shovel on the ground and leaned on the handle. "I live here." She tipped her head at the house next door to Cookie's. "You're not from this neighborhood, are you?"

"No." I realized how odd it must look, to see a stranger standing in the snow outside an empty house. I was lucky no one had called 911 to report me. "I knew Cookie, though. I just . . . stopped by." Which didn't explain anything, really, but I didn't have anything better. "I brought Cookie home the night she got sick. She was—"

"Then you must be Beth Kennedy. Did you get the box? Sorry I took so long to mail it."

I blinked. "You sent me the box?"

"And the letter." She half laughed, half didn't. "All a little weird, right?"

"Yes," I said emphatically, which made her laugh full out.

"That was Cookie. I'm Deirdre Gale, by the way. Cookie said you own that children's bookstore downtown? I should stop in one of these days. I don't have any kids myself, but I have nieces and nephews of assorted ages all over the country."

"Stop by anytime," I said. "So, about that letter . . . ?"

"Yeah, that postmark probably threw you, didn't it?" She smiled, and I suddenly realized that I was talking to a very beautiful woman. Midthirties, tallish, dark hair curling around the edge of her ski hat, high cheekbones, straight nose, full lips. The kind of woman who, if she had the right kind of parents, grew up confident and competent. The kind of woman who would work in a people-oriented field. A doctor, maybe, or a—

"I'm a field engineer," she said. "I travel a lot for the Madison firm I work for. Right now we're testing a new windmill design, and the winds up in Alaska are being harder on the bearings than we'd figured."

— or anything except what she actually was. So much for the stereotypical engineer, from which mold Marina's introverted DH was cast. "That sounds . . . interesting," I said vaguely.

"Probably not," Deirdre said, "but you're nice for saying so. Anyway, I was up there when I heard that Cookie had died and I mailed the letter right away. The box was here, so I couldn't get that out until I came home. I was going to drop it off at your bookstore, but the same morning I put it in my Jeep, the project manager for an installation in Chicago called all frantic about the detail sheets not having enough detail."

She rolled her eyes. "I had to go straight there and hold his hand until he felt better. That took a couple days, so I just mailed the box. I kept meaning to call you, or stop by to explain all this, but . . ." She paused and, for the first time in our odd conversation, didn't seem to know what words to say.

"It's all a little weird," I said.

"Yeah." She blew out a breath. "More than a little. Getting mail from a dead woman must have freaked you out."

"They say new experiences are good for you."

"They say we should eat more vegetables, too, but I never seem to have room after finishing the french fries and cheeseburger."

I made a mental note not to repeat this conversation to my children. "You had that letter with you in Alaska?"

She nodded. "Last fall Cookie asked me to start carrying it around. Said it was her own private insurance policy and that if anything happened to her, to send it to you right away."

Last fall? Curiouser and curiouser. "And the box?"

"She gave me that a few weeks ago." Deirdre brushed snow off the sleeves of her coat. "Around Christmas."

"Do you know what's in it?"

"Don't know. Don't want to know. It was Cookie's business, and if she'd wanted me to know, she would have told me."

I studied her. "You were more than her neighbor, weren't you? You were a friend."

"Well, sure."

"I'm glad. I'm not sure she had many."

Deirdre frowned. "She had you."

"We were more acquaintances than friends."

"Then . . . ?"

"Why the letter? Why the box?" I shook my head. "I don't know. That's probably why I'm here. Thinking and wondering why."

We stood quietly, watching the snow fall onto Cookie's quiet house.

"The other neighbors are saying she was murdered," Deirdre said suddenly. "Do they know who?"

"I don't think so. Not yet, anyway."

"It's not right," she said forcefully. "Cookie was a nice person. She didn't deserve to be killed like that."

Nobody did, I thought. "They'll figure it out," I said.

"First time I met Cookie," Deirdre said, "was maybe a week after I moved in. This is the first house I've ever owned, and I was all excited about pulling weeds and mowing the lawn—can you believe it? Anyway, I was out front about to yank out these funky-looking red weeds when Cookie gave this horrible, high-pitched shriek." Deirdre grinned. "I came this close to pulling out the most gorgeous peonies."

I laughed. "No wonder she shrieked."

"She was old enough to be my mother, but after that, we were friends. She took care of my house when I was out in the field, and she'd air everything out when I was coming back. She even got milk for my fridge and made sure there was something to eat." Deirdre's voice went distant. "She loved to hear my field stories. She couldn't get enough of them. She did so much for me, and all I ever did for her was shovel her driveway when it snowed."

"You did more than that," I said. She started to shake her head, but I knew I was right and kept going. "You did a lot more than that. You were her friend, Deirdre. You were her friend, and that counts for more than anything."

She sniffed. "Do you really think so?"

I did. And I also thought I was very glad to have met her. Maybe Cookie had been a difficult person to like, but she'd had at least one friend. A good one. Suddenly, I felt a lot better about the charge she'd laid on me.

I'm depending on you to figure out what happened.

I will, I told her silently. *I will.*

Chapter 15

Thursday passed with a flurry of semi-emergencies that ranged from Jenna's not being able to find spare laces for her hockey skates to Yvonne's car not starting and my favorite book distributor sending us boxes of absolutely the wrong books. There might be fifty shades of gray, but none of them were suitable for a children's bookstore.

I found the laces in the basement behind the shelves over which Jenna draped her equipment, I drove to Yvonne's house and used my jumper cables to start her car, and I got the books retaped and sent back before Lois could do more than say, "Hey . . ."

Friday went much the same way with slightly different semi-emergencies, but the weekend was a restful mix of hockey, sledding and an evening movie with Pete, then Sunday church and a lazy Sunday afternoon sliding into an even lazier Sunday evening.

It had all been just what the doctor ordered, and I bounded into the store on Monday with a song in my heart and a smile on my lips and stayed that way while I worked on the computer up front.

When Lois scuffed in, she gave me a sour look. "There are two kinds of people in the world. The ones who are perky on Monday mornings and the ones who are annoyed by the ones who are perky on Monday mornings."

But I was ready for her and handed over a steaming mug of Irish breakfast. "Drink your tea. And weren't you the one who was singing 'Oh, What a Beautiful Morning' last Monday?"

She sipped at the tea. "Yeah, but that was because I'd just thought up a good one to pull on Paoze."

"I think those days are done." Not so very long ago, Paoze had turned the tables on Lois and she was itching with revenge. "He's not nearly so gullible as he was, and we know who to thank for that, I think."

"Yeah," she said into the mug. "Talk about being hoisted by my own petard. What's a petard, anyway? And why would anyone be hoisted up on one?"

"They were basically bombs. They were used in the sixteenth century to blow gaps in castle walls. To be hoisted by one was to be caught in the explosion and be blown backward."

Lois looked at me. "You know the oddest things. And now that I know the answer, I think I was happier before."

"Knowledge is power."

She put her face back into the mug. "Knowledge is a dangerous thing."

Since she knew as well as I did what the actual phrase was, I moved on to Benjamin Franklin. "An investment in knowledge pays the best interest."

"To know is to know that you know nothing."

"Knowledge is true opinion."

She frowned. "Okay, I have no idea what that means."

"Me, either." I grinned. "And it's about the only thing I remember from my college philosophy class."

"Waste of three credit hours, if you ask me."

While I didn't exactly disagree with her, I felt obligated to defend my choice. Luckily, before I got any further than opening my mouth, the phone rang and I reached to pick it up. "Good morning, Children's Bookshelf. How may I help you?"

"Did you hear?" Marina demanded.

"Hear what?"

"It's all over the scanner."

"This is a children's bookstore," I said. "Having a police scanner going all the time isn't part of the atmosphere I want to create."

"Ha. Kids would love it."

They would. So would Lois; I could see a gleam in her eye at the mention of the nonpossibility. "What happened?"

"Cookie Van Doorne's house was broken into."

"It . . . what?" My knees suddenly felt as if they might start bending the wrong way.

"Beth? Beth!" Lois grabbed my shoulders and shoved me into a chair. "What's the matter? Is that Marina?" She yanked the phone out of my hand. "Marina? Lois. What did you tell Beth? Her face is looking as white as her legs do in early summer."

I heard Marina's voice sounding squeaky and concerned.

Lois peered at me. "She's still upright, but . . . hey!"

I took the phone back. "Do you know what happened?"

"Are you okay?"

"Fine. Just had a little . . . head rush, that's all." I wanted to stand up to prove it, but opted for the better-safe-than-sorry theory. "Do you have any details? What happened?"

"Nah." Her disgust came through the phone lines with no problem. "Can you get any info out of Gus?"

"He wasn't in church yesterday. Winnie said if his temperature isn't down today, she's taking him to the doctor."

"Wow, that's not like Gus."

No, it wasn't. "I'm sure he'll be better soon."

"I heard Todd Wietzel was down for more than two weeks."

That wasn't what I wanted to hear, so I moved back to the original subject. "What happened at Cookie's house?" Lois made a chirp of surprise and I waved her to silence. "Was there damage?"

"Not sure. All I know is the police were called to her address. The house has been empty for a while. Maybe it was someone looking for easy pickings. Either that or" — Marina lowered her voice an octave — "or the killer was looking to take away evidence that implicates her."

"Cookie died three weeks ago," I said. "Why would anyone break in now?"

"Maybe somebody did something that made her think there was something in the house."

"That's what . . ." I stopped.

"What?"

I sighed. If I didn't tell her now, she'd hound me until I did. "I went over there after the PTA meeting the other night. Cookie's neighbor and I stood outside talking for quite a while."

"Outside?" Marina half shrieked.

"In the snow?" Lois asked loudly.

"Why on earth didn't you go straight home?" Marina asked.

"For a recovering exhaustee, you're doing some pretty stupid things," Lois said severely.

I waited out their scolding. "You don't think me being there had anything to do with the break-in, do you?"

Marina made a gagging noise. "Quit taking yourself so seriously. You were there Wednesday night. This happened last night. If there's a connection, I don't see it."

I wasn't sure I did, either, but still . . . "Say, where were you all weekend? I tried to call you a couple of times, and your DH said you were out." I kept on asking silent questions. Why did you leave the PTA meeting so fast? Why aren't you sending me rude e-mails half a dozen times a day like you normally do?

"What? Uh-oh, sorry. There's a kid crying. Gotta go. Come talk to me after Mother's Day, okay?"   •

I let Lois pepper me with questions about Cookie's house for a few minutes. The ten thousandth time I answered "I have no idea," Lois muttered something about today's youth and stomped off to the graphic novels to read manga until she felt better.

Flossie came in just before lunch and the three of us spent the afternoon in separate parts of the store, the better to avoid conversation, my dear. Not that I was trying to avoid talking to Flossie. I would have enjoyed a nice, clearheaded chat with the woman who'd become one of my favorite people in the world, but doing so without incurring the wrath of Lois was currently a bit of a problem.

I was considering firing everyone, including myself, selling the store, and getting a less stressful job, perhaps as an air traffic controller, when the front doorbells jingled and Isabel Olsen came in.

"Hi, ladies!"

Her smile was so wide that I felt myself smiling back in pure reflex. "Hey, Isabel. What's up?"

"I'm looking for a present for Avery's birthday."

"How old is she now?" I asked. Six, maybe. Not seven. Well, maybe she could be seven, but it didn't seem possible.

"Eight, can you believe it?"

The definition of "impossible" shifted yet again. "Not really. What's she reading these days? *Magic Tree House*?"

Isabel nodded. "And I've started reading the Narnia books to her and Neal."

"Has she tried the Amelia Bedelia books?"

Isabel's face lit up. "Oh, wow, I *loved* those books when I was a kid! They'd be perfect for her. She could read them by herself, even. Do you have the very first one? I'll want that one for sure and—" Her happy face dissolved into mush. She bent over and clutched at her stomach, moaning.

From behind, I took hold of her shoulders to steady her. "Isabel, are you sick? Let me get you to a chair and—"

"Bathroom," she croaked. "I need to"—she swallowed audibly—"to . . ."

There was no need for an explanation. I steered her toward the back of the store and opened the bathroom door. "Do you want me to stay with you?"

"No," she croaked. "Thanks, but I'm . . ." In an awkward rush, she assumed the kneeling position and leaned over.

Quickly, I shut the door behind her. Lois and Flossie were both hovering.

"What's going on?" Lois asked. "Is she okay?"

Through the thin door came the unmistakable sound of retching. One of these days I really needed to get a solid door. It wouldn't stop all the noises, but it would help mask the worst ones.

"Flu?" Flossie asked.

I shrugged. "She seemed fine when she came in."

"That flu going around can take you quick," Lois said. "I remember reading about the epidemic in 1919. Or was it 1918? Anyway, perfectly healthy people got sick one day and were dead the next."

The three of us looked at the door. "No one around here has died from flu," I said.

"Not that we know about." Lois took a small backward step. "Have you actually seen Gus in the last week? Maybe he's dying, or even dead, and Winnie can't bring herself to tell anyone."

"That's ridiculous," Flossie said, but her voice held the tiniest of quavers.

"Of course it is," I said loudly. Or at least I meant to say it loudly. It came out as more of a croak. I cleared my throat and went at things from a different direction. "If this flu was that bad, we'd have heard public health warnings."

More retching noises reached us and Lois inched back a little more. "Did you listen to any news this morning?" she asked. "Watch any television?"

I hadn't. And judging from the expression on Flossie's face, she hadn't, either.

The toilet flushed, the sink ran, and poor, sickly Isabel flung open the bathroom door and bounded out with the energy of a toddler. "Hey, ladies. Is this the line for the ladies?" She giggled.

I squinted at her. So did Flossie. So did Lois, and it was Lois who first pointed her finger and said the words. "You're not sick. You're pregnant!"

Isabel's blush was a giveaway. "What makes you think that? Maybe I have a little flu. Or some twenty-four-hour bug."

"No one," Lois said, "who is sick enough to ride the porcelain bus could possibly look as perky as you do right this minute."

Isabel wiped the smile off her face. Or tried to. As soon as it was gone, it started inching back. Up her chin, through her mouth, onto her nose, and into her eyes. "I'm not perky," she said.

I put my hands on my hips. Lois followed suit, and an amused Flossie made three. "You are so perky," I said, "that you could be coffee."

Flossie caught on and joined in. "You're so perky that you're putting daffodils to shame."

"You're so perky," Lois said, "that . . . that you should be a jumping bean."

We looked at her. She shrugged.

But Isabel didn't care about the horrible analogy. "Don't tell anyone, will you? Any of you?"

I glanced at my staff, then gave her midriff a questioning look. "Even if we keep quiet, people are going to know eventually."

She giggled. "You're funny. Of course we'll tell people. We'll have to, pretty soon. It's just that we haven't told Kirk's parents yet. We're going to make kind of a production out of it, take them to the country club for dinner this weekend. We'll order a bottle of wine and when Kirk's dad starts to pour mine, I'm going to put my hand over my glass and say, thanks, but I can't."

It was a cute idea, and I said so. "I didn't know you and Kirk were members of the country club."

"Kirk got us the membership for Christmas," Isabel

said. "It's been so much fun going out there. Did you know they have this humungous brunch buffet on Sunday mornings? They make omelets to order and slice off prime rib while you wait and there's this huge table of nothing but dessert."

She sailed off into a description of the chocolate-covered macaroons, but my brain wasn't *ooh*ing and *aah*ing. I'd eaten at that buffet many a time with Evan and gave it a lot of blame for the weight I'd gained while dating him.

While Isabel was talking about the different varieties of cheesecake, I counted backward in time. When she paused to take a breath, I asked, "How long have you been getting morning sickness?"

"Afternoon and evening sickness, you mean?" She made a face. "About three weeks. We've been trying to get pregnant for a few months, but I wasn't sure until that PTA thing, the PTA in Review."

A clue, Watson, a clue!

Isabel didn't notice that my ears had perked. "That was the first night it was really bad," she said. "I was in the bathroom most of the night, doing, you know, my thing. But I told people I was in the back of the kitchen because I didn't want anyone guessing I was pregnant. Not until we knew for sure."

Lois nodded. "Bad luck to say anything until the doctor says it's okay."

"That's what I think." Isabel's head bobbed up and down. "Last week I got in to see my obstetrician, and she said everything looks good." Happiness poured out of her skin. "Isn't that just the best news?"

She and Lois started exchanging pregnancy stories, Flossie started to look politely bored, and I got out my mental list of suspects, found a mental pencil, and crossed off Isabel's name.

Lois spent the rest of the afternoon reminiscing about pregnancy. I liked children and had found being pregnant a deeply powerful experience, but hearing about someone else's gestation was a lot like listening to someone talk about their golf game.

Flossie was the smart one. Somewhere in the middle of Lois's first trimester with her second child, she stopped even pretending to listen and announced she was going to clean the workroom. It took me until the second trimester of the third child to edge away. "That's fascinating, Lois, but I need to work on . . . on the computer."

When Jenna came in from school, she buried herself in her math homework. At closing time she came back from the Green Tractor carrying two plastic bags and grinning. "Lasagna," she said. "With bread sticks and salads. This is healthy food, right? There can't be anything wrong with this dinner."

Nothing except the refined flour, fatty cheeses, and tomato sauce that was no doubt heavy on the salt. "It could be worse." I took one of the bags from her. "Let's go home," I said, and suddenly home sounded like the very best possible place in the world to be. What could be better on a cold February night than to be home with my children?

The sun was just sinking below the horizon when we pulled into Marina's driveway. Jenna stayed in the car and fiddled with the radio while I ran into the house.

Marina was in the kitchen pulling fresh Parker House rolls from the oven. "Look," she said, brandishing the sheet pan. "Ze ah zings of beauty, are they not? Ze crust is a perfect light brown, ze texture is zublime, yes?"

"Your French accent needs work," I said, "but they look wonderful. And we need to talk. Soon." I called for my son, who, from the sound of things, was in the family room playing Wii bowling with Zach. "Oliver? Time to go!"

She put the sheet pan on the range top and put her fingers in her ears. "La-la-la, I can't hear you until Mother's Day."

Right. "Why is it that you can get me to agree to six weeks of forced inactivity but I can't get you to talk to me for four months?"

She grinned. "Because you're a much nicer person than I am."

On the short ride home, Jenna continued to sit shotgun while Oliver sat in the backseat. He was in question mode tonight and went at it as if he'd spent the day putting together a list.

"Mom, how come people are mean to each other?"

After I'd tackled that one the best I could, he moved on to the far easier "Mom, why aren't birds sitting on wires electrocuted?"

My answer about electrical currents and grounding was followed by a question about the necessity of learning fractions, followed by a stumper question. "Mom, what's time?"

"That," I said, pushing the button to open the garage door, "will have to wait until after we eat dinner. Oliver, can you carry in the bag with the salads? Jenna, you get the lasagna, please."

They clambered out. I opened my car door and was

collecting backpacks and my purse when I heard a sound that chilled me to the bone.

"Mom? *Mom!*"

This wasn't the normal Mom call made when the toothpaste cap fell into the toilet. This was a call of pure panic.

I dropped everything and bolted for the open door. My children were standing in the middle of the kitchen, eyes wide, staring at a room that bore no resemblance to the marginally tidy space we'd left that morning.

Cupboard doors were open. Food and dishes and pots and pans were strewn all across the floor. Through the study's open door, I could see papers and books covering the carpet. The bookcase was tumbled over and the desk drawers were upside down on top of it all. I could only imagine what the rest of the house looked like. The rest of the house . . .

"Back to the car." I pointed at the door to the garage. "Now."

Our house, our home, our haven of safety had been ransacked, and for all I knew, the ransacker was inside.

Chapter 16

I'd never been more prouder of my children. They obeyed me without asking any questions, running back to the same seats they'd vacated less than a minute earlier, and buckling themselves in, in less time than it takes to tell.

I slid behind the driver's seat, shut the car door, and clicked the door locks shut. I started the car as the garage door rumbled open and backed out with only a scant glance for traffic.

"Where are we going?" Jenna asked in a small voice.

There was no question, no question at all. "Mrs. Neff's," I said. "Jenna, can you get me my phone, please?" She fumbled through my purse and handed it to me. "Kids, you should never drive and use a cell phone except in an emergency, okay?"

"Are we in an emergency?" Oliver asked.

"A midlevel one." I'd been trying for a light tone, but was pretty sure I hadn't reached my goal. I tried again. "We're okay, but the house is a bit of a mess."

"We didn't check on Spot," Jenna said, swallowing. "Or George. We left without making sure our pets were okay."

"Sweetheart, I saw Spot. He was in the laundry room, sleeping on a pile of dirty clothes." Yes, I was a horrible mother for lying, but I was not going to have my children be in that house until the police made sure it was empty of intruders. "And there's no need to worry about George. Cats can smell trouble better than tuna fish. He probably won't come out of the back of my closet for a week."

I pushed the speed dial and waited until Marina answered. "Hey. Something's happened and we're headed back to your house. No, we're fine. I'll tell you about it when we get there." I blinked at her question. What did we want for supper? I looked at Jenna, then looked into the backseat. "How about lasagna?" I asked shakily, because my children had returned to the car still carrying the food-filled bags.

An hour and a half later, I stood in the middle of my family room with Spot at my side, looking at what had, that morning, been a cozy place with upholstered furniture, a gas fireplace, a television, and shelves full of board games and children's books and crayons and paints and markers and stencils and glitter and glue.

"Mrs. Kennedy?"

I started. The kind—and very young—Officer Sean Zimmerman was looking at me. Judging from his expression, it seemed certain that he'd asked me a question and I hadn't answered. "I'm sorry, Sean. What did you say?"

He gave me a smile that was probably supposed to comfort me, but instead made me want to pat him on the head for trying so hard to be a good boy. "That it's going to be hard to tell, but do you think anything is missing?"

Missing? What was missing was the sense of security that I'd taken for granted. What was missing was the confidence that nothing truly bad would ever happen in this house. What was missing was my children's innocence that had been dumped on the floor and ground into the carpet along with the silver glitter.

I closed my eyes for a moment and, when I opened them, was faced afresh with the mess my house had become.

Sean, notepad in hand, encouraged me along. "I saw your computer is still here, in your study. Your TV is still here. And the DVD player. Did you have a PlayStation or an Xbox?"

Not unless you-know-where had frozen over. "They play those games when they're at their dad's," I said vaguely.

He nodded. "Okay, how about other electronics? I ask because that's what gets stolen from houses most often. Handheld stuff. Do you let the kids take their smartphones to school?"

I half smiled. I didn't let the kids have a phone at all, a matter that was becoming more and more a point of contention with my daughter. And it was then, for what reason I couldn't fathom, that I started crying. Tears gushed out of my eyes, down my cheeks, and into the corners of my mouth. "Sorry." I wiped at my face with the heels of my hands. "This is . . . all very strange."

"Don't apologize," Sean said. "You've doing fine. Matter of fact, you're doing great. Do you want to sit a minute?"

The front door creaked open, then slammed shut. "Beth? Beth!" Pete rushed into the room, his booted feet leaving scattered bits of snow behind him. "Sweetheart, are you all right? The kids?" He pulled me into a rough hug, holding me tight, cradling the back of my head, kissing my hair. "I got here as fast as I could. You're okay, right?" He held me at arm's length, searching my face. "You look a little funny. Let's sit you down."

"I'm okay." And somehow, suddenly, I was. "The kids are over at Marina's. They're fine." They were probably doing better than their mother. "Spot's fine and George is under my bed and showing no desire to move."

"Are you sure you're okay?" Pete thumbed a wet tear off my face. "Like sure sure? You're not being all Beth-like and saying you're fine when you're really not?"

"How about, I'm mostly fine?"

He smiled and I found that I could smile back. "Okay," he said. "That I'll believe." He embraced me again, whispered something that I couldn't quite hear, then kissed my forehead and released me.

"Officer Zimmerman." Pete held out his hand and the two men shook. "What's the story?"

Sean related the bare facts. That I'd called 911, that Sean had taken the call and, with the help of a second officer, had come to the house, lights flashing. They'd gone through the house quickly and found it empty of any intruders. Now it was just Sean and me, and now Pete, standing in the middle of the aftermath.

"How'd he get in?" Pete asked.

"Broke the window in the back door. No footprints in the snow, so he must have walked right next to the house where there isn't any."

I grew an instant dislike for the deep roof eaves I'd previously liked.

"Fingerprints?"

"The county is sending over their guy," Sean said. "He'll be here soon."

Pete nodded, but we all knew it was unlikely they'd

find any fingerprints that would be useful. "Well," he said, looking around, "it could be a lot worse."

I gaped at him. Worse? How could it be worse?

Then I realized that he'd taken off his friend-of-the-victim hat and put on his professional forensic cleaner hat. Because he was right, it could have been worse. A lot worse.

Every shelf and cabinet in the house had had its contents tossed to the floor, but the milk was still in its jug, the toothpaste was still in its tube, and the glue was still in its bottle. Though it was a horrible mess, a few hours of tidying and vacuuming would take care of it.

"You know," Sean said, "this looks a lot like Mrs. Van Doorne's house did the other day."

Pete and I exchanged glances. "Oh, yeah?" he asked.

Sean nodded. "Like someone was looking for something. Mrs. Kennedy, did you know Mrs. Van Doorne? Can you think of anything that connects the two of you?"

I shook my head. "She wasn't much more than an acquaintance."

He looked at me. "I've seen the letter she sent you. The one asking you to help find her killer."

At that particular moment, I didn't care if the president of the United States had asked me for help. The only thing I wanted was to get my house back together and my children back under my roof, safe and sound. "Sorry, Sean. She may have asked, but I don't know anything." I gestured at the surrounding chaos. "Can I start cleaning?"

It was midnight before Pete and I got the house back to anything that resembled normal. When he said he'd finish it the next day, I got all sniffly and said thanks so much for the offer, but of course you don't have to do that.

He handed me a tissue and said he knew he didn't have to, but he wanted to and to let him help, for crying out loud, that cleaning up crime scenes was what he did for a living and that he wouldn't sleep right until my house was back to normal.

I told him, in that case, I was practically obligated to let him finish up. He agreed, hugged me, and sent me back to Marina's to sleep in a sleeping bag on her family room floor, Jenna at my right and Oliver at my left, the three of us huddled together in one large lump of displaced Kennedys.

The next morning we dressed in clothes I'd shoved in a duffel and brought from the house. Marina's outstanding breakfast of scrambled eggs and sausages, the sort of weekday breakfast I only made time for on birthdays, went down into the stomachs of my children with ease. I, however, pushed the eggs round and round and cut the sausages into successively smaller and smaller pieces until my breakfast didn't resemble anything close to human food.

Marina took my plate away. "Try this," she said, and gave me half a piece of lightly buttered toast. I chewed at it from one side, then the other, and eventually got it all down.

"Thanks," I said in a low voice, for the three kids were chattering about a hot new rock group. The Lizard Withers? That couldn't be right. "For everything," I told her. "You're the best friend anyone could want."

She batted her eyelashes and handed me another piece of toast. "Eat up, buttercup, or I'll call Lois and give her my version of what happened last night before you get to the store."

It was a very real and powerful threat, so I ate up.

The kids clung to me a little when I dropped them off, though it could have been the other way around. But it was certain that Jenna kissed my cheek before she got out of the car, something she didn't normally do. When it was Oliver's turn to leave, he unbuckled his seat belt and sat a moment, staring at his knees.

"Are we going to sleep at home tonight?" he asked.

It was time for Mom to have all the answers, and she wasn't sure she had any, let alone the truckload he deserved. I knew Oliver missed sleeping in his own bed, and I also knew he was scared to go back into the house. I knew he was nervous about Bad Guys, but I also knew he was concerned about his stuffed animal collection. "Spot will miss us if we don't."

My son nodded. "Yeah. And George, too."

I doubted that very much, but went along with the fiction. "Pete is finishing up the cleaning today. By the time he gets done you won't even know that anything happened."

"Bet we do," he said quietly.

Oh, my son, of course we'll know, and I am so very sorry you've had your innocence stolen from you, so very sorry . . .

"Know how we'll know?" he asked.

"How?"

He turned to face me. "The bathtub will be really, really clean."

My mouth dropped open. "Oliver!"

He giggled, launched himself at me for a hug, then jumped out and ran up the long sidewalk to the school.

I was still smiling when I got to the store, and the smile stayed until Lois arrived. Since Flossie was due to arrive soon after, I waited until they both had hot drinks in hand to tell them what had happened.

"Oh, my dear!" Flossie, not a woman prone to public displays of affection, put down her coffee mug and enfolded me in a long, warm hug. "How dreadful for you. And the children? What a shock that must have been."

Lois thumped me on the shoulder. "Maybe you should go home today. Take it easy."

I explained that Pete was still finishing up, and they both agreed that letting the man take care of the cleaning was a wise move. "Like car detailing, only for houses," Lois said, toasting me with her mug of Earl Grey. "You go, girl. Whatever it takes."

So it was with a relatively light heart that I sat down at my desk. I powered up the computer and stretched out my legs while I waited for the screen to come to life. That minute or two wait was the time I often used to prioritize my daily tasks, and it was at this point I realized that calling my former husband and telling him about last night should be high on that list.

I slid down a little in my chair as I imagined the conversation.

"Beth," he'd say, "please tell me you locked the house before you left."

Yes, Richard, I locked the house.

"If there have been a rash of burglaries in the area, you should install an alarm system. Let me e-mail you a listing of reliable companies."

No, thank you, Richard, I don't think an alarm system would do much good now that the house has already been ransacked.

"You think that lightning can't strike twice?" He'd chuckle, then recite the statistic of how often it actually does. "Do you really wish to risk those odds with the children?"

I slid down a little farther in the chair. My left foot touched something.

What the . . . ? I sat up and looked underneath the desk. A cardboard box sat there, staring up at me.

Cookie's box. I'd completely forgotten about it. Sean's question of last night rushed into my head. "Can you think of anything that connects the two of you?"

Why, yes, Officer Zimmerman, I can.

I tugged at the box and dragged it out into the light of day. How was it possible that I hadn't remembered Cookie's box?

But even touching it was making the back of my neck twitch with unease. And that might explain why I'd forgotten about the box last night. There was only so much creepiness my brain could tolerate in one day; having my house ripped apart had been yesterday's allotment.

I hauled the box up onto my desk. Opened one flap. Opened the other. Peeked between the two inside flaps.

"It's just stuff," I told it. "There's nothing inherently creepy about any of you."

Except the doll. I'd never liked dolls with eyes painted permanently open, and that included Barbie and Raggedy Ann. Infant dolls especially should have eyes that closed. Babies needed sleep.

I fingered the flap. Sleep would be good. I hadn't had much last night. After tiptoeing into Marina's house and crawling into the sleeping bag, I'd lain awake thinking dark thoughts that didn't match well with my mom/children's bookstore owner/PTA president persona. Anger. Revenge. Paybacks. What little sleep I did get was restless and hampered by the fact that I was sleeping on a floor. A carpeted floor, to be sure, but still a floor.

"Quit lollygagging," I muttered, quoting my grandmother, and opened the box.

One by one, I took out the items Cookie had placed inside and put them on my desk. A Christmas ornament. A flat white paper bag. A high school graduation photo that looked about fifteen years old. A brochure for an African safari. A hand towel. A ceramic figurine of a football player. The doll. A snow globe. A small arrangement of silk flowers. A vegetable peeler, a one-dollar bill in a plastic bag, a toy boat, and a royal blue coffee mug.

I put the box on the floor and studied the stuff on my desk until my eyes hurt. If there was any meaning, it was escaping me. I arranged the items this way and that, looking for a message, a hidden communication, anything. I rearranged everything to be alphabetical. Rearranged everything by material. By season. Sorted by approximate price. By age of the likely user. By color. By size. Nothing I did got me any closer to a conclusion.

I was rearranging the items by shape when Lois burst into the room.

"Beth!" she shrieked, flapping her arms.

Oh, dear. Fluttering arms meant Lois was in full panic mode, something that happened maybe once a year. "What's the matter?" I asked.

She tugged at her hair. "It's almost time for that preschool class to show up. I forgot all about it. Fifteen little kids will be wanting to spend their money on stickers and we're short on dollar bills and dimes and I need to restock the sticker rolls and the stencil books and Flossie's helping, but—"

I was already sweeping my new desk decorations back into their box. "Don't worry about it. I'll go to the bank."

"You will? Really? Oh, bless you." She threw me an air kiss. "Mmm-wha! You're the best boss ever." She hurried out of my office, leaving an invisible trail of angst in her wake.

In an hour, Lois would be ashamed of her panic attack and try to convince us it had never happened. She was lucky Paoze wasn't working this morning; he would have been able to recite her babble word for word.

I put on my coat, then took a bank bag and stuffed some bills from the cash register into it. Looked inside, and stuffed a few more in. Little kids were the only people in the country who could be relied upon to pay for their purchases in cash.

Outside, the gray of early morning was progressing into a gray midmorning, and judging from the sky, it was going to be a gray noon, a gray afternoon, and a gray evening. A gray night, too, though it would be harder to tell at night what the clouds were—

"Hey, Beth."

I stopped looking at the sky and looked at the person standing in front of me. "Deirdre. How are you this morning?"

Cookie's neighbor glanced at the sky. "So far, so good, but I hear there's a storm coming."

"Headed anywhere exciting?" I nodded at the adjacent storefront, the one travel agency left in Rynwood.

She looked puzzled, and then her face cleared. "No, I came out of there." She nodded at the local stockbroker's office. "I have an account here, but I might be switching. Can you recommend anyone?"

Clearly, Deirdre didn't know how much money children's bookstore owners made. Or, more accurately, didn't make. The store was doing well, but I wasn't ever going to make enough money to think about putting it into anything even remotely risky. "Sorry. Can't help you with that."

We chatted a little more, then started the good-bye phrases that polite people use. "Well," I said, "it was nice to—" I stopped cold. The box. "Did anyone else know that you sent me Cookie's box? Did you mention it to anyone?"

Deirdre shook her head. "No, I . . . Wait. Hang on. The day I got back from Chicago, I dropped the receipt in the grocery store. I was getting milk and eggs before I headed home. That new vice principal picked it up and handed it back to me. I could have said it was for you from Cookie. Sorry. I really don't remember."

I might have mumbled a good-bye, but I might not. Probably not. I don't see how I could have, because my brain was too busy with the unwelcome knowledge that Oliver's Ms. Stephanie had abruptly moved to the very tippy top of the potential killers list.

The century-old bank lobby echoed with too many voices. If the building's designer had intended to create an impressive space, he had succeeded, but at a price. Every employee in, and customer of, the marble-floored, plaster-ceilinged, many-pillared, granite-countertopped, wood-walled bank suffered from auditory overload just by walking in the door. The acoustics were such that, if you had a mind to, you could overhear every conversation in the room.

It seemed odd, in a bank, not to have even a semblance of privacy while conducting financial transactions, but maybe that hadn't mattered when the building was built.

Thinking about it, I unzipped my coat. Back in those days, coats had been buttoned. Back then, women and men alike had worn hats when in public. Back then, ladies had worn gloves. I did a little mental math. If Cookie had started working at the bank when she was, say, twenty-five, she would have started working here in the late seventies. Back in the days of bell-bottoms and—

". . . Van Doorne."

I whipped my head around. Who . . . ? Then I recognized Mrs. Tolliver. Auntie May without any of the humor, Lois had told me years ago, and she was right.

Over near the high counter where people filled out deposit and withdrawal slips, the elderly and very upright Mrs. Tolliver was once again speaking her mind. "Not to speak ill of the dead," she said, "but that woman didn't have the gift of friendship. She didn't have friends as a girl and she never managed to gain more as an adult. I ask you, what kind of woman doesn't have a single good friend?"

She paused, waiting for a response. Her companion stood behind a pillar, invisible to me, and spoke too quietly for me to hear anything more than a low voice. A male voice.

I edged closer.

"Don't be ridiculous." Mrs. Tolliver's chin went up. "I know everyone in this town. If Cookie had had a friend, I would have known."

Deirdre. She didn't know Deirdre.

"Well, perhaps not every single solitary person," she said. "But I know everyone who counts, and Cookie wasn't on friendship terms with any of them. And how can you, of all people, defend her?" Mrs. Tolliver demanded. "After what she did to you? You can't tell me you shed a tear when she died."

I edged even closer.

"She was doing what she thought was right," Alan Barnhart said quietly. "No, I didn't grieve when she passed, but I can respect her actions. She had great courage, born of her convictions, and wouldn't the world be a better place if we all had that kind of passion?"

"Passion." Mrs. Tolliver thinned her lips. "There is no dignity in passion. Without dignity, there is no self-respect, and without self-respect, there is no honor. Honor is what's important. It's the only thing that ever has been."

A bank teller called. "Mrs. Tolliver? I can help you now."

"Honor," she repeated, and walked away, head erect.

With his back to me, Alan watched her go. I could almost see his mental shrug and knew exactly what it meant. It was far easier to agree to win an argument with Mrs. Tolliver when she wasn't in the same room.

Another teller opened up her window. "Good morning, Alan," she said, smiling. "What do you need today?" He said something I couldn't hear. "A safe-deposit box?" she asked. "Easy enough." She told him the annual fee and slid a piece of paper across the counter to him. "Other than the fee, all you have to do is fill out this form."

I watched Alan nod, then take the pen offered to him. He held the pen at an odd angle, and an old memory pinged. As Alan wrote, the top of the pen wobbled. It wobbled wider and wider, then fell with a clatter. Alan laid his hands flat on the counter. He stared at the fingers that had betrayed him, not hearing the concerned questions of the teller.

You didn't kill her, I thought. Only I must not have simply thought it, I must have said it out loud, because Alan turned to me, his eyebrows raised.

I smiled. "How about a quick cup of coffee at the Green Tractor?"

Ten minutes later, we were in the diner's back booth, warm mugs in hand.

"You seriously suspected me of killing Cookie?" Alan's raised eyebrows created lines in his forehead.

"Not really." I wrapped my hands around the mug of tea Ruthie had set in front of me. "But since you were helping out in the kitchen that night, your name had to go on the suspect list."

"You know that Gus talked to me," Alan said.

I hadn't known, but since I hadn't heard anything from Gus since he'd gotten sick, I wasn't surprised.

"So how do you know I didn't do it?" Alan asked. "After all, you could be wrong. You could be sitting here with a murderer."

But I was shaking my head. "Nothing Cookie did made any real difference to you. She didn't get you fired, and her whispering campaign about your store didn't hurt your business, not on a permanent basis. You overturned everything she did. And you defended her to Mrs. Tolliver."

Over his raised mug, he studied me. "Maybe I was just doing that to deflect suspicion."

"Maybe." I studied him right back. "But you couldn't have opened that pill bottle, not with your arthritis. You can barely hold that mug right now, can you? And in the store the other day, it was arthritis that made you drop that plate, wasn't it? That's why Alice was so worried—it wasn't the cut so much as the disease."

His wife was worried about him; she was worried about what was going to happen to him, about how his life was going to be changing, that soon he might not be able to do the things he loved to do. Just as my father hadn't been able to go fishing by himself in the years before he passed away.

"Alice could have opened the bottle for me," Alan pointed out.

I came back to the here and now. "Yes, but she didn't. You wouldn't have asked her to do something like that."

"But, anyway," Alan said, "we're aspirin people. Maybe some ibuprofen every once in a while, but not acetaminophen. We haven't had any in the house since Alice read an article about how dangerous it is."

I smiled. That sounded like Alice.

And that was the end of Alan being a suspect.

When I got back to a store crowded with preschoolers, a harried Lois gave me a look that could kill. Luckily my winter coat had magical powers and the blow bounced off me and fell to the floor along with the snow that had fallen on me while I was walking back from the Green Tractor.

"Where have you been?" she whispered fiercely as she yanked the bank bag out of my hand.

I would have told her, but I could tell she wouldn't be a receptive audience for my story, so I pulled off my coat and got to work.

*　　*　　*

When Jenna and I stopped at Marina's that evening to pick up Oliver, she was on the phone with what sounded like, from Marina's end of the conversation, a very uncooperative customer service representative from her credit card company.

I mouthed, *Call me.*

She nodded at me while saying, "But I've never been to Boca Raton. How could I possibly have purchased over seven hundred dollars' worth of lingerie at a Nordstrom? I mean, sure, I would like to, but I have four kids and the last time I bought a fancy bra was in 1987."

Two hours later, when I was in the study balancing the checkbook and the kids were in the family room arguing over what DVD to watch, Marina knocked and came in, stomping snow off her boots and making shivering noises. "Snowy and blowy and cold. Looks like we're actually going to get that storm they forecasted."

"I thought you were going to call."

"Not after Zach and the DH decided this was the perfect night to start repainting his bedroom. You know what the smell of primer does to me."

Five minutes in an unvented room and she'd get a splitting headache. Ten minutes and she'd start zoning out. Fifteen and her speech would be slurred. I didn't know what would happen at twenty because she'd never lasted that long, but there was no way it would be pretty.

I turned on the teakettle. "Did you get your new lingerie straightened out?"

"My . . . ? Oh, right. The stuff I didn't buy. All taken care of, thanks. Now, what was it you wanted to talk about?"

"We have to cross Isabel and Alan off the suspect list," I told her.

"Ooo, you have information!" Marina's face lit up.

She scraped back one of the chairs from the kitchen table and plopped down into it. "Spill, my friend, spill!"

So I told her about the bank and Mrs. Tolliver and Alan and how he'd defended Cookie and how he'd been dropping things and his arthritis and how he'd fought Cookie's efforts and won.

Marina went into Southern belle mode, her fallback persona. "Ah do declare, the man is a saint, bless his heart. Is theah anyone else who could be so kind as to defend his tormentor?"

"Unlikely."

"And what about deah Isabel? Ah'm glad to hear that sweet thing is not a murderah, but why do we know so?"

Since Lois and Flossie and I had promised Isabel that we wouldn't spread the news about her pregnancy, I needed a cover story for her innocence that would satisfy Marina. Unfortunately, I hadn't come up with anything. "It's a secret," I said lamely. "Next week I'll be able to tell you, but not right now."

I'd expected her to protest and wheedle and beg. Instead, she nodded. "Okay. But you'll tell me as soon as you can?"

Who was this woman sitting at my kitchen table and what had she done with my best friend? "Well, sure." I stared at her and might have gone on staring for quite some time, but the teakettle started its shrill whistle and turned my attention away from the alien who'd taken up residence in Marina's body.

I bustled about, brewing up mugs of decaffeinated tea, and by the time I brought the drinks to the kitchen table and sat down, we were talking about the budding storm and what the chances were of the school superintendent calling off school the next day.

Then I knew I had to tell her what I didn't want to think about. "There's something else," I said in a low voice. Jenna and Oliver were down the hall and in another room, but kids' ears have an amazing capacity to overhear whatever part of a conversation interests them.

Marina laid her arms on the table and leaned close. "Can I guess?" she asked in an equally low voice.

"No," I said, and talked over the top of her pouting protest. "Remember I told you about a box I got from Cookie, the one with all the odd things inside it?"

"Yeah, what's that all about, anyway?"

"Haven't a clue."

"No, I mean why did Cookie send it to you in the first place? You hardly knew the woman."

I'd been wondering the same thing. "When I took her home that night of the PTA in Review, she went on and on about all the murders I'd helped solve. Yes, you helped, too," I quickly added, "but you weren't in the car, so it was just me. From her letter, it didn't sound as if she had a lot of confidence in the police, so maybe she sent me the box thinking it would help me figure out her killer."

Marina squinted. "Sounds like something Cookie would think. Matter of fact, sounds like something I'd think if people were after me." She grinned.

I rolled my eyes. "This morning I ran into Deirdre Gale, Cookie's neighbor, the woman who sent me the box."

"Deirdre did it!" Marina thumped the table. "She and Cookie were fighting over . . . over a fence line and—"

"And she was in Alaska when Cookie was poisoned."

Marina's face lost its animation. "Really? Dang. I mean . . . you know."

I did know. Each person on our short list of suspects was someone we'd known for years. The thought that the person who'd murdered Cookie might be a relative stranger was a much more comfortable thought.

"You sure she was in Alaska?" Marina asked. "Maybe she sneaked into the kitchen when no one was looking. Maybe she's stealthlike in her movements and . . ."

I was shaking my head. "She works for a big Madison engineering firm. I called, said I was from the airline and needed to check on some flight dates for one of their employees regarding a baggage claim. She was in Alaska."

Marina grinned. "Clever you, thinking up a story like that. Say, did your ears turn red? I mean, it was kind of a lie, you know."

My ears had burned for an hour afterward, but I wasn't going to tell her that. "So when I saw Deirdre today, I asked her if anyone else knew that she sent me the box." I sighed. "And it turns out that Stephanie Pesch probably knew."

"Stephanie?" Marina's voice was loud with surprise.

I made frantic shushing gestures. "Shhh," I said, and gave her the details.

"Huh." Marina stared into her tea. "Our new vice principal just went to the top of the People Who Might Have Killed Cookie list. I don't like this, not one little bit."

"You're not alone." We talked over what I'd learned about Stephanie, about how Cookie had driven away her own daughter, and about how the argument at the bank showed how much Stephanie still hated Cookie.

Marina sighed. "Are you sure Deirdre couldn't have done it?"

"No possible way. There's not—" I stopped and looked down the hall. Once again my children were arguing, but this particular argument carried a different tone.

A *crash!* reverberated through the house.

Marina's eyes went wide. "What was what?"

But I was already on my feet and hurrying down the hall. "The front door," I called over my shoulder. Although why the door should have banged open, I had no idea. Then, as I went past the empty family room, I realized I had no idea where my children were. "Jenna? Oliver?"

I rounded the corner and went into the living room, where a cold rush of air was sweeping through the entryway and snaking its frigid way into the rest of the house. I grabbed the door handle and had started to slam it closed when I saw my daughter's dim figure disappearing into the dark white of an evening snowstorm.

"Jenna!" I called. "Come back!"

Either she didn't hear or she didn't pay attention. One step more, two, and then she was gone into the night.

Marina was at my side. "What on earth? Where's she going?"

I didn't know, but I was going to find out. I ran to the kitchen for my coat, for Jenna's coat, because she was out in that storm without it—*oh, Jenna!*—for my cell phone. "Oliver? Oliver!" I shouted.

But he was gone, too.

Chapter 17

"Beth, stop it!" Marina grabbed my arm and pulled me around to face her. "You can't spaz out. Not now. Deep breath, okay?"

I stopped screaming my children's names. Nodding, I pulled in a deep breath. The air rushing into my body interrupted my panic attack and let my brain start working. "Okay," I said. "Okay. I'm good. Now let's go."

"Boots, gloves, hat." Marina flung open the closet door and handed me articles of clothing. "For you and for the kids."

Taking the time to dress myself warmly felt like an impossible delay, but I knew she was right. I pulled my cell from my purse and pushed Pete's number. "I'm going to follow Jenna's tracks. You go ahead and look for Oliver in your van. Take their stuff, okay?"

Marina, a coat under each arm and two boots in each hand, gave me an awkward hug. "We'll find them, Beth. Don't you worry. Ten minutes and we'll all be back inside." She released me and hurried outside as Pete answered the phone.

"Hey, sweetie. What's up?"

As quickly and concisely as I could, I told him what had happened. "Can you help?" I asked.

"In the truck and headed your way."

Just knowing that he was coming made the tight band of fear at my neck ease the tiniest bit.

"But I'm in Madison," he was saying, "and you know what the weather's like. I'll call when I get closer and I'll find you. You called the police?"

"Next thing." We made quick good-byes. As I dialed the three numbers, I wondered at my knee-jerk reaction to call Pete first and law enforcement second, but pushed the thought away as I pulled on my boots. When the 911 dispatcher answered, I gave her the information with only a few stuttering sobs breaking up the telling. "And now I'm going out to look for them," I told her, pulling on one glove, then the other.

"Ma'am, please wait at your house until an officer arrives."

"Yes," I said, "I know I should wait, and it's silly for me to go out into that storm, but my children are out there and there's not a snowball's chance in you know what that I'm going to wait inside while they're out in that cold." I zipped up my coat.

"Ma'am, please—"

"How long until an officer can get here?" I asked.

There was a short pause. "Ma'am, children in danger are placed as the highest of priorities."

Which wasn't any kind of real answer. "How long?" My question was nearly a shout.

"All officers on duty have been called to an accident on the expressway. It may be some time before—"

"Thank you." I hung up, jammed a hat on my head, and ran out the front door.

*   *   *

The wind beat at me as if it had no intention of stopping. The treetops tossed and churned and roared, sounding like distant waves coming to get me, coming to get my children, to suck them up and pull them away and—

"No!" I shouted into the wind. "They're going to be fine!"

Jenna's and Oliver's footprints, though only minutes old, were nearly obscured by the blowing snow. The panic that had overtaken me earlier came back with a sharpened vengeance, only this time Marina wasn't here to help me snap out of it.

Deep breath, I told myself. *Don't be afraid. They can't be far. Besides, Pete will be here soon. The police will be here soon. Plus, maybe Marina has found them already.*

But my cell phone was in my hand and she hadn't called.

I shoved the panic down into a small imaginary box and nailed the lid shut. When the kids were warm and dry and hugged and kissed and given punishments that would last until they were thirty years old, that's when I'd think about panicking. Until then, my children needed me. I had to use my brain; I had to focus.

So I did.

The snowy tracks showed that they were moving south and east, away from the downtown area, out toward the edge of town, out away from the friendly streetlights and toward the—

No. Don't worry about the swampy areas out that way. Don't worry about the ice that might not be thick enough to support their weight. Don't worry about what might happen. Think.

Even as I was worrying, I rushed ahead, losing the

tracks every so often, but making ever-widening circles until I found them again.

Where on earth were they going? Had Jenna gone out to find Oliver? Where was Oliver going? Why hadn't she come to me?

Over and over again I lost my way. Over and over I found the faint trail. I went farther and farther out, where the gaps between the houses were wider and wider, where the howling wind pushed the fast-forming drifts higher and higher.

Oh, my dearest Jenna, where are you?

My sweet Oliver, why did you go out into this storm?

No. Don't think about it. Think about finding them. Everything else can wait.

I hurried on, following what I had to assume was Jenna's trail. The possibility that someone else could be out in these conditions wasn't one I was going to consider. Jenna was ahead of me and I would find her. I would find Oliver. I was their mother and I would find them.

My cell trilled. Hope leapt in my heart and I thumbed the button to talk. "It's me," Pete said. "Where are you?"

I gave him the name of the street. "About halfway between the house and that swamp on the edge of town."

He made a noise of surprise. "You're about a mile out already. Hang on, sweetheart. I'll be there in five minutes."

When the line cleared, I called Marina and told her my location. "I'm still on Jenna's trail."

She whistled. "That far? That's getting close to that stinky swampy place that—" She stopped. "Right. I'm a few blocks over. I'll move closer and keep on the grid pattern until you tell me different."

I told her that it might be a while before the police showed up. "But Pete is almost here."

"We'll find them," she said, no question in her voice.

Because I wanted to believe her, because I needed to believe her, I did. "Any minute now," I said, and hung up. But after I did, a wave of loneliness battered at me. A dark and vacant future yawned in my face, taunting me with its emptiness.

"No!" I wanted to beat at the wind with my fists, to scream at its howls. "No," I said more quietly. If we hadn't found them by now, it could only mean that they were still moving, that they were still okay.

Of course they were. They had to be.

I hurried through the snow as fast as I could, tripping and falling and getting up again, not caring that my lungs were burning, not caring that my fingers and toes had lost all feeling, not caring that I'd lost my hat half a mile ago.

They were fine.

I'd find them.

The houses were far apart now, and set back from the road. I lost count of the times I'd thought I'd seen a vague Jenna shape through the gusting snow only to run close and find that it was a mailbox or a small tree or nothing at all.

So when I saw something far ahead of me, I tamped down the excitement.

It's probably just another mailbox. Don't get your hopes up, don't assume it's them, don't . . .

My cell rang. "I see something," Marina said. "The light's crappy out here, but I think they might be crossing that big field—you know, the one where kids take kites? I'm at the far end, but I think maybe it's them."

For a second I couldn't talk. "I see something, too." My phone beeped. "Hang on, Pete's calling."

"Beth, that big field—"

"We know," I said, breaking into a jog. "Call Marina. You can't drive straight across with all the snow, but figure out which way they're headed. I'm going after them."

Even before I'd hung up the phone, I started running toward the two shadowy shapes. Running toward my children, ignoring the knee-deep snow, feeling myself pulled toward them, feeling the last gasps of fear whispering in my head, chasing them, needing them . . .

"Jenna?" I hurtled forward. "Oliver?" But their names were more a gasp than a shout. "Jenna!"

The taller of the two shapes stopped. Turned. "Mom?"

Relief almost dropped me to the ground. I staggered a few steps, then finally, at last, reached my children. I held their shivering bodies close. "We have to get you out of this weather right now." I turned on my phone and hit REDIAL. I couldn't remember who I'd last called, Marina or Pete, but it didn't matter. "I have them. We're almost to the road on the east side of the field. Can you—"

"No!" Oliver shrieked. "I have to warn her!" He pulled out of my arms, dodged away, and ran.

I stared at his back for a fraction of a second, then rushed after him. "Jenna," I called over my shoulder, "get into Mrs. Neff's car. Or Pete's."

But my daughter was at my side and running with me. "I'm really sorry, Mom," she said earnestly. "I couldn't stop him. He kept running ahead of me, just like this, so I went after him. I didn't know what else to do. I'm really sorry."

"Don't worry," I said, panting out the words between short breaths. Our swinging hands brushed up against each other's, and I grabbed her bare hand, squeezing it tight. I wanted to stop and pull off my gloves and force them onto her hands, but there wasn't time because my son, her brother, was running as if the dogs of war were on his heels.

We followed him out of the field, down a street, and up a long driveway to a small ranch house. Headlights came from both directions, bathing the three of us in light that created long, sharp shadows.

A car door opened, then another. Pete and Marina pounded up the driveway after us.

Oliver scrambled up the front stoop and banged on the door. He gripped the handle, couldn't turn it, released it, and started pounding again. "Open the door!" he shouted. "I have to tell you something!"

As I ran toward him, he kept on banging and shouting, making more of a racket than I would have thought possible for my shy and quiet son. I had no idea whose house this was, and no idea what was going on, but a few steps more and I'd have Oliver and we'd go home and—

The outside light flicked on and the curtain in the large window next to the door moved.

"Oliver!" I called, but he didn't turn. What on earth was the boy doing?

The front door opened and bright light from inside outlined the shape of a woman. "Oliver Kennedy! What are you doing out there without a coat?" She looked past my son. "Mrs. Kennedy?" She looked farther out and saw Jenna and Pete and Marina, all three slowing to a stop next to me.

"I think you'd all better come inside," said Stephanie Pesch.

For the first half hour, we shared no conversation beyond what was necessary to get the kids warm and dry.

Our entire group trooped into the small entryway, all

of us except Stephanie dripping snow onto the carpet in great plops. Stephanie looked at the shivering children, then looked at me. "I have two bathrooms. What does Mom say about a quick shower for these two?"

I did not want to believe this woman was capable of murder. "Thanks, Stephanie. That would be perfect."

Pete called the police department to let them know that what had been lost was now found. Jenna went into Stephanie's master bathroom, and Oliver took the guest bathroom. While the kids were running the hot-water tank empty, Stephanie gathered up their sopping-wet clothes and put them in her dryer. The two of us sorted through her collection of sweatpants and sweatshirts and found clothing that would work to keep the troublemakers covered until their clothes stopped tumbling.

I knocked on the door to the master bath and popped my head into the steamy room. "Jenna? Here are some things for you to wear."

"Okay," she said. "Thanks, Mom. Um, is Oliver okay?"

"He's fine, sweetheart."

When I knocked on the door to the other bathroom, opened the door, and mentioned the clothes, my son didn't say a word.

"Oliver?" I asked sharply. "Are you all right?"

". . . I'm good."

Something was off. Oliver wasn't being Oliver. I stood there, half of me in and half of me out of the doorway, undecided. "Well, okay. These clothes will be too big, but push up the sleeves. Your own things will be dry soon."

His wet head poked around the shower curtain. "What clothes are those?"

"Right here on the counter."

Drips of water coursed down his face. "They're Ms. Stephanie's clothes?"

"Well, yes. I know, they're girl clothes, but it's just a sweatshirt and a pair of sweatpants, so—"

He disappeared behind the shower curtain. The water turned off and a boy's hand appeared. "Can I have a towel, please?"

I left him to dry and dress and went down the hall to the kitchen. Stephanie and Marina and Pete were sitting at a round table, talking nonsense about the wind and the snow and about the biggest storms they remembered.

The talk broke off when Pete looked up. "Hey," he said, half standing. "How are they?"

Making sit-down gestures, I smiled at him, at Marina, at Stephanie. My children were safe and sound. All was right with the world. "They'll be along in a minute. Thanks again, Stephanie, for the clothes and the showers."

"No problem," she said. "I've always wanted to do search and rescue. Do they like hot chocolate?" At my nod, she stood and went to a slightly battered white refrigerator. She poured milk into a large glass measuring bowl and put it in the microwave to heat. As she opened cupboards and pulled out containers of cocoa and sugar, she said, "Sorry, but I don't have any marshmallows."

I hastened to reassure her that neither Jenna nor Oliver would turn up their noses at nonmarshmallowed hot chocolate and that she was, in fact, spoiling them for the packet hot chocolate I made them. Then I thanked her again for taking us in.

"And just as soon as my children get here," I said, "we'll be able to explain why we're here at all."

She stopped measuring out cocoa. "You mean you don't know?"

I shared glances with Marina and Pete. "Not a clue."

Hesitant footsteps came toward us. I looked up and smiled. "Ms. Stephanie is making hot chocolate for you two."

"Cool. Thanks, Ms. Stephanie." Jenna slid into a chair.

"Come sit on my lap, Ollster." I patted my legs and my son climbed up. He was getting so tall so fast. I leaned my forehead against the back of his head. "Now," I said. "How about telling us why you went out in the snow like that?"

He said something in a low voice.

"Sorry, Oliver. I didn't hear you."

His shoulders heaved. "I had to warn her."

"Warn Ms. Stephanie?" I asked. "About what?"

"About what you and Mrs. Neff were saying." He slid off my lap and stood in the middle of the kitchen's linoleum floor. "That Ms. Stephanie might be a murderer. You've sent bad guys to jail before lots of times. I had to warn her that you wanted to send her to jail forever and ever!"

I gaped at him. He'd overheard everything Marina and I had said. How could I have been so stupid? I'd known Oliver had a huge crush on this young woman. Why hadn't I realized his ears would swivel when we'd spoken her name? Why hadn't I anticipated what could happen?

Stephanie tinked a measuring spoon on the side of a mug, emptying it of its cocoa contents. "I've killed a few spiders in my time, but I don't think they send you to jail for that."

"No," I said, "they don't. Oliver's talking about . . ." I faltered. ". . . About something Marina and I were speculating about." Starting and ending a sentence with a preposition. Excellent work, Beth. "Wild speculation," I added lamely.

Pete stirred. "How did you know where Ms. Stephanie lived?" he asked.

"That computer Dad gave us for Christmas," Jenna said. "I was showing Oliver how to use Google Earth last weekend. You know how it works, right? We drove it all over Rynwood, and we looked up the houses of all our friends and teachers."

"Oh," I said faintly. And here I thought they'd been looking up answers to some of Oliver's homework questions.

"And how about you?" Marina tucked a lock of Jenna's towel-damp hair behind her ear. "Why were you out in the snow without a coat or boots or mittens or hat?"

"She went after Oliver," I said.

Jenna nodded. "I'm supposed to be helping take care of Mom. You said to, remember? And I didn't want her to worry about Oliver. I thought I could catch up to him and bring him back, but he kept running ahead of me. . . ." She dipped her head. "I'm sorry," she whispered.

I kept in the tears that threatened to pour out of me only by looking at my daughter's long face. "You did fine. You left a big enough trail that I could follow you," I said firmly. "You did a *wonderful* job."

She nodded, and a little bit of the pain eased off her face.

Oliver, on the other hand . . .

I looked at my son and had no idea what to do.

"Stephanie?" Marina asked. "Do you have some games the kids could play while us boring old adults have a little chat?"

I nearly fell upon her neck and wept with gratitude. Of

course Marina knew the right thing to do. She had four children, three of whom were fully functional adults, and she ran a day care business so successful that she had kids who weren't even conceived on the waiting list.

"Sure." Stephanie gave final stirs to the mugs of hot chocolate and handed them over. "I have a Wii setup. How about Mini Golf? Or Jeopardy!? And there's this I Spy game that's fun."

In less time than it would take to tell, Stephanie had the kids settled in the adjacent living room, close enough for me to hear their banter, far enough so that I didn't get distracted by every word they said.

Both Marina and Pete started talking, but I let their words wash over me as I forced my brain into action. When Stephanie came back to the kitchen, I was ready. Or at least as ready as I was ever likely to be in such an unexpected, awkward, and bizarre situation.

"In case you haven't figured it out," I said, "Oliver has a huge crush on you."

She sat in the last available chair. "I had a feeling."

Marina looked at her. "You probably get that a lot, right?"

Stephanie shrugged. "It never lasts long."

"Well," I said, "before you ask why we thought you might be a murderer, here's the explanation." I told her about Cookie's posthumous request and the far-too-short suspect list, and how and why she'd moved up to the top of the list after we'd learned about the argument in the bank.

"Okay," she said, "I can see all that, and I did despise that woman, but there's one problem."

"What's that?" I asked.

"I'm allergic to acetaminophen," she said simply. "I'm

so allergic I even have a tattoo." She held out her right fist and turned it over, revealing a tattoo on the inside of her upper wrist. Sure enough, it said she was allergic to acetaminophen.

"Well, there you go," Marina said, grinning. "I never really thought you were a good candidate for murder, anyway. It was Beth here who wanted you on the list."

Rolling my eyes, I thumped her lightly on the shoulder.

And so Stephanie was crossed off the suspect list.

When the kids were back into their own clothes, Marina drove on home.

"Thanks for everything," I said, giving Stephanie a hug.

"No problem." Smiling, she tousled Oliver's hair. "And thank you for trying to warn me. But next time, why don't you just call?"

"Yeah," he said, his face turning bright red. "That's a pretty good idea."

Pete and I helped the kids up into the backseat of his pickup, and we headed on home.

The four of us were quiet. I had no idea what the kids were thinking about, but I looked out on the white winter landscape and thought about all that had gone wrong and all that could have gone wrong and what I should and shouldn't have done.

I shouldn't have talked about Ms. Stephanie when Oliver was down the hall.

And should I have been talking about Stephanie at all? Was I really trying to help Cookie, or was I satisfying my own curiosity and puffing up my own vanity by attempting to do what was really police business?

Pete glanced over at me. "You all right?" he asked.

"I'm fine," I said automatically.

In the light cast by the dashboard, I saw him look at me again. Two words were all I'd said, but my delivery must have been off because I could tell he didn't believe me.

He reached out, gently pulled my hand out of my coat pocket, and gave it a squeeze.

In silence, we held hands the rest of the way home.

The right side of the driveway was deep with snowdrifts. Pete pulled up on the left side. "Exit to the left, please, folks." He opened his door and ushered the three Kennedys outside. "In you go. Your house is waiting for you."

I slid out of the warm truck and back into winter, smiling at Pete. I'd never thought about it like that before. Maybe that's what made a house a home: the knowledge that it was waiting, ready to offer comfort and calm and welcome. The violation of the housebreaking was nothing compared to what our house offered us.

"If you want," he said, "I'll shovel the driveway."

Dear Pete. I blinked away sudden tears. "You don't have to do that," I said.

He shrugged. "It's not that late. I don't mind and the wind's down. Hear it?"

I did. Or rather, I didn't. What I did hear was the far-off grumble of plow trucks. So much for the kids having a snow day tomorrow. I gave Pete a coat-encumbered hug. "What did I ever do to deserve you?"

"Oh, just about everything." He kissed my forehead and I melted. I loved it when he did that. It made me feel cherished and cared for and . . . and . . .

"Mom?" Jenna loitered just outside the door to the garage. "Can we have something to eat?"

Pete released me. "Go on. I'll take care of the driveway."

But I hung on to his hands, not wanting to let go. "You'll come in when you're done?"

"Sure, if you want."

I did want. I wanted it very much.

Inside, the kids remained unnaturally silent as I put together a sugar-laden snack of ice cream, hot fudge, and whipped cream. I even found a jar of maraschino cherries in the back of the fridge and perched one on top of each bowl.

They dug in, and I sat between them, watching, checking fingers and toes for signs of frostbite, checking for the shivers that might indicate hypothermia, and thinking that it was absurd to give them ice cream an hour after they'd almost frozen to death. Luckily, they didn't see the irony. Even luckier, they seemed perfectly healthy.

When they reached the bottom of the bowls, I said, "Oliver, teeth and jammies and bed. Jenna, teeth and jammies, but you can read for half an hour."

She shook her head. "I'm pretty tired. Can I just go to sleep?"

Again, unbidden tears pricked at my eyes. "Of course you can, sweetie. Oliver?" He'd been pushing his chair back, but froze when I called his name. "Oliver, we're going to have a long talk tomorrow."

He hung his head. "I'm sorry, Mommy," he whispered. "I was bad. I know I was. You're not going to get rid of Spot, are you?"

I blinked at him. "No, honey. Spot's part of the family." So was George, but a cat that spent most of his time

under my bed or in my closet didn't engender the same
kind of loyalty from a nine-year-old boy as a happy dog
did. "We'll talk about your punishment tomorrow."

Oliver's thin shoulders heaved and he nodded.

"Now give me a hug." I held out my arms and pulled
him tight. "I love you," I whispered in his ear. "Lots and
lots and lots."

"I love you," he said.

Jenna waited while he went upstairs. "Am I going to
be punished, too?" she asked, her face serious.

"Hmm." I put my elbow on the table and my chin in
my hand. "I think your punishment will be to go outside
into what was practically a blizzard, hunt down your little brother, and stay with him while running over a mile
in twenty-five-degree weather without a coat or boots
until someone comes to help."

She frowned. "But . . . that's what I did."

"Then I say you've been punished enough."

Her face lightened. "Really?"

"Really. But, Jenna? Please don't do it again. Once is
about all my heart can take."

"Sure, Mom." She giggled. "I promise never to go out
after Oliver in a blizzard again. Ever. And you know
what? Even if I can't be the best goalie on the team, I'm
going to try and do something else the best."

"What's that, honey?"

"I'm going to try and be the best big sister ever." She
leaned over to hug me, and once again, tears threatened
to pour out of me.

By the time Pete came back inside, I'd tucked the kids in
and kissed them good night. "All safe and sound?" he
asked.

"Snug as bugs in rugs."

"And how about you? Are you snug?"

I'd led him to the family room, where the gas logs were doing their best to give the illusion of a real fire. We sat on the couch. Pete put his arm around my shoulders and I put my feet up behind me. I snuggled into his side, breathing in the scent of outdoors that lingered on his clothes, breathing in . . . him. "All snug," I said.

He kissed my hair. "Anything else I can do, just ask."

"I have something I want to tell you."

His body stilled. "Okay."

"It's about Cookie." I felt him relax and wondered why he'd been tense, but went on. "I know she asked me to help find her killer, but I just can't any longer. Oliver and Jenna could have died tonight, and it's because of Cookie. Finding a killer is important, but it's not worth a hair from either of my children's heads. I'm done helping Cookie. The police will have to do without my help."

Pete laid his head against mine. "Whatever you do, I'm with you."

Dear, dear Pete. "Do you think I'm doing the right thing?"

"Only you know what's best for you," he said. "But I can suggest one thing."

"What's that?"

"Trust yourself."

We sat there, close together, wrapped in each other's arms, feeling each other's heartbeat, feeling affection and tenderness and . . .

I took in a small breath. "I love you," I whispered.

"And I love you," he whispered back. "So very, very much."

Chapter 18

It was easier than I'd anticipated to forget about Cookie's request because uppermost in my mind was caring for my children. Beyond the fear of a delayed case of hypothermia—which was impossible, but did we ever truly knew what was impossible?—there were psychological ramifications to consider.

My former husband pooh-poohed my concerns, of course.

"I don't know why you're so worked up," Richard said. The morning after the Adventure in the Snow, I'd called from the store and updated him on what his children had been up to. "They're fine, aren't they? I'll keep Oliver off the video games tonight and this weekend. That will be punishment enough."

"I'm worried that Oliver is going to have a hard time getting over his crush on Stephanie."

"You have to stop worrying so much," my ex said. "Why do women do that?"

Because we have to clean up the messes men make because they don't worry enough, I wanted to say. "Just pay attention to him, okay? He's getting too good at hiding his feelings."

Richard gave a patronizing chuckle. "That's what men do."

"He's not a man," I said sharply. "He's a nine-year-old boy."

"And he'll be getting his driver's license in seven years. Let him be who he is, Beth, not who you want him to be."

Anger jammed into my throat and kept my mouth from opening. Which was probably a good thing, because I would have gone into a long and strident rant about his own expectations, but doing so wouldn't have helped and could have made things worse. Instead, I said a stilted good-bye and hung up wondering how I could possibly have stayed married to that man for twenty years.

I got up from my desk and wandered out to the kitchenette. Owing to the odd confluence of a doctor's appointment for Yvonne, a sick grandchild for Lois, and an old friend of Flossie's who happened to be in town, Paoze and I were the only ones in the store.

When the microwave dinged, I took out my mug, dropped the soggy tea bag into a saucer to use again later, added a little milk, and went up to the front.

"Thanks again for coming in," I said to Paoze

He smiled. "I am happy to. It is a pleasure to work here."

"It's a pleasure to have you, and I'm not just saying that to be nice. I really mean it."

The books in his hands must have suddenly needed a lot of his attention, because he was studying them carefully. "Thank you, Mrs. Kennedy. You are very kind."

I made a gagging noise. "If I were really kind, I'd pay

you a lot more. Instead, I pay you a teensy bit above minimum wage, hoping that will somehow entice you to work hard and keep coming back for more."

The books kept needing serious inspection. "The reason I come back is not the wages."

Of course it wasn't. No one worked in a bookstore to get rich. People worked in a bookstore because they loved books. Game, set, and match. Which was why bookstore people tended to get along. It was the books that mattered, and . . . hmm.

"Paoze, last week I asked you what was going on between Lois and Flossie and you said you didn't know."

He rearranged the books. Now *The Indian in the Cupboard* was on top instead of *The Great Brain*. The new setup must not have worked for him, because he frowned, rotated them back to the way they'd been, and said nothing.

So the sideways approach wasn't going to work. No surprise there; Paoze was too smart to get caught so easily. It was time for a full-out attack. "They're not getting along and customers are starting to notice." Well, they might if the terrible twosome held an argument in front of a customer, but they were both too professional to do so. Still, the possibility existed. "If they don't stop arguing, I'm going to have to let Flossie go."

Paoze forgot all about the books and looked straight at me, eyes flared wide. "You will fire her? But she is so smart. She has increased sales far beyond what Marcia ever did, and the children love her."

I let out a heavy sigh. "Yes, but the store's staff has to work together. If they can't, well . . ." I shook my head with as much sorrow as I thought I could reliably fake.

Paoze turned the books over and over so much that I

started to be concerned that he'd wear the covers and I'd have to put them on the sale table. "I do not like to say," he murmured.

"Of course not." I patted his shoulder. "You're a good employee and a good friend. But I have to know what's going on."

"Yes, I see." He turned the books over a few more times. "I do not like to say," he said again, "and you will not like to hear this."

I blinked. "Okay. But I'm a big girl. I can take it." Because, really, how bad could it possibly be? This was likely something silly that had blown up big and neither one of them knew how to fix it. All I had to do was learn what is was and I'd be able to—

"They are arguing about you."

—to fix the situation with a few of Alice's cookies. Unless they were fighting about me, in which case I wouldn't have the foggiest idea of what to do.

His dark eyes were kind. "It is that intervention your friends had in January. Miss Untermayer thinks they should have left you alone, that you are smart enough to know when you need rest. Mrs. Nielson says that you don't always have the sense to come in out of the rain."

He stopped, but I waved him on. I knew a direct Lois quote when I heard one.

"When Mrs. Nielson sends you out of the store, Miss Untermayer ..." He hesitated. "She describes how she feels about people interfering in another's life without being asked. Mrs. Nielson replies that sometimes people need to be interfered with, and Miss Untermayer asks how Mrs. Nielson would feel if someone interfered in her life."

I could picture the scene as if it were unfolding in

front of me. Both of them shouting at each other, hands on hips.

Paoze sighed. "When you return to the store, they change their words to be about books. I am sorry, Mrs. Kennedy. I did not want to tell you, but I do not want Miss Untermayer to be fired."

"It's all right," I said vaguely.

"They are only fighting because they both care about you so much," he said. "They will stop when this intervention is over. This is soon, correct?"

I nodded, or at least I think I did. Because it was hard for me to hear his new words because his old ones were repeating themselves over and over inside my head.

"They are only fighting because they both care about you so much."

Slowly, so very slowly, I went back to my office, wondering what I'd ever done to deserve such wonderful friends.

Halfway there, I stopped cold, right in the middle of the graphic novels. Because I'd just recognized the real problem: how was I going to tell Lois and Flossie the jig was up without getting Paoze in deep trouble with both of them?

The rest of the day rushed past, followed by a busy Thursday and a customer-filled Valentine's Day Friday. As music, the ding of the cash register drawer opening on a steady basis might not have been the stuff of Grammy Awards, but it did more to warm my heart than anything the Foo Fighters had ever done.

I was a little sad that Pete and I wouldn't be spending the evening together, but he'd had a rush call to a job up in Wausau and wouldn't be back until Saturday noon. Of course I understood, I'd told him, and made plans with

Marina instead. Her DH wasn't big on what he considered coerced holiday celebrations.

During the extremely short midafternoon lull, Yvonne asked if I'd heard that Gus was back to work.

"Not that I know of," I said.

"No, I mean he is back. When I was out at lunch, I saw him."

"Really?" At church on Sunday, Winnie had said her husband was a mess and that she wasn't going to let him out of the house until he could do fifty push-ups. Not that I believed she'd actually make him do fifty push-ups. Twenty-five would probably do the trick. "How did he look?"

Yvonne shook her head. "Weak. Pale. Like he should still be in bed."

I started to ask if he'd be at work all afternoon, but the front bells jingled, half a dozen grandmotherly-looking women walked in, and the moment passed.

At closing time, the store was still crowded with customers. I shooed Yvonne and Lois off home, locked the front door, flicked off the lights that turned the front window into a fairyland display of books and toys, and pleasantly told the browsers that store hours were over, but to take their time making their selections.

Ten minutes later, they were all still in the store and I was doing my best to keep from tapping my foot and glancing pointedly at my watch.

Ten minutes after that, I turned off the rear bank of lights. Most of them got the not so subtle hint, made their purchases, and left, but the last holdout didn't seem to notice the lights going off around her until I tapped her on the shoulder.

"Ma'am? Excuse me, but we're closing."

"What?" She took her head out of the book she was

reading. "You're closing?" She looked around, blinking. "Oh, my goodness, you're closed! How long have I been standing here?"

I glanced at her choice of reading material. *The Hero and the Crown* by Robin McKinley. "Forty-five minutes, I think. Good, isn't it?"

Red flooded across her cheeks. "I am so sorry."

Grinning, I said, "Don't worry about it. At least you started early in the evening. It was eleven at night the first time I picked it up. I'm not sure I ever did get any sleep."

She apologized all the way to the cash register and as I rang up the sale and only stopped when I started to put it in a bag. "Don't bother," she said. "I only live a few blocks away. There's enough light from the streetlights that I can read while I walk."

I laughed. "A woman after my own heart. Just don't forget to look both ways before you cross the street." I came around the counter and unlocked the front door to let her out.

"Come back when you're done reading. That author has written a number of books." Smiling, I waved her good night and closed the door as she waved back, the expression on her face thick with something that looked close to joy.

It didn't take long to do the closing-up chores. I looked at my watch. Twenty minutes until Marina was going to show up for our no-kids-allowed night.

Twenty minutes wasn't very long, but it would have to be enough.

I grabbed my coat, let myself out the front door, locked it behind me, and hurried down the sidewalk.

*　　　*　　　*

"Wow," I said. "You look horrible."

Gus glared at me. Or what would have been a glare if it hadn't been interrupted by his sudden need to take care of a nose that was starting to drip indiscriminately. When he was done blowing, he said in a voice so hoarse it was almost unrecognizable, "Why, thank you, Beth, I'm feeling much better."

"Uh-huh." Uninvited, I sat down. "Is that what Winnie says?"

"My wife and I have come to an agreement."

Sort of, I added silently. Both Winnie and Gus were very good friends of mine, and no way was I going to choose a side in that dogfight. "Well, it's nice to see you back in the office."

He blew his nose again. "Even if I look like something the cat dragged in?"

I bared my teeth and made dragging motions with my head. This made him laugh, which was what it was intended to do, and I smiled, very glad indeed that Gus was feeling well enough to be back at work, even though he probably shouldn't have been.

"So, what's up?" He pulled out a lower drawer of his desk, leaned back, and put his feet up on the drawer. "Winnie's going to drag me out of here in fifteen minutes, so you'd better talk fast."

Perfect.

I told him everything I could remember. About Isabel's pregnancy, about Alan's arthritis and his ways of coping, about Stephanie and her allergy to acetaminophen. About Oliver's crush, how he'd overheard Marina and me talking and how he'd run out into a winter storm to warn Ms. Stephanie. About how Jenna had followed him. About how I'd come far too close to losing both of them.

When I stopped, Gus didn't say anything. He just looked at me and waited.

"So," I said. "I'm done. No more investigating, no more poking around into things that aren't any of my business, no more doing what law enforcement has been trained to do."

Gus sighed. "Yeah," he said. "Glad the kids are okay, and I'm sorry to lose your eyes and ears, but I understand. Cookie had no business asking for your help, anyway. That's what we're here to do." He tapped his gold-colored badge.

In spite of my determination to walk away from all this, I felt a pang when Gus mentioned Cookie's request. "Right," I said lamely. "So . . . I guess I'll go."

"You and me both." Gus dropped his feet to the floor. "Winnie's going to have my . . . er, she's going to chew me out if I'm not at the back door in"—he glanced at his watch—"in negative two minutes."

I laughed and got to my feet. "See you at church on Sunday?"

"Count on it."

Outside, the cold air snapped my brain awake. Not that it had been sleeping, exactly, but it must have turned a little dozy inside the police station because I'd forgotten to tell Gus about the box. I should have plopped it on his desk as a kind of "Sorry I'm quitting on you, but here's this" gift. And I'd neglected to give him the one name Marina and I hadn't crossed off the list. "I forgot," I said out loud. I stopped in the middle of the sidewalk, ignoring the odd looks of the passersby.

I turned around and headed back, but a hand grabbed at my arm and held it fast.

"Oh, no you don't."

Marina looped her arm through mine. Using her weight advantage, she steered me around in a half circle and started walking us away from the police station. "No going back to wherever you were going. It's our official no-kids-allowed night and we don't even have half a plan for what we're going to do."

I tried to pull away. "Just give me five minutes. I need to tell Gus something."

She gestured to a battered minivan passing us on the street. "That Gus?" Through the side window, we could clearly see Gus as passenger and Winnie as driver, both of them waving. "When did he come back to work?" Marina asked. "Gotta tell you. He still doesn't look that good. Did you see that pansy wave he gave us?"

I watched the van tail off into the dusky evening. Tomorrow. I'd call Gus tomorrow morning. And if he wasn't in his office . . . well, this could wait until Monday. It was important, but it wasn't worth risking Gus's health.

Marina was still talking. "It's freezing out here. Let's get back to the bookstore and figure out what's on for tonight."

By the time we'd walked into the store's warmth, she'd already proposed hanging out in an airport bar, buying me an entirely new—and much more fun—wardrobe, driving to Chicago for pizza, and flying to the Bahamas.

I rejected all of her suggestions.

"Huh." She put on a thoughtful look. "Okay, if the Bahamas are out, how about Cancún? You and me, kid, in lounge chairs, umbrella drinks in our hands, sun on our faces, toes in the sand. What do you say?"

On the surface her tone was casually light, but I could hear the tension that lay underneath. You can't hide much from someone who's been your best friend for years. I opened my mouth to ask what was wrong, to tell her that I wasn't going anywhere until she told me what was bothering her, but then I remembered her vow about Mother's Day, a date I'd picked out of the air.

"Stupid air," I muttered. Why hadn't it told me to choose St. Patrick's Day? Or better yet, Valentine's Day, because if she'd agreed to that I'd already know what was wrong and we'd be dealing with the problem instead of doing our best to ignore it.

"What was that?" Marina asked.

"Stupid hair." I pushed back my flyaway strands. "I need to try a new conditioner, I think."

Her narrowed eyes were a definite indication that she didn't believe me, but before she could call me on the lie, there was a pounding at the front door.

"It's Claudia Wolff," Marina whispered loudly. "Hide!"

"Too late. She's already seen us."

"We can pretend we didn't hear her." Marina talked fast, tugging at my coat sleeve. "We can pretend we didn't see her. We didn't turn on any lights. We can plead complete ignorance. Plausible deniability, right?"

"Deniability is for weenies," I said, moving toward the door. "Buck up."

"But I don't want to talk to Claudia."

I stopped and stared at her. "Was that a whine?" Marina was many things, a number of which were annoying, but the one thing she wasn't was a whiner. "Are you feeling okay?"

"I'm fine," she almost snapped. "I just don't want to talk to Claudia. She's bound to say something that will ruin the mood for our entire evening. Don't do it, Beth. Just don't."

But my ingrained be-nice reaction was already kicking in. "I'm sure it won't take long. I won't even open the door all the way." With a twist of the wrist, I unlocked the front door and cracked it open. "Hey, Claudia, you know we're closed, right? Marina and I are just— Ow!"

The door hit my hand, which, in the classic "For every action there is a reaction," was shoved back and hit my face. It startled me more than hurt me, but Claudia showed no concern about which it might have been.

She burst through the door, her breath going in and out in fast puffs. "Do you know what I heard?"

For years I'd believed the old teacher's mantra, that there are no stupid questions. Tonight could be the night I changed my mind. I locked the door. Again. "Why, no, I don't, Claudia. Why don't you tell us?"

She ignored, or didn't hear, my sarcasm. "I was at Sabatini's just now, right? My family had dinner, and I was heading out to get some shopping done while my husband took the boys home. I went to the restroom before I left, and you'll never guess what I heard."

"You're right," Marina said. "We'll never guess. You win, we lose. See you later, Claudia. Have a good—"

"It was Kirk Olsen." Claudia's face was flushed, and I suddenly realized it wasn't from the cold. "He was talking to what's his name—the guy who owns Sabatini's."

"Joe," I murmured. Joe Pigg, actually, but if she didn't already know that fun fact, I wasn't going to spread it around.

"Yeah, Joe, that's it. Anyway, they were in—oh, what do you call it?—back there where the entrance to the men's bathrooms are in that little space. Ah, what is it?" She frowned, the narrative halted for want of the right word.

"Alcove," I supplied.

"That's it," she said. "They were in that alcove, yucking it up about something, and that's when Kirk said what he said." She looked from me to Marina and back, clearly waiting for one of us to beg her to go on. When she couldn't stand the wait any longer, she rushed back into the story. "Kirk said that with Cookie dead, the town's safe for men who know what they want."

A tingle ran up my back, ending in a knot of tension at the base of my neck.

Claudia's cheeks were now stained bright red. "Don't you see? Kirk must have killed Cookie! Why else would he say stuff like that?"

Marina sniffed. "If you're so sure Kirk did it, why haven't you called the police?"

"I'm on my way to the police station," she said. "But then I saw you and Beth in here, and I had to stop to say that you're not the only crime solver in this town." She put on a triumphant smile. "I can catch killers, too, and I figured this one out first. All by myself."

She went on, but I stopped listening.

It really was Kirk.

Our short list, the list we'd joked about and not taken very seriously, the list we hadn't wanted to be right, it had been right all along.

Kirk had poisoned Cookie.

He'd added acetaminophen to her coffee and let her go home to die.

I wanted to close my eyes against the reality. I didn't want to know this awful truth. I wanted things to go back to the way they'd been, with Cookie a slightly annoying acquaintance and Kirk a slightly overbearing PTA member who thought a little too highly of himself and enjoyed bragging about his cars and vacations a little too much.

But though I certainly didn't want Kirk to be a murderer, too many signs were pointing straight at him. But . . . *why* was he? Why on earth would he have done such a thing? What could have driven him to such a horrible crime? Why would he have killed a woman, a mostly mild-mannered bank teller who—

The "why" suddenly clicked into place.

Stockbrokers make money on commission. Deirdre said he wasn't that great a stockbroker. Kirk couldn't have been making much money, yet he'd been buying cars and trips and country club memberships.

He'd been stealing from someone. And Cookie had found out.

I tuned back in to my surroundings. Marina and Claudia were in a face-off, neither one brooking any opposition.

"It was poison," Marina said loudly. "That means the killer is most likely a woman and—"

Claudia leaned forward. "I don't care about most likely. I know what I heard and—"

"And you think just because of that one conversation, you know what's really going on?" Marina snorted. "Please. Finding a killer takes a lot more than eavesdropping. It takes courage and smarts and . . . and all sorts of things. And what it really takes is knowing your suspects. Your suspect is a man and just that alone makes you wrong, right, Beth?"

I didn't want to say she was wrong, not in front of Claudia. "We don't know anything, not for sure."

"Come on, Beth," Marina scoffed. "Tell her that the killer is a female. Tell her she's wrong."

Claudia put her chin up. "Tell her *she's* wrong. Tell her I'm right about Kirk."

"Oh, please." Marina laughed. "There is no way that you're right. No way at all. Right, Beth?"

I suddenly felt like a referee in a hockey game, trying to keep apart two players who, more than anything else in the world, wanted to rip each other's arms off.

"Tell her, Beth." Marina stood, hands on hips, a small smile on her face, sure of me.

The small ache in my heart grew five sizes. "I think . . . you're wrong."

She frowned. "You mean Claudia's wrong."

I shook my head slowly. "No, I'm sorry, but I think she's right."

Marina went very, very still. "You can't mean that."

"Kirk Olsen is the last one on the list," I said. "He's the only one left who could have killed Cookie. And I think he did it because—"

She wasn't listening. She was too busy buttoning up her coat buttons and pulling on her gloves. "Fine. If you want to team up with Claudia here, you go right ahead. I'll be busy having fun instead of messing around with things that should be left to the police. Have a good time."

"Marina, don't—"

She walked away from my words, unlocking the front door with a twist of her wrist, and headed off into the dark night.

"Well." Claudia smirked. "You and Marina having a little tiff. I never thought I'd see the day."

It wasn't a tiff—it was more like the end of an era.

I blinked back tears. "Anyway." The word came out weak and soggy. I coughed and started over. "I think you're right. I think Kirk Olsen is Cookie's murderer."

Claudia crossed her arms and smiled. "I knew you'd see it my way."

Not what I was thinking, but whatever. "Kirk may be the murderer, but you need more proof than an overheard scrap of conversation that could be interpreted in many different ways." Claudia glowered, but I kept going. "Plus, what you have is all hearsay. What you need is evidence. If you can find even one piece, the police will listen to you. Without it, there's no proof of anything."

"But—"

"The police can't arrest anyone without solid evidence," I said firmly.

She pouted, something I rarely found attractive in children, let alone grown women. "Then we need to find some," she said.

"We"? There was no "we" in this scenario. I was done investigating; I'd hung up my hat not half an hour ago.

"Yeah," Claudia said eagerly. "We can do this. I'm sure of it. With my know-how and a little of your experience, we can tie up Kirk Olsen in knots and hand him over to the cops with a bow on top."

I got a visual and immediately tried to erase it out of my head. "Claudia, I'm not investigating anything. I have a store to run, a PTA to lead, and, most of all, two children to mother."

"What about all those other times?" she demanded. "So you'll hunt down killers with Marina, but not with me? Is that what you're saying?"

I sighed. "What I'm saying is leave it to the police. That's what they do."

"In Rynwood?" She snorted. "When's the last time they solved a murder without outside help?"

"They'll figure it out just fine," I said.

"And what am I going to do in the meantime?" Claudia asked. "Now that I know this about Kirk, I have to do something with it." She eyed me. "I bet you know something about Kirk that you're not sharing. Don't shake your head at me, I can tell you're holding back. If it's not about Kirk, then it's about Cookie."

I was still shaking my head. "I don't know anything, really I don't. Nothing except . . ."

The box.

Chapter 19

"What box?" Claudia asked.

Why is it that the things I most wanted to keep to myself, I often gave away? It couldn't be a Freudian slip because there was nothing subconscious about my wish to keep quiet about the box, but there was bound to be some name for what I'd just done. Though "stupidity" covered it nicely, perhaps there was a multisyllabic term that was a bit more precise and—

"What box?" Claudia asked again, this time with heat in her voice.

I looked at her. If it had been Marina, I might have sent up a distraction that she would have recognized as a distraction in a heartbeat, but she would have let it go because she understood that sometimes you just don't push, that respecting someone else's wishes is more important than satisfying your own curiosity, that—

"Beth Kennedy, if you don't tell me what box you're talking about I'm going to . . . to . . ."

To what? To make my life miserable? She'd already done that at least a dozen times over the years. What was one more?

". . . to start a petition to have you kicked out as PTA

president." She put her nose in the air and smiled triumphantly.

I laughed out loud. "Go right ahead. Being president isn't nearly as much fun as you think it is."

"But you wouldn't like it taken away, now, would you?" I wouldn't, and she saw it plain on my face. "You like being in charge and you like having things go your way and—"

I'd had enough. "And I don't give in to blackmail."

Her mouth dropped open. "What are you talking about? I'm not blackmailing you. I wouldn't do such a thing. How could you think I'd do something like that? Just because you would doesn't mean I would. I can't believe you!"

I sighed. Again. "Maybe blackmail wasn't the best word. How about coercion?"

"They're the same thing. And I can't believe you'd accuse me of either one. All we're doing is having a friendly conversation."

She went on and on while I considered my next move. Which should come first, grabbing a dictionary and shoving the definition of "coercion" under her stubby nose, or raising my voice to drown out her analysis of my flawed character by giving her a detailed description of her own?

But since I'd been raised to be a Good Girl, I kept quiet and let her rant. A sneak of a smile slipped out, though, and Claudia stopped abruptly.

"What's so funny? What are you smiling about?"

Since I'd been mentally starting the second page of my outline titled Claudia's Character, outline item D, Child-Rearing Weaknesses, I cleared the smile off my face and said, "Don't you have shopping to do?"

Her eyes narrowed to small slits. "You're not going to tell me about that box, are you?"

Spending time with Claudia always ended up with me using my weekly allotment of sighs inside of ten minutes. I tried to stifle this one, but didn't do a very good job.

"You're sighing at me," she said accusingly. "I hate it when people do that."

I bit down on my inclination to say, in that case, maybe she should consider some behavior modification. "Cookie sent the box to me. I have no right to reveal to anyone else what might prove to be some very private belongings."

Claudia snorted. "What private things could Cookie have? She was a bank teller."

"She was a person," I said quietly. "And every person deserves respect."

"Yeah? Well, I'm a person. Do you respect me?"

Her question caught at me. I did not respect Claudia. I did not hold her in high regard, did not admire her, and, in a general way, did not appreciate anything she'd ever done.

"You think I'm an idiot, don't you?"

"Of course not," I said automatically. Narrow minded, petty, and shortsighted, but an idiot? No.

"Yes, you do." Claudia nodded.

I sighed. There wasn't much I disliked more than people telling me what I thought. "No, I don't."

"Yes, you do, and you're sighing again. Do you know how that makes me feel?"

My best defense against Claudia had always been silence, but tonight that strategy wasn't doing the trick. "Claudia—"

"It makes me feel like an idiot, is how it makes me feel!"

"I'm sorry that you feel that way. I—"

"Are you really sorry? Or are you just saying that?"

What I was sorriest about was that we were having this conversation at all. "It's getting late. Why don't we—"

"Oh, sure, cut off the conversation when you're losing. That's what you always do, isn't it? You're big on stacking the deck in your favor, aren't you? Setting yourself up for the advantage, you're really good at that."

Maybe someday I'd understand what she was talking about, but I hoped not.

"You think you're so smart, don't you?"

Clearly, she'd never heard the story about the fax number, either.

"And there's that smile again, so superior." She made a gagging noise. "You're no smarter than I am. And I'm going to prove it to you and to everyone else in this town. I'm going to prove that Kirk Olsen murdered Cookie. I'll figure it out all by myself. I mean, if *you* can find killers, it can't be that hard."

She flounced off, a difficult thing to do in a thick winter coat and heavy boots, and banged through the front door that Marina had left unlocked.

Marina . . .

Oh, my friend, what has happened to us? What is happening?

I stood in the quiet store, listening to nothing, doing nothing, thinking about things I'd said but shouldn't have, about things I should have said but didn't, thinking about lost opportunities and missed chances, about who I was and who I wanted to be.

For the last fifteen minutes I'd been a doormat for Claudia. Was that who I wanted to be? No. Was that anyone I wanted Jenna and Oliver to be? No again, with feeling. Lots of it.

I zipped up my coat and hurried out the door, pausing only to arm the security system and lock the door. I caught a glimpse of her at the end of the block. "Claudia!" I called, but she reached the corner, walked across the street, and turned left. I trotted down the sidewalk, a rising wind in my face, and when I got to the corner myself, I saw the back end of Claudia flick out of view behind the building.

It was like chasing a cat, I thought. But at least I had a good idea where she was going, unlike a cat-chasing episode. The only reasonable place Claudia could be headed was the city parking lot.

"Gotcha," I muttered, and half walked, half ran through the alley behind the stores until I reached my car. Wherever she was going, I'd follow. Whatever she had to say, I'd talk over her. Maybe she wouldn't listen—probably she wouldn't—but at least I'd tell her all those things I'd swallowed over the years in the effort to be polite. From now on, she'd have to find someone else to be rude to. I wasn't going to roll over for her ever again.

The very thought made me sit tall in the driver's seat, shoulders square and chin proud. Maybe all that time my mother had spent telling me to sit up straight would have been better spent telling me how to stand up for myself.

I drove down the alley and cut straight across the side street and into the parking lot. She had to be here somewhere; surely she couldn't be gone already. . . . There! On the far side of the lot, turning right.

Huh. Turning that way meant she wasn't driving out to the mall and she wasn't going home. Where . . . ?

But it didn't matter where she was going. If she was

going to . . . to her mother's house, I'd follow. If she decided to drive to Milwaukee, I'd follow. If she was going to the moon, I'd follow.

She drove through downtown, and when an oncoming car lit the interior of her SUV, I could see that she was holding a cell phone to her ear. *Talking when driving, Claudia? Not safe, not safe at all. Do you do that when your boys are in the car? Tsk-tsk-tsk.*

With the wind buffeting the car, I followed her into a residential area and was close behind when she turned and then turned again to go around a block-sized neighborhood park, and didn't let the gap between us widen by a single foot as she barreled down a long street, then made a fast turn and—

And I suddenly knew where Claudia was going.

I let off on the gas pedal and took my time turning onto a short side street, then turning right onto a treelined street of older houses. A few ranches, a few two-story homes, and a few Cape Cod houses. Half a block later, I spotted Claudia's SUV parked exactly where I'd expected to see it.

Right in the middle of Cookie Van Doorne's driveway.

I parked on the street and walked up the short driveway, cold wind tugging at me from every direction. What on earth did Claudia think she was going to find out by staring at a vacant house? Yes, I'd done it myself not so long ago, but that had been because I hadn't wanted to go home to a kidless house, not because I'd thought I'd find something that would prove who killed Cookie.

The front tires of Claudia's SUV were deep into a snowdrift. I came around the driver's side and followed in her footsteps. Unfortunately, Claudia was a little shorter and her feet a little smaller than mine, and using her steps to break trail ended up being more annoying than helpful. When I came around the corner of the house, I saw Claudia crouching at the back door and jiggling the door handle.

"What are you doing?" I asked.

Claudia shrieked, jumped, and whirled around. When she recognized me, the fear that had been on her face turned into a scowl. "What are you doing here? And look what you've made me do. I've dropped my card. It's ten bucks for a replacement. If I can't find it I'm sending you the bill."

"What card? A Valentine's card?" Not that delivering a Valentine's Day card to a woman who'd been dead for weeks made any sense at all, but who knew what lurked in Claudia's mind?

"Don't be stupid." She hunkered down and felt around in the snow with both hands. "My credit card. Well, my ATM card, if you want to get technical about it, and I bet you do, don't you?" She shot me a fast, fierce glare, then turned her attention back to the snow. "It's more flexible than the credit cards, and flexibility is what you need."

I frowned. "Why do you need a flexible card?"

"Jeez, Beth, are you really that stupid? To get into . . . Ha!" Triumphantly, she held up a small rectangular piece of plastic. "Found it, no thanks to you." If she'd had laser vision, her gaze would have peeled the flesh off my skin. "I would have been done with this ten minutes ago if you hadn't come along."

The wind kicked up a skirl of snow, almost obscuring Claudia from view. It was a nice moment, in many wa but when the snow fell back, I saw what she was doing. "Claudia, stop! You can't do that. That's breaking and entering. That's illegal. That's—"

With a faint *click*, the door popped open. Claudia crowed happily, and stood up. "Please. Are you honestly going to tell me you've never opened a door with a credit card?"

Why was it such a bad thing to be good? "I've always lived in houses with dead bolts. Credit cards don't work to open those."

"You have to be the most boring person in the world." She pushed the door open and reached inside to turn on the light. "I'm going in. Call the cops if you want, but you know they won't get here for at least fifteen minutes, and by then I'll be gone."

"Claudia, you—"

But she was already inside. A *whoosh!* of wind pushed me forward a step, then another, and then I was close enough to see into the kitchen, close enough to see Claudia opening drawers and cupboard doors.

A wave of revulsion passed through me. Cookie would have hated to see someone else pawing through her belongings. I might have logged off from investigating her death, but I wasn't going to let Claudia rummage through her personal things without supervision. Someone had obviously taken the time to clean up after the house had been broken into the other day. To have things disturbed a second time was just plain wrong.

I hurried up the back steps, did my best to bang the snow off my boots, went into the kitchen . . . and did a classic double take.

"Wow . . ." I blinked once. Twice, then three times, but kitchen still looked the same way it had when I'd walked into the room. There was nothing out of the ordinary about its bones: counters, refrigerator, range, coffeemaker, sink under a window, table with chairs. No, that was all very normal. I supposed with a name like Cookie, you'd get your fair share of cookie-shaped gifts, but this was . . . "Wow," I said again.

Cookie-shaped magnets covered the refrigerator. More cookie-shaped magnets covered the range. Framed photos of cookies covered every inch of wall space and the cabinet doors were decoupaged with magazine photos of cookies. The drawer handles were metal cookies. The clock was a large plastic cookie. The wall calendar featured cookie recipes. The table's place mats were a cookie print.

Chocolate chip cookies, Oreo cookies, oatmeal cookies, meringue cookies, peanut butter cookies, sugar cookies, chocolate cookies, cutout cookies, no-bake cookies, butter cookies, Snickerdoodles, gingerbread, jam thumbprints, Lebkuchen, Springerle, Russian tea cakes, every cookie I'd ever seen or tasted was represented, plus dozens I didn't recognize.

The slam of a shutting drawer woke me from my cookie-induced stupor. Claudia had finished her examination of the silverware and was moving on to the cabinet under the sink. I unzipped my coat in the semiwarm air. Cookie's son must have left the heat set to around fifty degrees to keep the water pipes from freezing.

"What do you think you're going to find?" I asked mildly. Ten minutes ago, my goal had been to tell Claudia that I wasn't going to let her walk on me ever again. Thanks to her burglary skills, my priorities had shifted for the time being, but I was going to have my say before the night was over.

"I'll know it when I see it." She slammed the cabinet door shut.

What exactly she might expect to find under there, I wasn't sure, so I went ahead and asked.

"It could be anything and it could be anywhere," she snapped.

"'It'?"

"You know. The smoking gun, the purloined letter, the candlestick. The whatever-it-is that will tie Cookie to Kirk Olsen. You go ahead and find it, if you think you're so smart."

What I thought was that she'd been watching too much television. "Seems to me," I said, "that the police would already have looked through the house, trying to find that very thing." If it existed.

The utensil drawer slammed shut, rattling the spatulas and tongs within. "Well, if they did, it didn't do them any good, did it? And they're mostly men, aren't they? How would they know if there was something in a woman's house that wasn't right? Men don't know spot cleaner from window cleaner."

Pete did, but I kept the thought to myself. As Claudia continued to poke through Cookie's belongings, I tried, and failed, to come up with a scenario that resulted in cleaning supplies providing a link to a killer's identity. Perhaps I was lacking in imagination. Maybe I needed to watch more television. For all I knew there could be a *CSI*-type show dedicated entirely to cleaning supply murders.

"*Now* what are you smirking about?" Claudia was frowning at me.

Like I was going to relay that thought out loud. "Nothing."

"Nothing, she says." Claudia sniffed. "Laughing at me again, aren't you, just like always?" I started to object, but she ran right over my words. "I get so tired of you, I can't stand it. Well, this time I'm the one having the last laugh!" She swept out of the kitchen.

Sighing, I followed her into the small dining room. Nothing in the china cabinet must have had Kirk's name on it, because she was in and out of the room in short order. The only thing in the living room that got any of her attention was the coffee table, which was piled high with cooking magazines.

Claudia glared at me while she picked up a magazine and flipped through the pages. "Cookie could have written a note, you know. Where better to put a secret note than out in plain view?"

To me, plain view would have been the middle of the dining table, but what did I know?

From the living room she went to the tiny study and plopped herself down in the desk chair. "There's bound to be something in here," she muttered, opening drawers and pawing through papers. "I should have looked here first."

I leaned against the doorjamb. Not so very long ago, in the house of another murder victim, I'd done the very same thing Claudia was doing. If I recalled correctly, I hadn't found anything of value in the desk. However . . . "Have you seen any photo albums?" I asked. "Those might tell you something."

Claudia's head jerked up. "You leave them alone. I'm doing this myself." She cast a wild glance around the room, jumped to her feet when she spotted a bookcase, and grabbed a small pile of albums. "Got them! They're mine!"

They were Cookie's, or rather photos of Cookie's children, but I shrugged. "Have at them."

She flicked on the desk light and sat facing me, the pages of the photo album tipped so I couldn't see the contents.

Whatever. I shifted, trying to make it a very comfortable doorjamb, and thought about Kirk, and Cookie, and how she might have come to realize he was stealing.

She was a small-town bank teller, and people tended to walk themselves into ruts without realizing it. Maybe Kirk had taken his deposits and withdrawals to Cookie for years. Maybe she'd seen that he was making largish deposits. Not deposits bigger than that magic ten-thousand-dollar mark that alerted whomever those large deposits alerted, but enough large amounts that she'd grown suspicious. Maybe she'd asked questions. Maybe she'd asked a few too many questions.

And maybe that was how Cookie had learned so much about the people she'd hinted at in the hospital, the people who—

"Nothing." Claudia slapped the photo album shut. "Just pictures of babies and little kids." She got up, dumped the albums back onto the bookcase, and shouldered her way past me.

Next thing I heard was her footsteps tromping up the stairs. Before I could make up my mind to trail after her, she was headed back down.

"Cold up there," she muttered. "And it was just her bedroom and the rooms her kids must've had. Not that you could tell. They look like guest bedrooms that haven't been used in forever."

"I told you it would be hard to find anything." I stifled n eye roll. Or so I thought.

"I'll figure this out if I have to tear the house apart!"

"Claudia, I'm not—"

"Shut up," she said, pushing past me. "Just shut up."

It was time. I stood straight. "Don't talk to me like that. I don't deserve to be treated as if—"

"Yeah, yeah. Save it for later."

She thumped back to the kitchen and I came after her. "I will not save it for later," I said. "For years you've assumed the worst of me when all I'm doing is trying to be polite."

"Polite?" She snorted. "Those smirks aren't exactly going to get you the Polite Person of the Year Award. You just think you're nice. Deep down inside you're just as mean as anyone else." She flung open the basement door, hit the light switch, and headed down.

I was hot on her heels. "What gives you the idea that I think I'm better than you? I've never thought that."

"Don't lie to me!"

My face felt hot, and for once it wasn't from embarrassment. "Don't call me a liar."

She flounced away from me and started poking around the room. It was a typical old-style basement: unfinished, completely utilitarian, and slightly damp. Three sets of ancient wooden shelving lined one wall, the shelves filled with plastic tubs written with black marker on one end. St. Patrick's Day Cookie Cutters. Easter Cookie Cutters. Fourth of July Cookie Cutters. One shelf held a few tools and laundry detergent for the nearby washer and dryer; otherwise it was all cookie cutters, all the time. I hadn't realized there were that many different kinds of cookie cutters in the world.

"Then don't lie." Claudia opened one of the many boxes labeled Christmas Cookie Cutters, looked inside frowned, then slapped the lid back on. "My kids know they're going to catch big trouble if they lie to me. Guess your mother didn't teach you as good as I teach my boys."

"How can you possibly know if I'm lying?" It was almost a shout. "You hardly even know me."

She made a *pfft* noise. "I've known people like you all my life. People like you think a college education makes you better than people like me. Well, you're wrong, dead wrong."

I stared at her. My grandmother, who had been one of the smartest people I'd ever known, hadn't even graduated from high school. I had many vices, but educational snobbery wasn't one of them. "You have this all wrong. I don't—"

"See, there you go, telling me what to think." She stalked over to the basement's dark corner and crouched down to peer at the underside of the stairway. "I don't know where you get off, telling me I'm wrong. My feelings are just as real as yours."

"But they're based on erroneous information!"

She made a gagging noise. "Erroneous. Puh-leese. No one talks like that. Or no one should." She stood and walked to a relatively new furnace. Looked behind that, looked behind the hot water heater, looked behind a folded-up Ping-Pong table, looked behind the washer and dryer. "And you're not even from here," she said. "That bookstore has been in Rynwood forever. Why you think you should be the one to run it, I don't know."

"Probably because I'm the one who paid for it," I said dryly.

"Oh, sure," she huffed. "Now you're throwing all your money in my face."

"All what money?" A discussion with Claudia was an exercise in exasperation. "Where do you get these ideas?"

"Please." She faced me, arms crossed. "You live in that great big house in the nicest part of town. You own that bookstore. You dress nice. Your kids dress nice. Your car is nice. Why is it that people who have money always want to pretend they don't?"

I had no idea what people with money did, because I certainly wasn't one of them. "What are you talking about? If I look as if I dress nicely it's because I take care of my clothes since I can't afford to buy new. The clothes my children wear are mostly purchased by their grandparents. I only live in that house because my ex-husband pays a big share of the mortgage, and there's a huge loan on the bookstore."

I was waving my arms around and shouting. "Do you know the last time I went on a vacation anywhere but to my mother's? Before Jenna was born. Do you know the last time I bought a new car? Even a new used car? Seven years."

Her mouth opened, but I was in full rant mode and didn't let her get a word in.

"We go out to eat once a month, and that's usually for pizza. We don't get anything more than basic cable television, and our Internet access speed is slower than molasses in February. Soda is a treat for us and I only buy store-brand cereal!"

A male laugh whirled me around. Standing at the bottom of the stairs was Kirk Olsen.

And he was pointing a gun straight at me.

"Store-brand cereal," he said, chuckling. "That's practically cruelty to children. You'd think those kids would rise up in revolt."

Claudia let out a squeak. "He's got a gun! Beth, do something!"

Though I'd had a gun pointed at me before, that experience wasn't making this one any more comfortable. "Do something?" I asked. "Like what?"

"You're the smart one," she snapped. "Or so they say."

"Sorry," Kirk said. "She's going to do what I tell her."

"Why's that?" Claudia asked.

"Because I'm bigger and stronger than either one of you. And," he said, smiling, "because I have a gun. Beth, there's a roll of string on that shelf over there. Claudia, put your hands behind your back and let Beth tie your wrists together. Slowly, now."

I didn't move. "They'll catch you, you know. Someone's bound to have seen you."

"Not a chance," he said confidently. "I followed you both here, then found a nice dark spot a couple blocks away. It's cold and windy, and I didn't see a soul. And even if I had, with my hood up not even my mother would have recognized me."

"Marina knows," I said.

He laughed. "Not the most credible source, though, is she? She probably had this one as a suspect," he said, gesturing to Claudia. "Now, tie her up already."

The steel that rang in his voice compelled me to do his bidding, but the stubbornness in my spine kept me from moving. "No," I said. "Claudia and I are going to walk out of here. Killing us won't help."

"Guess we're going to have to agree to disagree about that." Kirk took two swift steps toward me. I ran, tried to run, tried to stay out of his reach, but he was too big, too fast, too tall. His free hand grabbed hold of my wrist and wisted it up behind my back.

I cried out in pain, then hated myself for the pathetic bleat.

"You'll do what I say," Kirk said pleasantly. "Won't you?"

People who say they can ignore pain either have a much higher threshold for pain than I do or they're nuts. All I wanted was to end the agony that ran hot through my shoulder, back, and arm. "Yes," I gasped.

He released me, and I stumbled forward into Claudia's glare. Her expression intimated that I was stupid, incompetent, and going to get us killed. I wanted to tell her to jump right in with her own bright idea to save us, but didn't. Couldn't, really, because I was still gasping from pain.

"Tie her up," Kirk ordered.

I grabbed the string and started to formulate a plan. Tie Claudia's hands together. Take the scissors that were also on the shelf and move as if to cut the string, but drop the string on the floor. Kirk's eyes would be distracted for a moment. I'd stab his arm with the scissors, he'd drop the gun and I'd pick it up. Beth saves the day, Claudia is forever grateful, and my children go on to live happy and fulfilled lives.

"Make it good and tight," Kirk said.

So much for tying Claudia loosely, giving her a chance to escape.

I held her wrists together, her skin cold under mine, and wrapped the string around and around.

Something prodded me in the back. Since I was still wearing my coat, I was able to pretend it was his index finger. "Tighter," he said.

"You know, you're just making this worse."

"Not a chance."

He said it calmly, which gave me the willies because how could anyone sound so normal when holding a gun practically to someone's head? How could he sound normal when he was obviously planning to kill us?

I shook my head. "No, this is much worse. With a good attorney, you could have passed off Cookie's death as an accident. It's hard to see how bullet wounds in people with their hands tied behind their backs could be anything except murder."

Claudia squeaked again.

"If you're not stupid," Kirk said, "there won't be any bullets in anybody."

"She's the stupid one." Claudia moved her head around to glare at me. "If it wasn't for her, we wouldn't be in this mess."

How she figured that, exactly, I wasn't sure. So much for the solidarity of sisterhood in the face of danger. "I like the idea of no bullets, but I like the idea of living even more."

"Sorry about that," Kirk said, chuckling.

"Are you sure? We can't negotiate on this?" I tied a square knot and made a show of looking for something to cut the string with. "Surely we can work out some sort of arrangement," I said, reaching for the scissors. "It's always worthwhile to talk, don't you think?"

Kirk snatched the scissors away from the tips of my fingers. "Women," he growled. "Always talking when it's the doing that's important." He brandished the scissors and opened and closed the blades with a loud *snick*. "Like Cookie. If she'd kept her mouth shut, none of this would have happened." He snipped the string, put the scissors back on the shelf, and grabbed the ball of string from my hand.

"Turn around," he ordered, giving me a shove of encouragement.

Always eager to oblige someone holding a gun, I turned around. Claudia was staring at me, eyes wide, face pale. I tried to give her a smile of encouragement, but all I could manage was a pathetic, trembling effort that wouldn't have fooled a two-year-old.

I winced as Kirk wound the string around my own wrists. "What did Cookie say?" I asked. "What didn't she keep quiet about?"

"Like you don't know." He tied a knot in the string, wrenching it so tight that my fingers were already tingling. "She comes to me for investment advice, and then she's too stupid to take it. Not what you'd call an ideal client. She kept wanting to invest in funds that were *meaningful.*" He snorted. "A nosy nut case, that's what she was. And you're following in her nosy footsteps."

Some of this made sense . . . but not really. "What are you talking about? I barely knew Cookie."

"But you have her insurance."

"Her . . . what?"

Kirk jerked my hands up and backward. I did my best to keep from crying out in pain. Didn't do a very good job.

"Don't pretend you don't know about the box." His voice bounced off the hard floor and walls, pounding my ears with words I didn't want to hear. "I know you have her box. She told me about it, said it was her protection against people like me, said if anything happened to her, it would go to someone who would know what to do with it."

Stupid. I was truly stupid. Why hadn't I studied the box more thoroughly? Why had I let myself be creeped

out by its contents instead of using it as a tool to find
Cookie's killer? "You don't know that she was talking
about me."

Kirk used his size and weight to push Claudia and me
into the far corner of the basement, back where the furnace lived. "Right. Everybody knows how you're the one
who figured out who killed Agnes Mephisto. And Sam
Helmstetter. And all those others. You were the obvious
choice, so I've been keeping a watch on you."

My insides went wavery. He'd been watching me?
Eww.

He kicked at the backs of our knees and forced us to
collapse to the floor. He hauled us around so Claudia
and I were back-to-back, and started wrapping the string
around our bodies. Then he cursed. I turned my head just
enough to see that he'd run out of string. Hallelujah!
With nothing left to tie us up with, he'd have to—

"Got it," he muttered, destroying my surging hopes.
He took two fast steps to a shelf that held a long length
of inch-wide webbed strap. After he'd attached it to the
furnace and around our upper bodies, he grunted, and
said, "When I saw what's her name, that girl who drives
the UPS truck, stop and hand you a box that obviously
wasn't heavy with books, I had a feeling. So I flagged her
down and made up some story about expecting a box
just that size, and was she sure it wasn't for me from a
Van Doorne, and she said I had the right return name,
but it was for Beth Kennedy."

Truth. If I told him the truth, surely he'd believe me
and let us go. "Kirk, honestly, I don't know what's in it. I
mean, I opened it, but what's inside doesn't make any
sense."

"Don't lie to me!" he shouted. "It's not in your house.

I know it's not because I looked, so it must be in your store. If you hadn't installed that stupid alarm, I would've got hold of the box days ago. It's your own fault you're in this mess." He loomed over me. "Where is it?" he demanded, pointing the gun at my chest. "In your office, isn't it?"

Fear beat at me with a hot, searing breath. I didn't want to tell him the truth, yet I was such a horrible liar that I couldn't lie and be believed. On the other hand, there was a partial truth that could work. "Yes," I whispered.

"What's the security code?"

I swallowed and told him.

Claudia, who'd been uncharacteristically silent, let out a shriek that came near to piercing my eardrums. "You have to let us go!"

He crouched down and grinned at her. "Actually, I don't." Whistling, he stood and fiddled with the furnace.

"What are you doing?" Claudia asked, her voice pinched and high. "Beth, don't elbow me. I want to know what he's going to do."

He chuckled. "Beth knows. Don't you, Beth?"

I'd known ever since he dragged us to this side of the room. "It's a gas furnace," I said tonelessly. "He's going to let the gas escape into the basement."

Ten percent, I'd read. All it took was ten percent of the air in a building to be replaced with a combustible fuel and it would be at the explosion point. "When . . ." My mouth was too dry to talk. I worked up some moisture and tried again. "When the furnace turns on again, there will be a spark, and the spark will combust the gas."

"Bingo!" Kirk laughed. "Turns out that it's true what they say, that no knowledge is ever wasted. Here I thought all those summers my dad made me work for his heating-and-cooling company were pointless, but by golly, I was wrong."

He made a few rattling noises, whistling all the while. "Well, I think that will do it." Then, hands in his pockets, he stood there, looking down on us. "With you out of the way, it'll be easy enough to get that box. Get rid of that and I'll be home free."

A smile lit his face. "Happy landings, ladies," he said, winking. "Thanks for making this so easy for me."

Then he left.

Chapter 20

We listened to his heavy footsteps climb the creaky stairs, cross the kitchen, and leave the house. A thousand thoughts rushed into my tiny brain, thoughts that ranged from concern about the tingling in my fingers to a far-from-idle curiosity about the psi in the gas service line.

Claudia shifted in a way that tightened the string around my wrists, immediately changing the tingling to numbness. "What does 'combust' mean?" she asked.

New thought: Claudia Wolff was not the person I would have chosen to be tied up with. "Explode," I said.

She gasped. "You mean we might blow up?"

"There's no 'might' about it," I said, "not if we don't figure a way out of this."

"But I don't want to die. And I shouldn't be here anyway. This is all your fault, Beth Kennedy, I hope you know that."

Of course it was. Nothing bad that happened to Claudia was ever her fault. I hitched myself around to try to add some play to the bonds that connected us and only succeeded in making them cut into me even more.

Claudia began to weep. Noisily. "I don't want to die."

I didn't, either. Maybe someday I'd be ready for the

inevitable, but not today, not with so many things left to do. Not with my children still young and needing me, not when a happy future with Pete was waiting.

My companion's tears turned into shuddering sobs. "I'm not ready to die. My boys need me. I don't want to die, not here, not in a basement, not with you."

I stopped my efforts to untie the strap Kirk had wound around us. "What do you mean, 'not with me'? There're worse people in the world you could be tied up with, you know."

"Because . . ." Claudia hiccupped out a sob. "Because you hate me! I don't want to die next to someone who hates me."

Oh, for Pete's sake. "I don't hate you."

"Well, you sure don't seem to like me."

I looked at the furnace. This would be an excellent time to find a sharp corner. Unfortunately, all I could see were the rounded corners of an energy-efficient furnace. Too bad we weren't tied up to an old octopus-style plant—one of those surely would have had something sharp to cut the string around our wrists. "I'd say the feeling is mutual."

"I knew it," she sobbed. "I knew you didn't like me."

What I didn't like was the idea of my children being left without a mother. Especially after I'd sworn off investigating to prevent that very thing. "Claudia—"

"Of course you don't like me. You're so smart and so together and you're not afraid of anything. No matter what I do, I can't be as good as you at . . . at anything." She dissolved into fresh tears.

I stared across the room, seeing the distant tubs of cookie cutters, but seeing nothing.

All these years, I'd taken Claudia's snide remarks and

rude behavior as a commentary on my inability to work well with others, on my shyness, on my reluctance to engage in confrontation, on any number of my personal flaws and failings. All these years I'd been wrong. Beth, the myopic non–Wonder Woman.

"I always thought you were the one who hated me," I said. "When I hired Yvonne, you picketed my store. For a couple of weeks, I thought I was going to go out of business."

"That bookstore is my favorite place ever. All I ever wanted is to own that store, but you bought it out from underneath me." She sniffed. "I hated to see you run it into the ground, making all those bad decisions. It made me so mad that I had to do something."

My head might explode ahead of the basement. "You didn't like the Story Project idea. You fought me tooth and nail every step of the way."

"I know," she wailed. "I wanted to see you fail at something. Anything! Everything you touch turns to gold. Everything you try just . . . just works out."

"You're kidding, right?"

She shook her head. Or at least that's what it felt like. Back-to-back as we were, it was hard to know for sure. "Look at you. Everybody likes you. You're president of the PTA. All your project ideas make more money than Fort Knox. You could have had that hottie, Evan Garrett. Your kids are smart. The bookstore is doing great. You have a new boyfriend. You even solve murders!"

As she listed my few successes, I thought about all my failures. Then, instead of just thinking about them, I started reciting them. "I have a failed marriage. My relationship with my mother is strained at best. Dust bunnies live under my bed. I can't bake bread to save my life, and

I haven't the foggiest idea how to change the ring tone on my cell phone."

More sniffs. "Really?"

"And I'm scared of pretty much everything."

Sniff. "You? No way."

"Every hour of every day," I said honestly. "And my sense of humor is always getting me into trouble. I have all these funny things going on in my head, but they're too stupid to say out loud."

"Huh." There was a long moment of silence. "So it's not like you're laughing at me on the inside?"

I shook my head. "More like I don't want you laughing at me."

A large sigh gusted out of her. "I wish I'd known this a long time ago."

"Yeah, well."

Inside the furnace, there was a loud *click!*

Claudia went still as stone. "What was that?"

Fear slithered around my neck, choking me so tight that I couldn't get the words out. "The thermostat," I finally managed to say. "It's . . . the furnace is going to turn on."

"Nooo!" Claudia screamed.

I shut my eyes. *I love you, Jenna. I love you, Oliver. Oh, Pete . . .*

And the furnace roared to life.

The metal against my shoulder rumbled. Hot air blew through the furnace, through the ductwork and out into the house.

Where was the ka-boom?

I opened my eyes. There should have been an earth-shattering ka-boom, but all that was happening was a normal heating cycle. My face went wide in a huge smile. Not dead. We were definitely not dead yet and wouldn't be for years and years. All we needed was to loosen the strap that held us together, break the string that was cutting off the circulation to my hands, stop Kirk's gas leak, and get out of the house without creating a spark.

"Aren't we going to blow up?" Claudia asked.

"Not yet." I sniffed. "Smell that? The gas is leaking, but there's not enough in the room yet to hit the combustion point. We have time."

"How long?" Her voice quavered.

No idea, is what truth demanded I tell. However, telling the whole truth and nothing but the truth doesn't necessarily get the best results. I pushed my mind away from the philosophical question of convenient morality, and said, projecting as much confidence as I could, "Long enough."

"How do you know?"

"Because . . ." Because thinking we didn't have enough time to escape would render me a helpless puddle of tears, and that wouldn't do anyone any good. "Because the psi— that's pounds per square inch—of gas flow hasn't yet reached the saturation point. We're okay until the next time the furnace cycles on."

"Really?" Claudia asked.

Actually, I had no idea what I was talking about, not for sure, but having two of us being teary puddles was pointless. "Sure. The furnace won't spark again for . . . for quite some time."

Claudia squirmed. "Ow. That string hurts. How are we going to get out of here?"

"That's an excellent question."

"You don't have a plan?"

"Not yet." I had some inklings of something that might work, but a full-fledged plan? Not even close. "Do you?"

"Me?" She sounded surprised. "I thought . . . I mean . . . I figured you would, that's all."

"Sorry. I got nothing."

There was an odd sort of heaving at my back. "Claudia, are you okay?" Which was a stupid question, but I didn't know what else to ask.

"You, you . . ."

More heaving. I frowned and tried to look over my shoulder. "Are you laughing?"

Her muted giggles became outright laughter. "Yes," she gasped. "I shouldn't be. We might die any second, and I know what you said about having lots of time was to keep me from being too scared, but I just assumed you'd have it all figured out."

"Well." I strained against what now felt like wire around my wrists. "You know what assuming can do."

Her laugh faded into a snort. "When we get out of this, we don't need to tell anybody how dumb we were, do we?"

When we got out, she'd said. Maybe being tied up with Claudia wasn't going to be the death of me. "I won't if you won't."

"And I won't if you won't." She giggled. "We should pinkie-swear."

I wriggled my hands around as best I could. "Can you reach?"

"Almost." She gave an *oomph* of effort. "There. Is that your pinkie?"

My throat was too dry to talk. I coughed, then said, "I don't know. I can't feel my fingers anymore."

"But I can. Why can't . . . ?" Then she remembered. "You tied me. Kirk tied you."

"Yeah. Well." Neither one of us stated the obvious fact that Kirk had tied me up a lot tighter than I'd tied Claudia. "Is there any chance you can wriggle your hands loose?"

She struggled, grunted, struggled some more. Panting, she said, "I loosened it a little but I can't get free."

Not a huge surprise, but it would have been stupid not to try. I looked longingly at the faraway scissors. "I don't suppose you carry a pocketknife, do you?" I felt the shake of her head. "Scissors?" Lots of moms carried scissors in their purses. You never knew when you'd need to cut bubble gum out of someone's hair.

"In my purse," Claudia said. "But it's in my car."

"That's where mine is, too. Along with my cell phone." I was definitely not prepared for an evening of escape.

"We could try and, well, kind of muscle ourselves free." Claudia started rocking back and forth. "Maybe we could break something that will—"

"Stop," I said sharply. "Doing anything like that might make sparks."

She stopped abruptly. "Right. Sorry. I wasn't thinking."

And that somehow reminded me that Claudia hadn't heard me put all the pieces together. "This is all because Kirk has been embezzling from his company. Cookie must have figured it out because she was his regular teller at the bank. She must have seen all the deposits he was making into his account."

"He was the worst broker in the business," Claudia said. "Everybody in town knew that. Why didn't Cookie tell the police if she thought he was stealing?"

"I don't know." What I suspected was that Cookie believed more in the eye-for-an-eye-and-a-tooth-for-a-tooth style of punishment. That she preferred her own style of justice to what the court system could hand out.

Behind me, I felt Claudia's shoulders sag. "Okay, then," I asked briskly. "There are two primary issues we need to deal with. One is that we're tied up here with no one to rescue us and no one to hear us even if we scream all night. Two is that gas is leaking into this basement, and if we don't escape, we'll succumb to either gas fumes or the impending explosion."

Claudia gave what sounded like a small snort. "That's what you do when you're scared, isn't it? Talk in long sentences and use big college words."

"Sorry," I said. "I don't mean to sound snotty. It's just something I do to distance myself from difficult situations."

"You're still doing it," Claudia said, with a slight giggle. "And you don't have to apologize. It's kind of cute, in a weird and geeky sort of way. Now that I know why you do it, I mean. I always thought you were just showing off."

Claudia Wolff was telling me not to apologize? Surely the world was indeed coming to an end.

But I didn't want to think about that.

"Do you have anything in your pockets?" I asked. "Pants pockets, coat pockets?"

"Nothing that will help us. How about you?"

"A couple of tissues." I thought a moment. "And there might be a peppermint."

"Come to think of it," Claudia said, "there might be a pen in one of my pockets."

"If I stretch," I said, "maybe I can reach into your pocket and get it."

"What good is a pen going to do us?"

"I only tied one knot in the string around your wrists." Unlike Kirk, who had tied numerous knots in my string. "All we need to do is break one of those strands and your hands will be free."

"That makes sense," she said in a dubious tone. "But still, how is a pen going to help?"

"No idea. But I've lost almost all feeling in my fingers, so if I don't try soon, I won't be able to try at all."

There was a short silence, punctuated by rhythmic blowing noises from the furnace and the thumping of my own increasingly frightened heart. "Okay." Her voice was small.

She guided me with her voice. "A little to the right . . . No, the other right. That's it. Keep going, you're almost there . . . Okay, that's it. Is there a pen?"

My fingers were so lifeless that if there'd been a live mouse in Claudia's coat pocket I wouldn't have felt it. "I'm not sure." I hitched myself closer. But there was nothing in her pocket to be found.

"No pen," I said.

The smell of gas insinuated itself through my nasal passages, up into my brain, and permeated my thoughts with despair. I sat up straight. No. I was not going to let despair win. I was not going to give up and I was not going to die. Not tonight.

"Your other pocket," I said. "Let me try. You never know what a mom might have stowed away. You might have something you forgot about in there."

Claudia shifted around to make my access as easy as possible. "I suppose," she said listlessly. "But I'm sure it's empty." She started to say something more, but her words faded off to silence.

Which worried me, because Claudia always had something to say. A cramp in my shoulder that had formed when reaching for the pen reappeared in a slightly different location, but I timed my grunt of pain with a stretching motion so I wouldn't scare anyone, including me. "Are my fingers in the right place?" I asked. "It's hard to tell."

"A little to the left. Okay, that's it. Just reach in."

My fumbling fingers weren't cooperating in the least, but I shoved them forward, hoping for the best, praying for the best, and tried to distract myself with inane conversation.

"Moms find all sorts of weird things in their pockets. Someone should do a research paper on it. Wonder if I could get a grant."

"I really smell gas now," Claudia said.

"Oh, Claudia," I breathed. "Oh, my dear Claudia."

"What? What?"

"You have boys. You have three boys." Named Tyler, Taylor, and Taynor, but I wasn't going to think about that right now.

"I'm not sure . . ."

My smile, which she couldn't see, was big and happy. "Thanks to one of your boys, you have a toy car in your coat pocket." My lifeless fingers hadn't been able to tell what it was, but when I'd slid it up to the insides of my wrists, my skin had identified the shape.

"It was broken," Claudia said faintly. "There was a sharp piece. I didn't want Taynor playing with it. He might have cut himself."

And in doing so, she'd saved us. "I'm going to pull it out, okay?"

We made the transfer oh so carefully, and Claudia immediately started sawing away at the string around my wrists. "I can't tell," she panted, "if I'm using the sharp part."

"Keep at it," I said. "It'll cut. Just keep at it."

"I can't," she said weakly. "This isn't getting us anywhere. For all I know I'm using the wheel to cut with."

"You can," I told her. "You can and you will. Say it after me. 'I can do this.'"

"Beth—"

"Say it! 'I can do this.'"

"I can do this," she said in a monotone.

"Now say it with feeling. Say it three times."

"I can do this." She sighed. "I can do this. I can do this." But on the last one, her voice grew stronger and she kept going. "I can. I *can* do this, can't I?"

"Yes," I said. "You can."

She went back to the sawing. "I can do this." Each word synchronized with a stroke. "I. Can. Do. This. I. Can—"

My wrists fell apart and my hands dropped to the floor. "You did it," I whispered. "You did it just fine."

She whooped. I used the stubs at the ends of my arms—stubs that had once been my hands—to push myself to a half crouch. "Claudia, can you grab the end of my sleeve? If I pull out of my coat . . ."

With *oof*s and grunts and a fair amount of sotto voce cursing, my thick winter coat slithered off my arms and onto the floor. I lifted my arms and started squirming out from underneath the strap Kirk had tied around us.

Inside the furnace, there was a loud *click!*

Chapter 21

    ·

"Beth?"

    I wanted to tell Claudia not to worry, to let her know that it would be okay, to tell her things would be fine in the end.

    But there wasn't time.

    There was no time to talk, no time to think; there was only time to act, and I had to act and move fast, faster than I'd ever moved before, because if I didn't, there would be no time left for either of us.

    "Beth!" Claudia shrieked.

    In one simultaneous motion that I could never have achieved if pure panic hadn't been pushing me, I shoved the strap up over my head and propelled myself forward, a sprinter starting the race of her life.

    How long ago had that heart-stopping *click* been? One second? Two?

    No time . . .

    I lunged across the room.

    "Beth!"

    Abandoning reason and using instinct alone, I launched myself into a full-length horizontal stretch, arms out high above my head, reaching and lengthening every muscle and every joint and every cell in my body.

Have to get there, have to reach, have to make these useless fingers be useful, have to . . . have to . . . have to . . .

With my eyes focused hard on the object of my desire, I extended my hand, reached . . . reached even farther . . . and pulled the furnace's plug out of the wall with a satisfying *thwip!*

I crashed to the floor.

"Beth?" Claudia asked tentatively. "Are you okay? You sounded like you might have hurt yourself. And, um, are we going to be okay?"

No matter how much gas leaked into this room and no matter how low the temperature in the house dropped, without electricity, the furnace would never turn on. "Hang on."

Carefully, oh so very carefully, I walked to the nearest window. I was wearing rubber-soled boots, but if there were stones lodged in the boot treads, a spark could undo us. I stood below the small window and looked up at the single pane. No crank to wind out a casement window, no side-by-side panes to slide, not even an old thumb latch to open. To open it, I'd have to break the glass.

Gas was heavier than air. Would breaking the window do us any good?

Behind me, Claudia coughed and I realized how strong the gas smell was.

Maybe breaking the window wouldn't do any good, but it couldn't hurt. As long as I didn't create a spark, of course.

I stood on my tiptoes, bent my wrist, and bashed at the glass. Sharp tinkles fell away and fresh air rushed at me as did the lessons from middle school science class.

Gas is heavier than air. Cold air is heavier than warm.

The new air would mix with the gas, and if not dissipate the gas completely, it would buy us enough time to get free of the house.

"We're almost out of here," I told Claudia. I paused to suck in one long selfish breath, then went to grab the scissors. Just before I picked them up, I stopped short. My fingers were still merely lifeless sausages at the ends of my hands. If I tried to pick up the scissors, I'd drop them on the floor. The metal scissors. On the concrete floor. With a lot of gas still floating around.

Not a good idea.

Hmm.

I looked at the scissors for a long moment. Thought hard. Got a plan.

"Careful," I muttered to myself. Using my elbow, I slowly slid the scissors off the edge of the shelf. They plopped nicely into the coat pocket I was holding open with the other hand. "Here," I said, walking over to kneel behind Claudia. "Can you reach into my pocket? If you can get hold of the scissors, you can use the blade to—"

"To slice the string," she said, reaching backward with her strung-together wrists. She slid her working fingers around one of the scissor handles and pulled it out of my pocket. One, two, and three easy sawing motions later, she'd cut herself free.

"Hallelujah!" She raised the scissors in her hand and hauled back to toss them across the room.

"*No!*" I jumped in front of her upraised arm, only it was too late; she'd started her throwing motion and couldn't stop.

The pointed blade sliced through my coat, through my sweater, through my shirt, and into my skin. I gasped. Searing red-hot pain. Burning white pain that was turning wet with . . . oh, eww. "Don't drop the scissors," I managed to say. "Whatever you do, don't drop them."

With one hand, Claudia pushed the strap up over her head and was free. "I cut you! Why did you jump in front of me? You're bleeding. Oh, Beth, you're bleeding!" She laid the scissors on the floor and hauled us both to our feet. "We have to get out of here. That gas smell is still way too strong. Come on."

She put one arm around my waist.

"The scissors," I said, trying to explain. "The gas. They might have sparked."

Claudia stopped. Looked back at the innocent household object that had come so close to sending us to kingdom come. Looked back at me. "So you saved us twice," she said seriously, starting us walking again.

If she'd been Marina, I would have said that I'd really only wanted to save myself, though since she'd been there with me, there hadn't been much choice. But it was Claudia and she didn't exactly understand my sense of humor, so I said, "Yeah. Well."

"Can you make it up the stairs? I'll help. . . . There you go." She came up behind me, supporting me, half pushing me, which was completely unnecessary because I could tell my wound wasn't that deep. "You know," she said, "when I cut you free and you were moving really fast, I thought, well, I thought you might be running away and leaving me alone."

I stopped dead, halfway up the stairs. "Oh, Claudia. I never would have done that. Never."

"Yeah. I should have known better. Um, thanks."

Hot embarrassment flamed my face. Happily, Claudia was behind me and couldn't see. "Don't mention it." Please don't. But I knew she would. She'd tell her hus-

band and her children and her friend Tina and her friend
CeeCee and . . . I sighed.

"You sure you're okay?" she asked.

"I will be." Eventually, I'd be fine.

"So now what?"

"We call Gus."

After listening to my short but concise explanation of
the evening's events, a hoarse Gus asked me where we
were.

"In Claudia's car," I said. With the doors locked. Claudia had insisted on looking at my cut before I called.
After cleaning up the blood and sticking bandages on
me, she'd pronounced that I didn't need to go to the
emergency room. It was nice that we agreed on something.

"And her car is where?" Gus asked.

I frowned. What difference did it make as long as we
weren't in the basement about to die? "In Cookie's
driveway."

"You need to leave immediately."

My frowned deepened. "We're fine. We even have the
doors locked." I forced out a chuckle. "You know, just in
case."

"Get out of there now!"

I blinked. Gus had used the chief of police voice on
me. He wouldn't have done that unless he had a very
good reason. "Okay," I said. "We'll—"

"Go to the police station. Don't worry about calling
the gas company. I'll take care of that and the neighborhood evacuation. Just leave. Now!"

He was gone. I handed Claudia the phone. "He wants
us to go to the police station."

"What for?"

And that's when I remembered what had happened a couple of years ago. How a gas leak in a house had caused an explosion that had flattened the house and taken walls out of the houses surrounding it. How the explosion had caused structural damage to houses in the next outer ring. How people had died.

"It'll be more comfortable there," I told her. "This might be a long night."

The nice Officer Sean Zimmerman greeted us at the door. When we were settled, decaf coffee in hand, he started asking questions. He was still asking questions when I needed to take a bathroom break and he was still asking questions when Gus came in.

"Haven't you finished yet?" Gus pulled a chair up to the interview table and sat heavily

"Almost, sir." Sean scanned his notes, then looked up. "So after you cut the string, disabled the furnace, broke the window, and got out of the house, you called Chief Eiseley from Mrs. Wolff's car. Is that correct?"

Claudia and I nodded.

Gus put one elbow on the table and rested his chin on the heel of his hand. "Sean, did you ask them why they were there in the first place?"

"Yes, sir, I did. Mrs. Wolff said, and Mrs. Kennedy corroborates, that they were making sure the house was secure. They said . . ." He checked his notes. "They said that they'd been at the bookstore. During a conversation about the PTA, they'd started to worry about Mrs. Van Doorne's house being empty for so long, and they decided to check on it."

"Uh-huh."

Gus didn't sound convinced. Which wasn't surprising, since Gus had known me for a long time, but Claudia and I had come up with a story and we were sticking to it. Not a bad story, really, and it was almost true.

Well, it was a little bit true.

"So what happened?" Claudia asked. "Did you get him?"

Gus folded his hands. "Mr. Olsen is in custody and being held at the county jail. Evidence is being collected. Your statements will be of great assistance to the investigation."

Later, I would learn that Gus and a fellow officer had burst in on Kirk at his stockbroker's office. Since he hadn't been able to get into the bookstore—thanks to me giving him last week's security code—he'd taken out his frustration on an innocent back door by denting it with his fists and feet. When they'd found him in his office, he'd been online, booking a safari trip to Africa.

Later, I would learn that Kirk had embezzled more than two hundred thousand dollars from his clients and from his employer. Later, I would learn that he'd been let go by his previous employer, Glenn Kettunen, because of accounting discrepancies. Later, I'd learn that Kirk had a storage locker full of brand-new golf clubs, new power tools, a new sixty-inch television, and a new boat.

I would learn all that later, and none of it would make me happy, because all I could think about was Isabel. The pregnant Isabel. What was she going to do without her husband? How was she going to manage? How would Neal and Avery and the upcoming baby manage without a father?

"You okay?" Gus asked.

I shook my head. Then nodded. I wasn't okay, but I would be. I'd feel much better after I got home and snuggled into my own bed with my cat and dog. And I'd feel even better after calling Pete, because more than anything, what I wanted was to hear his voice. "I'm fine. Can we go home?"

"Sure. We're done for the night."

I started to stand, then plopped back down. "My car is still parked near Cookie's house."

"No problem," Gus said. "I'll give you a ride."

But it was Claudia who stood and held out a hand to help me up. "Let me," she said, and smiled at me. A real smile that made her look almost like . . . a friend.

The next day was Saturday. I hadn't been scheduled to work, but after I found myself wandering aimlessly around the house with a dust rag for an hour without having dusted a single thing, I drove to the store.

A wide-eyed Lois and a shocked Flossie listened to my story of What Happened Last Night with only the occasional "Get out of here!" and "Oh, dear" for interruption.

When I finished, Flossie touched my arm. "And you? How are you?"

"I'm . . ." Fine, I almost said. But something held me back. Maybe it was the empathy in her pale eyes, maybe it was the kindness in her voice, and maybe it had something to do with not having called Marina last night. Whatever the reason, instead of the standard "I'm fine," what I said was "I'm not sure."

Lois blinked. "But you're always fine. Now you're suddenly not?"

"The social 'I'm fine' does not equate to truth," Flossie

said. "She says 'I'm fine' because that's what you want to hear."

"That's not true." Lois squared off to face her opponent. "Heck," she said, "I'd rather hear someone say, 'Oh, but that looks good on *you*' than hear Beth tell half a lie. A quarter of a lie. And I'd rather hear someone say—"

But by then I was out the door and walking down the street.

"Thought I'd see you this morning." Gus waved at his guest chair. "What's on your agenda today? Catch another killer?"

"I sincerely hope not," I said, unzipping my coat. Not this morning and, with any luck, not ever again. "And it's a little disheartening that I'm so predictable."

"Means you're reliable. Stolid. Trustworthy."

"Stuck in a rut. Boring."

He smiled. "Boring people don't break into empty houses to try and find a clue to a killer's identity." He held up his hands as I started my obligatory protest. "I know, I know. You and Claudia Wolff had a story, and you're sticking to it. Speaking of which, you and Claudia working together is unexpected. How did that happen to come about?"

"Bad luck, really." I rolled out the backstory of the previous night, then said, "What I don't understand is why. Why did Kirk . . . you know."

Gus leaned back in his chair and put his hands behind his head. "Cookie Van Doorne considered herself an arbiter. She was law enforcement, prosecutor, jury, and judge all in one handy package."

I frowned. "It sounds as if you knew this for a while."

"Oh, yes. Cookie's style of justice had not escaped our notice. I'm sorry I couldn't tell you about this earlier, but it wasn't knowledge I could release. Even to you." He smiled briefly. "Most of her 'projects,' as she called them, were relatively harmless, and, no, I'm not going to say who they were and what they'd done."

As if I wanted to know. Well, maybe I did, a little, but it would be best if I never knew anything about any of it.

"Anyway," Gus went on, "I told her that someday she was going to get herself into trouble. That if she didn't stop being a one-woman Justice League she was going to get hurt."

"But she didn't stop," I said.

"No." He sighed. "She didn't. At the time—last summer, I think it was—she smiled and said she had it all worked out. That she'd told all of her projects she had revealing information about them. That if anything happened to her, all the dirt would come out."

"And did she?"

"Have the information?" He shrugged. "I imagine she did, somewhere. But we searched the house top to bottom and didn't find . . ." He dropped his hands and his gaze sharpened. "What's the matter?"

"The box," I whispered.

"Box? What box?"

"The box Cookie had a neighbor of hers send to me after her death."

"A box you never thought to mention to me? No, wait. Never mind. I've been out sick, and you didn't want to show it to anyone else."

I nodded. "Plus, what's inside is . . . well, it's weird." I started to describe some of the contents, but he interrupted.

"And where is said box right now?"

I stood. "At the store. I'll go get it."

Chapter 22

As I hurried up the sidewalk, my purse started singing "The Good Old Hockey Game." I dug for my cell phone.

"Hey, Mom," Jenna said.

"Hey, yourself. How are you this lovely morning?" And it was a nice morning, I decided, looking around. The sky was clearing, and while it was too cold for many birds to be twittering, there were signs that spring was indeed coming. Not many signs, but warmer weather would be here soon. I was sure of it.

"Guess what happened."

"You got your weekend homework done already."

"Mom." She shaped the single syllable into approximately six. It might have been more, but I lost count.

"Can I have one more guess?"

"No," she said. "Coach called me this morning."

I stopped in the middle of the sidewalk. "What did he say?"

"I've told you about the new girl? Hannah?"

"At least once."

She blew over the trace of irony I'd let slip into my voice. "Our game this afternoon . . . um, you'll be there, right?"

"Of course I will. Pete and I both. And we'll be holding up signs with your name on them."

"If you do, I will die of embarrassment. Just plain die. Anyway, Coach says I'll be starting the game today."

I started to say congratulations, but she wasn't finished.

"I start first period and Hannah plays second period. Then whoever has the lowest goals-against number for the game will play the third period." She sounded pleased with the concept.

"That sounds reasonable."

"Yeah, it's a good idea. Hannah's a good goalie, too, so she should get a chance to play. Splitting the periods is about as fair as you can get, don't you think? Coach is pretty smart."

"He's the King Solomon of coaches." I thought for a moment about the wisdom of Solomon, then asked, "Your muscles won't get too tight sitting out a period, will they?"

"Mooom, don't worry so much."

Oh, my dear, you have no idea how much I worry. Every day of my life I will worry about you—about your safety, about your health, about your happiness—and there is no changing that. It's what moms do.

"I'll try," I said, which was a total and complete lie. "I'll see you this afternoon, sweetheart. Where's your brother?"

"Hang on." The phone clunked down and I was treated to what sounded like a battle from a nearby war zone. Odds were good that the kids were playing one of the video games their father had purchased for them, but you never knew. Maybe rival gangs had infiltrated Richard's condominium complex and—

"Hi, Mom!"

A teensy shred of worry wafted off into the sunlight. My children were fine and all was right with the world. Well, almost. "Good morning, honey. What did you three do last night?"

He launched into a bite-by-bite account of the take-out Chinese meal they'd eaten. I heard about the hot-hot-hot! bite of Szechuan chicken he'd tried from his father's plate and how funny shrimp look. I heard how much he liked the crab rangoons and how they'd played rock-paper-scissors for the last one.

"Who won?"

"Dad did." He giggled. "Dad used thermonuclear holocaust, but then he split the rangoon, so Jenna and I got half each."

Who knew so many King Solomons were in our midst? Certainly I'd never suspected my former husband of being one, but perhaps he was rising to the occasion as the kids grew older. "Sounds as if you had fun."

"I guess so."

His tone was a little distant. A new worry jabbed at me. "Oliver, are you feeling okay? You're not coming down with a cold, are you?" This was the result of his nighttime trek in the snow. Only a cold at first. Then it would devolve into flu, then pneumonia. He'd be hospitalized and it would be my fault for not being a better mother.

"I'm good," he said. "It's just . . ." He sighed.

My grip on the phone tightened. "What, honey? Whatever it is, you know you can tell me." Hundreds of concerns flashed through my brain. He'd broken his dad's computer and was afraid to tell him. He wanted to take up the bassoon. He wanted to take up go-cart racing. "Talk to me, Ollster," I said gently.

"Mom?"

"Yes, honey?"

"What's better for a girl, to have brown hair or to have yellow hair?"

I started walking again. This was his question? "I'd say hair color doesn't matter at all."

"Yeah, but what's prettiest?"

"Beauty is in the eye of the beholder," I said.

"What does that mean?"

"Different people think different things are pretty, just like different people like to eat different things. Your dad likes spicy foods. You don't. Either way is fine."

"So I can like yellow hair best?"

"It's fine to prefer blondes, but what counts more is if the girl is nice."

"I think," he said dreamily, "that Mia Helmstetter has the prettiest hair of anyone in the whole school."

"You . . . do?"

"Do you think she might ever like me someday? I mean, when we're grown up and stuff?"

I smiled into the phone, smiled at my son, smiled at the whole world. "Anything is possible, Oliver. Anything."

My smile lasted down the block, across the side street, down most of the next block, and through the front door of my bookstore and into its warmth. Then it stopped. Lois and Flossie were at it again.

"I have no idea why you think the writings of J. K. Rowling are any comparison to the outstanding prose of Katherine Paterson," Flossie said, frowning at Lois, who didn't miss a beat.

"A little angst is fine," she said, "but bring a little humor to a story, will you? Life isn't all dark and dreary. I don't care who you are or what's happened to you. You need to lighten up sometimes."

Flossie kept on. "It's the job of a storyteller to tell the story. If the story isn't amusing, there's no need to add levity for the sake of levity."

"Oh, yeah? Uh . . ." Lois faltered, then got her second wind. "What about *Tom Sawyer*? Didn't you say that's your favorite young adult book ever? Maybe it would have been better if Twain had taken out all that stuff that makes you laugh."

I saw a dark expression fall across Flossie's face. Oh, dear. Lois had crossed a line. Making fun of someone's favorite childhood book was something you just did not do. Not in my store, anyway. I put my fingers in my mouth and blew.

The piercing whistle had the desired result. The two women stopped arguing and turned to face me.

"What's the matter with you?" Lois asked, scowling. "We're just having a friendly disagreement."

"Yes." Flossie nodded. "Very friendly. I can't imagine a friendlier disagreement."

"I know exactly what you're disagreeing about," I said, "and it's time to stop."

Lois's scowl kept going. "So you want us to stop talking about books. That seems a little much for a bookstore."

"You're arguing about me and you're going to stop. I am not an issue in a tug-of-war, I am not a bone of contention for you two to growl over, and I will not tolerate another argument."

There was a short silence. "Paoze," Lois muttered. "I'm going to wring his skinny little neck."

"You say anything to him about this and I'll fire you."

"Oh, come on, Beth, you— " Lois stopped and gave me a long look. "You would. You really would."

"Wouldn't want to, not in the least, but I also can't have you two going at each other whenever I'm out of the store. Now, I'm going back to my office." I cast about for a plan. Found one and smiled a slightly evil and Lois-like smile. "By the end of the day, I would like everything taken off the tops of the bookshelves, dusted, and put back. A much easier task if you work together, yes?"

Though I dearly wanted to watch the expressions on their faces, I didn't want to ruin my exit line, so I spun on my heel and marched to the back of the store.

I closed my office door, but not quite all the way, and before I even got down on my hands and knees to pull Cookie's box out from under my desk, I heard the murmur of voices. A slow, strained murmur at first, but then a smooth one.

Smiling, I grabbed the cardboard flaps and tugged. It would all work out. Lois and Flossie would go back to being friends and the bookstore would go back to being a happy place.

I sat in my chair and started moving items from the box up to the top of my desk. A Christmas ornament. A flat white paper bag. A fifteen-year-old high school graduation photo. A brochure for an African safari. A ceramic figurine of a football player. A doll. And another dozen or so items that meant absolutely nothing to me.

I fingered the photo of a young man I didn't recognize, and wondered.

This was the revealing information she'd been killed over? This was her insurance policy? A box of innocuous items that couldn't mean anything to anyone but her?

I kicked at the box. How stupid to be murdered over something like this. I kicked again and knocked the box on its side. What a stupid, tragic waste of what could have been.

A rustle of paper made me blink.

I leaned down and picked up the box. Had . . . ? Yes. A piece of white notebook paper had slipped out from beneath the inside bottom flap. I jiggled the box and three more sheets fell down.

Then four.

Five.

All with line after line of handwriting on them.

Suddenly, I wished the feeling hadn't come back to my fingers, because I knew I didn't want to touch those papers. Didn't want to see them, didn't want to read them. They couldn't contain anything I needed to know.

Averting my eyes, I gathered up the sheets in one hand. I'd shred them, that's what I'd do. I'd cut them up into tiny pieces and . . .

A sheet fluttered to the floor. I grabbed out and, catching it, read the name at the top of the page.

Kirk Olsen, it said. *He has embezzled money from his employer and has agreed to repay it all. I have given him until the end of January to do so, and while, to date he has not, I expect to . . .*

For the first time ever, I regretted my ability to read quickly. I folded the paper shut.

Only there was more writing on the back. More names.

Marina Neff.

Marina . . .

I smashed the paper into a tight ball. Every single one of those horrible papers went back into the box. I slapped the flaps shut and knew, without a doubt, what I had to do.

I slung my purse over my arm and carried the mostly empty box out to the alley. Out in the chill air, my resolve hardened into a vow of immediate action and I set the box on the pile of snow next to the recycling Dumpster. This would work out fine.

Cold whipped down the back of my neck as I dug through the bottom of my purse, the final location for any item I ever wanted. I fingered through tissues and car keys, pens and checkbook, wallet and bandages. Was that . . . ? I felt the small square of pressed cardboard. Why I had it, I wasn't quite sure, but everything in a purse is useful at some point.

I turned my back to the wind, tore a match out of the Sabatini's matchbook, and lit it. The flame flared large, then shrank to a friendlier size. Crouching, I touched the match to Cookie's handwriting. Marina's name lit up from behind, then, as I watched, was eaten away by the reaching orange light.

The papers burned. The box burned. And I watched the small blaze with a clear conscience. Yes, I could have given Gus the complete and full contents of the box, but to what end? Cookie's murderer was in custody. Everything in the box would have been the word of a dead woman against living denials. Besides . . .

Footsteps tapped slowly down the alley. I looked up, readying myself for the lies I'd have to tell, but then I saw who it was. "Hey," I said.

"Hey." Marina plodded up, coming to a stop an arm's length away.

Besides, thanks to my total and complete inability to

look away from printed material when it was in front of my eyes, Kirk Olsen had been the only true lawbreaker in the group. Some names I'd recognized, some I hadn't, but none of them needed to suffer public humiliation for what they'd done.

Did Gus need to know that, as a child, Christine Kettunen had ruined Christmas for her four-year-old brother by telling him there was no Santa Claus? Did anyone in law enforcement need to know that a Randall Crowley had cheated on his high school physics final exam? Did anyone other than Cookie care that someone named Dale Faber had bet against the Green Bay Packers in their last Super Bowl appearance? Well, probably a lot of people, but it wasn't a crime, even in Wisconsin. And I was quite sure that no one needed to know about the vacation Randy Jarvis took at a nudist colony.

"What's that?" Marina nodded at the feathery ash.

"Nothing anyone needs to know about." I peeked into the Dumpster. Excellent. I reached in and pulled out a cardboard tube I'd tossed in yesterday. Using it in a stick-like manner, I poked at the flames, making sure each and every bit burned until it couldn't burn any longer.

Marina watched as I stepped on the last of the hot ash, grinding the powder into small bits, smashing it into unreadable oblivion.

"Was that from Cookie's box?" she asked.

I shoved my hands in my pockets. "She'd kept a list. It was in the bottom of that box. I didn't find it until just now."

"A list?" Marina sounded far away.

"Yes." And I was certain I'd never make another list in my life for fear of remembering the horrible one I'd just burned. "Kirk's name was on there."

"Mine, too?"

I nodded. When I'd read the notes about Marina, so much had become clear. I knew why she'd been acting oddly; I knew why she'd been distant. I knew why she'd been preoccupied and I knew why she hadn't told me about the woman I'd seen her with at the mall. And I thought I knew why she'd been sitting at her kitchen table sobbing, all those weeks ago.

"How did Cookie find out?" I asked.

Marina took a step forward and twisted the toe of her boot on the ash. "That time you saw us at the mall, remember? That was the second time we met. The first time was at a restaurant out by the airport, and for who knows what reason, Cookie was sitting behind us. I didn't know she was there, didn't know anyone was there. She heard .. everything."

"And later, Cookie called you. The day I found you crying."

She looked up at me, then away. "I couldn't tell you. I just couldn't. I didn't . . ."

I let out a deep sigh and tipped my head back. The sky was half blue, half clouds. Did that make it partly cloudy or partly sunny? There were so many things I didn't know. For instance, I didn't know the difference between deduction and induction. For years, I didn't realize there was a North American time zone east of the Eastern Time Zone. And, until fifteen minutes ago, I hadn't known that Marina, as a teenager, had borne a daughter and given her up for adoption.

"There was a letter, right before Christmas," Marina said. "She wanted to meet me. To talk about medical history, about her biological father, about family history . . ."

Her voice trailed off. Since I wasn't sure it would start up again without a push, I said, "She looks like you."

Marina nodded. "Of all my kids . . ." What sounded like a sob got stuck somewhere in her throat. She coughed. Coughed again. "Yeah. She does, doesn't she?"

"What's her name?"

The ghost of a smile showed on her face. "You're not going to believe this, but her name is Elizabeth."

"You're right. I don't believe it."

"But she goes by Liz."

"Okay, then I do believe."

Marina kicked at the ash again. "That day, at the kitchen table, Cookie said having a child out of wedlock was wrong, that I needed to be punished, to make amends. She'd said she'd tell me what I had to do. Only . . ."

Only Kirk had stepped in first.

It's our duty to make things right, Cookie had told me. It's black-and-white, she'd said.

But Cookie was wrong. Life was rarely black or white. I intended to live my life erring on the side of kindness, and I was going to do my best to teach my children to live the same way.

Kindness. Was there anything more important?

I heard Marina sniff. When I looked at her, I saw a tear trickling down her cheek. My best friend was in pain, and here I stood, hands in my pockets. Where was that kindness I thought was so important?

Coughing down my own sob, I stepped close to Marina. Put my arms around her, put my cheek against hers, and held her close.

"It was the worst thing I ever did," she whispered, "giving her away, but I knew it was the best thing. I tried to forget about it, about her."

"But you couldn't," I whispered back. "Of course you couldn't."

She nodded, hugged me back, then pulled away. "I'm so sorry, Beth. I wasn't sure you'd understand. You're so smart and strong all the time. And I know all about last night. Winnie called. So if you turn best friends with Claudia, it would only make sense. I wasn't there for you. I was at home sulking like a whiny teenager." More tears came down. "I was stupid when I was a kid and I'm stupid now, but I won't be able to take it if you look at me like I'm the stupidest person on the planet. I just won't and—"

"And will you stop already?" I asked. "I'm just as stupid, almost all of the time."

"Yeah, but that's just a front for how smart you really are." She sniffed, but one corner of her mouth turned up.

Suddenly, I knew it would be all right. Happiness bobbed in my heart, bouncing around like a bright yellow balloon. "We can both be really stupid and we can both be really smart."

"Hmm." Marina wiped at her eyes. "You might have something there. I mean, you can't be smart all the time. What we have to do is coordinate our stupidity." She twisted up a small smile. "You can have Mondays, Thursdays, and Saturdays. I'll take Tuesdays, Fridays, and Sundays. We'll split Wednesdays."

"Why do I have to be the one who's smart on Mondays?"

"Okay, we'll split Mondays instead of Wednesdays."

"It's a deal."

She stuck out her hand and we shook. "Friends?" she asked. "Forever and for sure?"

The sky had been clearing as we'd talked, and now the

last shred of cloud whisked out of view. A bright yellow sun shone down from a brilliantly blue winter sky. The day and the future were bright. My children were happy, I was happy, and Marina had come back to me.

I grinned. "Don't be stupid."